Stormwalker Series

Connections in Time

Seadon's Story

Book 2

S.G. Boudreaux

ISBN: 978-1-960091-05-5 (Paperback)
ISBN: 978-1-960091-06-2 (Digital)
ISBN: 978-1-960091-07-9 (Audio)

Zanchier Publications
Printed in the USA
www.zanchierpublications.com
www.SGBoudreaux.com
sgb@sgboudreaux.com

Publisher's Cataloging-in-Publication Data

Names: Boudreaux, S.G. (Shawna G.), 1970- .
Title: Stormwalker series : connections in time : Seadon's story : book 2 / S.G. Boudreaux.
Description: [Louisiana] : Zanchier Publications, 2025. | Series: Stormwalker series ; book 2. | Summary: Seadon Brinley and his family fall into a time portal while searching for his older brother Bain. Seadon finds himself in trouble because of decisions that he makes. His life for the next ten years is one of hardship. He finds escape and must learn a new way of life.
Identifiers: LCCN X | ISBN 9781960091055 (pbk.) | ISBN 9781960091062 (ebook) | ISBN 9781960091079 (audiobook)
Subjects: LCSH: Time travel – Fiction. | Self-actualization (Psychology) – Fiction. | Pirates – Fiction. | Conduct of life – Fiction. | Faith – Fiction. | Family – Fiction. | BISAC: YOUNG ADULT FICTION / Fantasy / General. | YOUNG ADULT FICTION / Science Fiction / Time Travel. | YOUNG ADULT FICTION / Family / General.
Classification: LCC PS3602.O93 2025 | DDC 813 B—dc23
LC record available at https://lccn.loc.gov/X

Old Castle Belarusel
Castle Montesario–Belarusel
Ruling Monarchy for the Territory
Montesario Lake
Jaraphite Mountians
Desert Portal
Point of Entry

Chapter 1

Seadon Brinley, along with his sisters, Wynne and Adda, and his parents, Wilkins and Harper, stood looking at the strange new world they had just entered from the light portal in Storm Valley. They had all voluntarily left their world of Zanchier to search for his oldest brother Bain, who they knew had disappeared through that same portal at some point over the course of the day.

Seadon marveled at the scenery before him. The strange construction of the pointed-topped buildings with their swooping sides, and the wide river which flowed through the center of the city. A sky ferry system hung across the river, transporting people from side to side, as well as boats that seemed to seamlessly glide along the smooth, reflective surface of the water. The yellow skinned people with their straight black hair, and almond shaped eyes reminded him of Cypress Ridge back home. Not that he got to see much of the village growing up but during the recent wars they had flown over the village several times.

The only difference seemed to be that the people of Cypress Ridge painted colorful skin markings on their bodies, and their attire was more of a colorful, flowing style of clothing. These people here seemed to have a more basic style of dress, yet their clothing wasn't like his own leathery, thick attire. He had to say, he was beginning to get a bit hot beneath the afternoon sun. It was much hotter here than back home in Zanchier. Seadon was suddenly drawn from his thoughts as he heard his mother's voice call to his father.

"Wil, can you see Bain anywhere?" Harper said, anxiously searching the throngs of people who skirted past them.

"I don't see him, Harper. And he would definitely stand out in a place like this."

"What do we do now?" Harper asked.

Wilkins looked around. "Well, first, we need to see about transferring our rhedon into a currency this world will accept so we can live. Maybe I can find a job to earn some money."

"Money?" Seadon asked.

"It's what they called rhedon in some of the cultures I visited when I was time-walking."

Seadon said, surprised. "I didn't know you time-traveled before, Father."

"Yes, unexpectedly, when I was an Operatives Specialist. That's why I was missing for five years. It took me a long time to figure out how to return to Storm Valley and Zanchier."

"Cool." Seadon nodded.

Wilkins and Harper turned and smiled at their son's reaction.

Harper addressed her three children. "All of you stay close. Wynne, you and Seadon keep a very close eye on Adda. I don't want any of you getting lost in this strange world."

"Yes, ma'am," they replied in unison.

"All though," Seadon added, "I am seventeen, Mother, I'm not a child. Wynne either, she's nearing fifteen."

Harper turned to her son. "Your point is what exactly?"

"That you don't have to worry about us," he said, sticking out his chin.

Harper gave him all of her attention. "And, based on your point of view concerning your age, who exactly is it we are currently searching for?"

Seadon sighed heavily. "I know, Mother. Bain is the oldest and nineteen, but we are capable of handling ourselves too, we aren't children anymore. We've fought in wars in Zanchier, and battled the Scaithers, flown airships, and ridden and controlled massive, wild creatures." He nodded at his two younger sisters when he mentioned their parts in the war.

Harper smiled slightly at her children's tough, independent spirits. "I hear what you are saying, but we are in a world that none of us know or understand. I just don't want to lose any of you again. Searching for Bain will be hard enough as it is."

Seadon nodded, turning his attention to the scenery once again as his thoughts overtook him. He understood his mother's anxiety over losing them. Especially since she and his father had been separated from them for nearly six years when they were young.

Both of them had been forced to serve in the military, but his mother had it the worst. She had been imprisoned for the better part of that time, and pregnant when she had been taken from them. She had been told that Adda had died in childbirth, only to find out five years later that she was alive and well. They had all been raised by Harper's parents, Derek and Gracelynn Fenore.

Although Seadon's grandfather, Derek, had turned out to be a criminal and responsible for his mother's imprisonment. His grandmother Gracelynn, however, had been their solid rock through those uncertain years. He missed her terribly at times, and wondered if she and his father's parents, Aaric and Neitha Brinley, would find peace far away from Zanchier. They and hundreds of other refugees had left Zanchier just minutes ago at the same time he and his parents and siblings had walked through the time-portal to search for Bain.

Seadon was pulled from his thoughts again as his father Wilkins turned and said, "Now, let's get to looking for your brother and see if we can find a place to sleep for the night.

Darkness will come soon, and we need to find a safe place to stay."

They all nodded and followed Wilkins through the crowd of people who were swiftly moving through the streets in all directions.

Seadon noticed that many looked at them oddly, likely due to the color of their hair and the different style of clothing they wore. He noticed that people seemed drawn to Adda's blond, spiral curls more so than his sandy blonde color or even Wynne's red hair. His father's hair was dark brown and his mother's was red like Wynne's. Their height and build seemed to get them noticed as well. Wilkins was a large man compared to the men here.

Even Seadon, at his own six-foot-height, with his shoulder-length, dirty-blond hair, and athletic physique seemed to draw the attention of those who passed by him. Seadon noticed his mother watching him and smiled at her.

Harper smiled back and continued to watch the effect their presence had on the people here. She was nervous about this strange world, but she had to smile to herself as Seadon seemed completely oblivious to the effect he often had on the young girls who giggled and stared after him. Seadon's head was still in the clouds where his beloved airships, and the life he left behind in Zanchier, still occupied his brain space.

Harper had to admit that she was happy about that at the moment. The last thing she needed was her teenage children to suddenly become interested in the opposite sex while time-traveling. That could well turn into a disaster.

They followed closely behind Wilkins as they snaked their way through the crowd toward a large open pavilion in the center of the plaza. One end of the building seemed to be a gathering place for people to sit, and the other had an elevated stage where theatrical performances were held like the ones that Seadon's Grandmother Gracelynn often put on back home. People began to gather in the center of the building, many occupying the seats facing the stage.

"Father," Seadon said, "it looks like something is about to happen soon. Can we see what it is?"

Wilkins sighed heavily. "I'm not sure that's a good idea, Son. We aren't familiar with the culture here. We need to step back and observe from a safe distance before partaking in the local entertainment. We're still drawing too much attention, some of which seems a bit hostile."

Wynne asked, "What do you mean, Father?"

"Well, it feels like these people are looking at us with distrust. Almost like they have seen us before and have a strong dislike for what we represent."

"How so?" Seadon asked.

Wilkins nodded toward a group of men who watched his family with too much curiosity for his liking. "Those men over there have not taken their eyes off of us since we walked in here. We need to find somewhere to hide for a little while until we can get a feel for the culture here."

Seadon watched the men his father had mentioned, and they did indeed give him some very distrustful glances. He felt his father tap him on the back and he turned as Wilkins steered his family out of the crowd toward some smaller buildings that lined a side street.

Wilkins found an empty shop with an unlocked door, and they followed him inside. Seadon turned to take one last look at the gathering crowds just across the street; his curiosity still piqued by what was going to take place. He shut the door slowly, continuing to watch the people before the door shut tightly closed.

Seadon's attention turned to what his father was saying.

"We need to try to find some clothing or robes like most are wearing to help us to blend in with the crowds."

Harper motioned toward the back of the room. "There are some boxes over there."

"Good, you search through those while Seadon and I keep an eye on the street. We don't know if anyone saw us come in here."

Harper nodded. "Come on girls, help me look through the boxes."

While Wynne and Adda followed his mother, Seadon and Wilkins found a spot in front of the dirt encrusted windows and, as best as they could, cleaned a small spot for them to peer out through.

"Father, why do you think we were drawing so much attention to ourselves? I mean, I know we're a little different, but the looks those men gave us were filled with dislike."

"I don't know Seadon, and until I find out, I don't want anyone leaving this building. We don't know what to expect, and we weren't exactly greeted with kindness or even pleasant curiosity. It was almost as if most people feared us."

"Why do you think that is?"

"Again, I'm not sure."

"Well, when you time-traveled before, did you experience anything like this then?"

"No, I can't say that I did. But I also never saw a place like this. Most of my travels, few as they were, were in average places. Don't get me wrong, I saw some beautiful and amazing places, but I was just an average guy. Bigger than some, smaller than others. However, you, your mother, and your sisters, with your light-colored hair, curls, and skin-tone vividly stand out in this world. We need to take extra precautions to keep everyone safe, and I'm depending on you to help me to do that."

"Yes sir." Seadon nodded, understanding his father's meaning that he needed to be on his best behavior.

As he watched the street outside, he thought about his life so far. He was used to being self-reliant. He was used to taking orders as part of the airship crew; but being told what to do, how to act, and where to go outside the academy, that was different. He had been in the Praxtingen Airship Academy since he was fourteen.

He had begged his parents to let him attend, and since his grandfather, Aaric had been head of the Loradin Secret Society and had a voice in his attendance, he had been allowed. He had always had a propensity for the airships and had been a favored prodigy of flight school. Most people didn't attend the academy until at least sixteen, and those were the fortunate ones. The average age of students at Airship Academy was eighteen to twenty. It had taken the older kids a lot of time to get used to the fact that someone so young attended along with them and even bested them at the tasks put before them.

Sitting on his hands waiting for things to happen was not Seadon's style. He preferred action and liked being involved in the excitement of life. He watched as his mother and sisters pulled promising clothing from boxes. He wasn't used to being responsible for others, and even though he loved his family, he felt like he was being held prisoner, unable to break free and do his own thing.

The past three years of war in Zanchier had made his mother even more clingy, and it was driving him crazy. He loved his parents, and he understood why his mother felt the way she did, but why must he be made to suffer her constant watchful eye just to make her feel better?

"Here, Seadon," he heard Harper say, startling him from his thoughts. "I think this cloak will fit you nicely." She held the garment up to his back to measure the size and length.

"Thank you, Mother."

Harper grinned at him and lovingly brushed his cheek with her hand. Seadon noticed the look in his mother's eyes as he took the garment. She often looked at him with a sad, wistful expression. Surely, once again, remembering how much of their childhood she missed.

Harper turned her attention to Wilkins, handing him a large cloak as well.

"Wil, we need to find some food. It's getting late and darkness will be on us soon. I'm sure the kids are starving by now."

Wilkins nodded. "I'll see if I can round up something for us to eat."

Seadon asked. "Can I come with you?"

Wilkins turned his head, beginning to protest.

Seadon quickly added, "Please, Father. I have a cloak, and I'll stay covered. I can't just sit here. Besides, Mother is trained in combat, and they are well-hidden."

Wilkins looked at Harper, who shrugged her shoulders. He turned to Seadon. "All right, but keep your hood on and stay close to me at all times."

"Yes sir."

They peered out through the small peep holes in the dirty window one last time, slowly opened the door as they scanned the area in front of the building, and slipped out of the door into the crowd; this time not drawing any attention to themselves.

Wilkins and Seadon walked unnoticed through the crowd still gathering in front of the stage. Seadon's curiosity began to grow stronger as more people filed into the large open-air pavilion.

Wilkins turned to him, handing him a loaf of bread. "Here, stuff this under your robe."

Seadon took the long loaf and tucked it securely beneath his arm while Wilkins discreetly grabbed some strange types of fruit and vegetables and hid them beneath his own.

Seadon spotted some sort of bottled drink and quickly hid several of them beneath his robe, wrapped tightly in his arms against his chest. The two of them headed back to where they had left his mother and sisters, looked around to make certain no one was watching them, and slid through the doorway into the building.

On the fringe of the growing throng of people, one large man with a metal arm and hand, his back leaned against the building, peered out over the crowd scouting for his newest crewmembers. Able-bodied young men ripe for the picking that would make excellent deck hands for his captain's newest venture.

Bosun Kaliel spied the two unusually large, cloaked forms sifting through the crowd. They were not the typical size of the indigenous people here in Chindaria. They appeared more typical in size to his own race of people. As he watched the two forms move through the crowd the smaller one turned to reveal a little of his face, of which appeared to be a very young man just the age he was looking for. He also wondered why the two men hid their appearance beneath the cloaks. Perhaps the Chindarians thought them to be part of the crew of the *Raik* already?

Kaliel would keep his eye on this one, which shouldn't be too hard just based on his size alone. He would try to get a good look at the other one, but based on what he could tell from the cloak on his back, he was older; his smooth, even movements trained like that of a warrior. He would avoid that one at all costs.

A man like that could interfere with his gathering. But the other one's movements were less seamless and more anxious, like that of a young man antsy for adventure. Kaliel grinned at the thought. He would give him adventure, for certain. Yes, this one was a prime candidate for the mission he was given by Captain Iramor.

Once a year, as Bosun, Kaliel was tasked with collecting new crew members for the *Raik* to replace those who died, were killed in service to their profession, or ended up somehow running away; though few ever managed the latter. The boys of Chindaria were easily snatched due to their smaller build; not being too much of a challenge for his deckhands to handle.

They made excellent crew members too as many were complacent and non-combative; at least, not once they got a look at him, and if he didn't pose a striking deterrent to mutiny, the threat of his cat o' nine tails across their backsides sealed the deal.

Kaliel made a mental note to return to this area before finishing his task to find the boy in the cloak. For now, he made his way around the edge of the crowd looking for young men who were careless, alone, or causing mischief then running for cover. Those were always the easiest to catch. Some of the Chindarians recognized him and his crew, pulling their children closer to them as he walked past.

This caused him to smirk. He had no interest in their little ones, only the ones left to themselves. That age of self-discovery, self-reliance, and selfishness. This attitude tended to capture him many a young boy, who when feeling carefree, found himself in a new world of servitude due to his carelessness. Yes, Kaliel loved this age of maleness, and breaking the spirits of the young men was part of what he loved about his job.

Chapter 2

Night crept by slowly as Seadon's family; now with full belly's; slept soundly, except for him. As he lay there on the floor staring at the ceiling, the night-time activities continued just outside the locked door of the abandoned shop. He could hear revelry, music, and some sort of explosives which screamed through the sky just before popping and making a crackling sound.

He looked over at his father and mother to make sure they were asleep, then crept to the window and looked out of the peephole. The crowd around the pavilion was still thick, and he could slightly make out images dancing on the elevated stage as colored lights moved about the underside of the pavilion.

Another explosion in the air snapped his attention upward. Colored lights shot out across the night sky in all directions. He glanced back over his shoulder again at his sleeping family before creeping over to the door, carefully opening it, and then slipping outside without a sound. He stopped for just a second, wondering if he should go back inside. His conscience and good sense told him yes, but his adventurous, rebellious side told him that looking around for just a bit wouldn't do any harm. He pulled his hood down even lower, and hunched over in an attempt to make himself blend in more with the crowd.

Seadon pushed his way toward the side of the stage to get a better look at the performance taking place. People playing instruments sat to the far side of the stage. Others dressed in costumes, which conveyed a large creature with wings and sharp teeth, four legs and a colorful body, danced around the back of the stage. The large drums and cymbals used by the musicians rattled his chest with each step the large creature took.

Four women dressed in colorful gowns and carrying swords danced in the front of the stage to the tune of flutes. Two young men carrying bows and arrows snaked around the women, dancing and chasing the large beast as stringed instruments plucked and matched their steps.

Seadon watched the crowd around him erupt in laughter and cheer every time the men chased the creature away. The colorful lights seemed to represent the coming and going of danger, and then the arrival of morning, then seeping into night once again, signifying that the battle on stage was taking place over the course of several days.

Seadon was mesmerized at the smooth movements, and perfectly timed, coordinating steps of the women in front. One particular dancer caught his attention. Her movements were more graceful than the others as she methodically performed for the audience, never looking up or out over the crowd. The dancers kept their eyes on the ground or the ceiling, chancing small glances at the creature that danced behind them. Her dress was long, and a smoky shade of lavender, and it floated above the stage with each step and turn.

He moved closer to the stage to get a better look at her, his movements in the crowd catching her eye as well. The closer he got to the stage the more her dark eyes shifted upward toward him. For just a moment his gaze locked with hers. Seadon felt like time stopped. Then suddenly her expression took on one of fear as her gaze shifted upward behind him. Seadon began to turn to see what drew her attention, but before he could fully turn, he felt something stick him in the arm and he suddenly went slack.

Harper woke with a start, looking around the room and counting bodies. One was missing.

"Wil, wake up. Seadon's gone."

Wilkins woke to the panic in his wife's voice and jumped to his feet, scanning all areas of the room.

"Maybe he just went to the bathroom."

Harper nodded, her nerves on end as her throat felt it might close up with anxiety and concern. She stood and followed Wilkins throughout the two-story building, calling quietly to Seadon.

They returned downstairs and Wilkins said, "Stay here, I'll go look for him."

"Wil," Harper said, placing her hand on his arm, "please be careful, and bring back our boy."

Wilkins could only nod before heading out the door. He scanned the crowd for his son as his thoughts overtook his mind.

He knew Seadon was curious and all boy. Wilkins remembered that age and wanted to kick himself for falling asleep. He should have known that Seadon would want to explore such a celebration in full swing only steps from his door. He had watched his all too adult-like children over the last few months as their lives and worlds had changed drastically from three years of war to a sedentary lifestyle.

He noticed that Seadon had grown restless and ready to be in the air once again, flying the balloons across the Zanchier landscape. Over the past few months life had slowed and become commonplace before the animal attacks had started, causing everyone to want to leave Zanchier for good with no safe place to live.

He sighed heavily. He couldn't yell for him; he could only look. Many of the people in the crowd wore long, hooded robes, making it extremely difficult to search.

He figured he would go toward the most activity so Wilkins headed in the direction of the stage, reaching it just as the show ended. He stood there, looking in all directions as the crowd began to disperse.

Wilkins looked up to see a young woman watching him. He nodded at her and she nodded back, watching him in a strange way. She slowly approached the edge of the stage toward him, concern evident on her face. Wilkins felt compelled to walk forward to speak with her.

She said in broken English, "You look for someone?"

Wilkins nodded, "Yes. A young seventeen-year-old man."

"Yes. You have the same eyes."

"You saw him?" Wilkins asked anxiously.

"Yes. Bad men take him."

Wilkins grew nervous. "What bad men? Took him where?"

She pointed toward the river. "Boats on water and sky."

Wilkins turned to look back at the river. He thanked her and took off as fast as he could toward the river's edge. When he reached the edge of the concrete wall where ships could tie up, there were only a few boats visible moored up to the poles. Wilkins ran the entire length of the wall, jumping down and looking through the boats tied there, much to the protests of those they belonged to.

He could hear other people shouting names, apparently calling for others that were taken.

He grew frantic and began yelling Seadon's name, the hood of his robe falling back. It began to entangle his arms and legs, and in irritation Wilkins threw off the offending cloak. He remembered what the girl said, water and sky boats. Wilkins searched the night sky, hoping to catch a glimpse of something in the moonlight, but it was too dark.

Just then he jumped at a touch on his arm. An old man, bent over from years of living, drew his attention.

"Come," he beckoned.

Wilkins frantically searched the water once more, unwilling to leave with the man.

The old man grabbed his wrist this time. "Come. I know for what you search."

Wilkins followed the man to an area where several others gathered, women weeping as men consoled them.

The old man gathered them around before he began. "Pirates stole our sons again. We must weep for our sons for they are now lost to us, forever."

Wilkins shook his head in disagreement. "What pirates? Where did they go? I need to find my son!"

The man looked at him with sorrow. "Your son is lost forever. Those taken never return."

"What do you mean? Taken where? Who took them?" Wilkins looked around at the other grieving families, which appeared to be about a dozen.

The old man pointed to the water and waved his hand over the surface. Wilkins watched as his arm lifted from the surface of the water into the air toward the stars. "The men who roam water and sky."

"How do I find them?" Wilkins peered down at the man.

"You cannot find these men. They come only to take and then go for many years."

"There has to be a ship I can rent to follow these men."

"Perhaps someone will take you, but most fear these ships and bad men."

Wilkins raked his hands through his hair and stared off into the night sky as fear for Seadon's life gripped his heart. He had no idea where to search, how to do so, or who to talk to. He would continue to question this old man until he could figure out how to find Seadon. Right now he needed to get back to Harper and the girls; to keep them close to him. They would find someone to take them to find these water and sky pirates. As he ran back to the shop, he wondered how he would tell Harper that yet another child was gone, and perhaps in more danger than the first. His sons, both of them, felt lost to him forever, and Wilkins would never be able to forgive himself for not being more diligent about watching over Seadon's restless heart.

Seadon woke to darkness, a groggy feeling consumed him. Moving slowly due to the spinning in his head and the nausea that dared overtake his stomach, he tried sitting up to gauge where he was. He could hear what sounded like stifled crying coming from somewhere relatively close and scanned the darkness, but his vision was slightly blurry as well.

Where am I, he wondered. He searched his mind for the last thing he could remember. He was at the celebration, watching a young woman dance. He remembered the color of her dress swirling and then her dark eyes connecting with his, and then sudden fear on her face. He touched his shoulder where he had felt a stab. There was no cut or blood. Someone must have drugged him with something. But why?

As his thoughts and vision cleared and adjusted to the dim light of the small room he was in, he began to make out other shadowy forms. They appeared to be other young men. Most still looked asleep, one whimpering in the corner, and another sitting with his back to the wall. Seadon's movement caught the boy's attention. They looked at each other, a question on Seadon's lips when a door above the stairway opened up and bright light exploded into the room, making those awake moan and quickly shield their eyes.

A booming voice yelled down at them. "All right boys, time to get up and get acquainted with your new lives,"

The shadowy form with the full sun at his back cast a dominating shadow into the room. He yelled the orders again, Seadon assumed, in another language which sounded similar to what he had heard others speaking last night. The others who were asleep jolted awake at the booming order. Slowly coming to as Seadon had, holding their heads and stomachs. Some even retching before standing.

The other boy who had been sitting against the wall looked at Seadon as he stood, then climbed the stairs. Seadon followed him as the others filed in behind him. As they climbed the short staircase upward, Seadon was shocked to find himself on the deck of a ship.

Men of all shapes, sizes and ethnicities stood around them, each wearing a weapon of some sort, many who were barefoot with dingy, dirty, bedraggled clothing. They all smiled knowingly at them, their grimy teeth, what was left, revealing a stark realization. They were on a pirate ship! Kidnapped. Stolen away in the night. Seadon and the other boys lined up, side by side in the middle of the deck, as the large man stood in front of them, his muscular arms crossed over his chest.

He was a large, dark-skinned man, with many tattoos, and black, wire-like hair that stuck straight up with wooden beads and a few small feathers braided into it. He had a square jawline, and large lips with two small hoops pierced into one corner of the lower lip. A large scar streaked from his temple, down his jawline toward his mouth. One arm was made of metal from just below the elbow and appeared to be fused to the bone as no straps to hold it in place were visible. It moved almost like that of a normal hand.

"I am Bosun Kaliel," he boomed, "And that—," He pointed up at another higher deck. "—is Captain Iramor."

The captain peered down at them, unflinching, as Kaliel continued.

"Welcome aboard the *Raik*. This vessel and the duties you will be given is your new life. Forget the people and places you know. They are no longer a part of you. You will do as instructed or you will face me. If I am not enough motivation for you to do your jobs without complaint, my cat o' nine tails will surely convince you otherwise. Pray you do not have to bear witness to her, she is not pleasant and will leave scars. But do not mistake my warning for concern. For there is nothing I enjoy more than training a young boy to be a man and Cattail is my preferred method of teaching."

The warning spurred anxiety in some and terror in others. The young man who had been whimpering earlier, tried desperately to control his tears, but with each shudder and whimper the teasing from the crew grew more intense until he was openly sobbing out of fear and regret. Seadon and the other boy that stood to his left watched as Bosun Kaliel turned his full attention to the boy who tried to control the shuddering that had overtaken his body.

The Bosun stopped directly in front of the short, round, boy which made him jerk to attention, stretching to make himself appear taller. The crew erupted in laughter until one look from the Bosun silenced them all. The Bosun menacingly glared at the boy who tried not to look at the man, averting his eyes to anywhere else.

The more the Bosun stared at him the more the boy shuddered and whimpered in fear. The boy threw his arms around his stomach, clasping his hands around his own arms to try to control the shaking. He suddenly leaned forward and retched all over the deck. The deckhands all burst out in laughter as the boy audibly cried out in fear. The Bosun looked at one of his crew with a raised eyebrow and several men quieted their laughter and grabbed mops and buckets and began cleaning up the mess.

Bosun Kaliel grabbed the boy by the neck of his shirt and pulled him upright, leaning forward until his face was mere inches from the young man's. The Bosun asked a question in the foreign tongue and the boy stuttered around his tears, what Seadon could only assume was his name. The Bosun said something else, and the boy seemed to grow more worried but appeared to be trying to calm himself down.

Seadon noticed the other boys in line seemed to grow nervous at whatever the Bosun said. The bigger one to his left, the one who matched Seadon more in size, began to grow angry. Seadon turned slightly to better see, as the boy at the end of the line still shook with crying, trying desperately to control himself.

Bosun Kaliel yelled, "Bring me Cattail!"

A crew member jumped into action while several others grabbed the whimpering boy and pulled him kicking and screaming toward the main mast.

Seadon watched in horror, realizing what the Bosun was about to do.

"Stop!" Seadon heard himself yell.

His words garnered the attention of the entire ship. Bosun Kaliel walked over to him and stopped in front of him, leaning toward him.

"Something you want to say, boy?"

"Can't you see he's frightened?"

"Yes, I can, and I plan to whip the fear out of him."

"Why?"

"Who do you think you are to question me boy! Since you are so concerned for him, perhaps you would like to take half his lashes. Tie him on the opposite side!"

Seadon tried to back away as he was grabbed by two large men, dragged to the mast, stripped of his shirt, and tied opposite the other boy.

"Five lashes each!" the Bosun yelled as he took the long whip in hand. It had nine shorter lengths of leather strips, each one knotted at the tip. "And be warned, I usually start with ten, but since this boy here has decided to help out and take five of them, you two can consider yourselves fortunate."

The skin of their backs was exposed for punishment as their arms wrapped around the mast, and their wrists bound with ropes. The two boys could see each other's faces around the mast, the other boy speaking something and shaking his head in objection. Seadon could make out that the boy was pleading with the unmoving Bosun. The boy then tightly closed his eyes and began what sounded like praying.

The Bosun laughed out loud. "Your God cannot help you now, boy."

Bosun Kaliel smirked at Seadon who was forced to watch as he laid five lashes across the other boy's back. The boy screamed out in pain, and with each strike all the boys flinched in reaction, some beginning to hyperventilate in fear and desperately tried to control themselves so as not to face the same punishment.

By the last whip of Cattail, the boy had passed out from the pain. Bosun Kaliel walked over behind Seadon and cracked the whip in the air, causing them all to flinch. He then began whipping Seadon. The first strike across Seadon's shoulders was searing pain as each of the nine tails lit into his skin in a different spot.

Seadon pulled against the ropes that tied him to the mast, the rough wood digging into his chest and cheeks. He gritted his teeth, a small agonizing scream hissing through his clenched jaw. He stood up to the strike, bearing the pain of it; not wanting to give the Bosun the satisfaction of hearing him cry out.

Just as he caught his breath the Bosun would lay another lash against his back, and the pain would increase as some of the tails cut into the last break in his skin. By the time the bosun was done, Seadon could barely stand. The searing pain in his back felt like fire burning him straight to the bone. But he had refused to scream or cry out, gritting his teeth tightly against the strikes, his forehead pinned to the mast, his grunts kept as inaudible as he could manage.

The Bosun walked up to him, leaned into his ear, and said, "You may be tough, boy, but there are no heroes here. Be warned, the next time you decide to interfere with one of my orders, you'll get ten lashes for your trouble."

Their hands were untied and Seadon slid to the deck as the other boy fell over, still unconscious from his beating. Seadon couldn't see his own back, but the other boys was very visible. Whelps raised up about an inch on his skin while others were split and bleeding. Seadon imagined his own back looked much the same. The other boys were ordered to help them both to their feet and taken to the ship's cook for cleaning up and bandaging.

Seadon laughed a little at the order. Why whip them to near death and then fix them up? He supposed they wanted them fit for servitude as quickly as possible. The boy to his left in line and another to his right stepped up to help him walk trying to be careful where to place their arms, neither of them wishing to touch the torn flesh of his back and shoulders.

The taller boy who had been standing next to him in line said, "Jonquin," and pointed to his chest.

Seadon understood it was his name. He nodded and pointed to himself saying, "Seadon."

The boys dragged them along, following one of the crew members of the *Raik*. When they reached the kitchen one deck below Seadon was nearly unconscious and the other boy had yet to wake.

The cook glanced up and said, "Well, what do we have here? I see the Bosun has already begun to divvy up the lashings." The cook walked over to take a look at their backs. "Only five each eh? The Bosun must be feelin' generous today." He smirked and chuckled. "Lay 'em down over there, boys," he said, pointing to a stack of burlap sacks against one wall. The boys dragged them over, laid them down, and left. After which, Seadon passed out from pain and exhaustion.

Chapter 3

Seadon awoke, his thoughts fuzzy and unsure where he was, until he moved and the searing pain in his back reminded him of what had happened. He tried to sit up and his back lit on fire, twinging in protest to his movements. He winced, involuntarily sucking in a deep breath as pain radiated across his back. He remembered the other boy and looked around, noticing him still passed-out and lying on a cot on his stomach. His red streaked back had been cleaned and the whelps had somewhat receded back to a smaller size.

"Well, it's time one of you woke up," he heard a voice say.

He scanned the dimly lit room realizing he was still in what appeared to be the ship's kitchen.

Seadon just nodded, not wanting to offend anyone else and get into further trouble.

The man asked, "Do you know where you are, boy?"

Seadon replied, "On a ship called the *Raik*."

"Yeah, and what got you and that one there in so much trouble right out of the gate?"

Seadon tried to stand up and nearly toppled over again, mainly from the rocking of the ship. The man chuckled. "You'll get used to the sea boy, and by then, you'll have to get used to the sky."

Seadon just looked at him curiously.

"Now, what got you two in trouble?" The man asked again.

Seadon thumbed toward the sleeping boy. "He was frightened and couldn't stop crying. He was going to be beaten, and I tried to stop it."

The man's face screwed up in what looked like understanding. "Well, boy, there ain't no reason in playin' hero on board the *Raik*. Next time you decide to do so, it'll be worse for ya. Bosun Kaliel don't play at words. If he gives an order, there won't be a warning if you fail to expedite it. Before you know it, you won't have a back left, so my advice to you is to do what you're told and keep yer head down."

Seadon nodded at the man. "Now that I'm awake, what am I supposed to do?"

"Well, since ya ain't fit for swabbin' the deck or learnin' anythin' up there yet, you might as well grab a knife and help with peelin' them potatoes for supper."

Seadon nodded, grabbed a small stool against the wall and sat down as the man handed him a knife. The man stopped short before handing it over and said, "Now don't be gettin' any ideas with this here knife, boy. There ain't nowhere to run. If you try, Bosun 'll likely just kill ya."

Seadon nodded and took the knife.

The man looked at him curiously. "You don't say much, do ya?"

"I'm not exactly in the mood to chat right now." Seadon tried to stretch a little and winced in pain again.

The man nodded in understanding. "The name's Cook. Not real original, I know, but it's easy for everyone to learn and remember my position on board."

"Seadon," he said, sliding the knife across the skin of a potato.

"Well, Seadon, even under the current situation, it's nice to meet ya. I got to say, I think yer gonna' be somethin' to watch. Yes sir, I think yer future is really gonna' be somethin', as long as ya don't go an' get yerself killed." The man laughed, a cackling sort of sound that started deep and ended in a high pitch.

"That's not something I plan on doing." Seadon nodded and continued his work.

It wasn't long before the other boy woke up, moaning. Cook walked over to him and gave him something to swallow to help ease his pain, then applied some sort of ointment to his back as the boy twitched and flinched in discomfort, beginning to whimper silently, appearing to pass out yet again.

When Cook finished, he shook his head at the boy. "I ain't so sure this one's gonna make it out here."

"It's not like it was his choice to come," Seadon muttered.

Cook turned to him and motioned for him to turn around. "Life's about decisions. Whatever he was doin' to get caught is on him."

Seadon swallowed hard, knowing that if he had stayed put with his family, he wouldn't be here either.

Cook continued. "Believe it or not, yer back, though it's bad and likely feels worse, ain't as bad as his. That fella' there is more on the meatier side than you and Bosun's cat o' nine did more damage to his hide than it did yers. Now, this salve is ta keep infection at bay, so put down that knife so ya don't stab me, and grab hold of the table. This is gonna' sting like the devil."

Seadon did as ordered. He lay down the knife, and no sooner than he grabbed the wooden table's rough edges, his arms stiffened in pain as his hands clenched the large worn table. His knuckles went white as he bore the pain and burning of the medicine.

"That stuff makes it hurt worse," Seadon hissed between clenched teeth.

"Yeah, but a nasty infection will put more of a hurtin' on ya than this here salve."

After Cook finished and the pain in Seadon's back lessened enough for him to sit up straight, he picked up the knife again and spent the next hour peeling potatoes and following Cook's instructions on preparing the evening meal.

When they had finished, they carried the pot of meat, carrots, and potato laden stew, and slabs of sliced bread to an eating area just around the other side of the wall. It had two long tables, with chairs stretching nearly the length of the ship.

Cook and Seadon stood behind one table, as men filed into the room from the upper deck. They each grabbed a bowl and spoon from the end of the service table and passed in front of them. Cook dished the stew into the bowls and Seadon passed out hunks of the sliced bread.

One younger man carrying a tray pushed through the crowd unapologetically, grabbed four bowls and spoons, and waited for Cook to ladle plenty of stew into each. Seadon noticed that no one protested. The man then stood in front of Seadon and Seadon laid four pieces of bread on the tray.

The man grinned. "Four more pieces, boy. Captain Iramor, First Mate Whiteclaw, and Bosun Kaliel get extra."

Seadon smirked. "Who's the other 'extra' piece for?"

"Me, boy. I'm cabin boy for the captain, first mate, and bosun, and as such I get extra too. And you best watch that tongue of yours or you'll be gettin' lashings daily." The greasy smile of the cocky man told Seadon he was not one to mess with. Seadon put four extra hunks of bread on the tray and the man walked away.

When the other boys who were taken approached from the end of the line, the larger one nodded to Seadon and said, "Where is the other boy?"

Seadon, surprised he spoke English, nodded to the wall behind him. "Still out, in the kitchen."

The boy acted like he wanted to say more, but Cook said, "Move along boys, yer holdin' up the line and I'd like to eat my own supper before it gets cold and the washin' up begins."

The boy nodded apologetically to Cook and moved on. After everyone was fed, Cook and Seadon returned to the kitchen to have their own meal. There wasn't much left in the pot. Cook woke the other boy and handed him a bowl and slice of bread.

Cook said in Chindarian, "Eat up boy, you'll need yer strength."

The boy hungrily took the bowl, thanked Cook, and scarfed down the food.

Seadon sat at the table while Cook pulled two full bowls and four large slices of bread from the stove and slid them onto the table.

He nodded to Seadon as he sat down. "There's benefits ta bein' the cook. I always put my food aside first before feedin' up the crew."

Seadon hurriedly ate the food, not realizing just how hungry he was. They ate in silence before returning to the other room to gather all the dishes and spoons. Cook gave Seadon and the other now slightly functioning boy, who introduced himself as Dowjun, large tubs to haul them back to the kitchen for washing. Seadon washed them in the sinks, while Dowjun dried them. Cook placed them in a cabinet and secured the latch.

He then turned to them and said, "Come along boys, I'll show ya to yer bunks. Both of you return here in the mornin' to get salve put on them cuts again. Seadon, you make sure he comes back 'cause I know he don't know English, and I ain't sayin' it twice."

"Yes Cook."

Cook led them through the eating room with the long table and up one flight of steps to the deck.

Seadon noticed the fullness of the moon looming high in the night sky. The seas were calm right now and the ship rocked slightly as the waves lapped against the hull. There were few people on deck at night, a stark contrast to yesterday afternoon.

Seadon realized that he must have slept for nearly twenty-four hours. On the upper half-deck where the ship's wheel sat stood a man who Seadon assumed him to be the first mate. Seadon's gaze followed the sails up to the crow's nest where one lone, barely noticeable, shadowy-figure leaned against the mast and whistled a sad-sounding tune that floated on the night breeze.

The ocean air felt good against Seadon's skin, cooling the burn and ache in his back, and at the same time tickling the irritated skin slightly causing Seadon to want to reach up and scratch it, but he knew better. He shrugged off the feeling and stretched a bit causing some of the scabs on his back to break and burn some. He needed to keep his skin and muscles from getting stiffer, and no matter how badly it hurt, he would keep stretching.

Cook took them to the bunkroom and walked them all the way to the end where a hand-full of beds were unused.

"All right, boys, pick yer berth and get some sleep. The day starts early on the *Raik*, and if yer caught sleepin' in, the Bosun 'll you punish ya even more." Cook chuckled a little then walked off. Seadon and Dowjun chose beds, lay down on their sides, and covered up with the rough musky-smelling blankets.

Seadon's mind was filled with the mess he had gotten himself into. And his poor parents; what must they be going through with worry over him? His mother was likely going nuts, and it was all his fault. He had no idea how he was going to get out of this mess. Even though his mother had smothered him, at least it had been out of love.

Now he would likely never see anyone again. His mother's worst nightmare was happening all over again, but at least he and his siblings were much older now and able to take care of themselves, mostly. If you call getting yourself kidnapped and flogged taking care of yourself.

Seadon sighed heavily, shut his eyes against his wandering mind and the pain of his back, and drifted to sleep for a night of fitful rest.

Seadon dreamed of the girl in the lavender dress, swirling on stage, the sword clasped firmly in her hands. Her back was to him and when she turned, her dark eyes penetrated deeply to his very soul. His heart pounded in his chest as she drew closer to him. When she was close enough for Seadon to reach out and touch, the sudden fear on her face as she quickly backed away jolted him from his slumber.

Why did she invade his sleep this way? She had been a very pretty girl, but what was it about her eyes that stirred something inside of him? Seadon slowly sat up and stretched his back. It was feeling better this morning. He wished he had a mirror to see what the damage looked like. If it looked anything like Dowjun's he had a pretty good idea anyway.

Seadon sat on the edge of his bunk, the first mate yelled down into the berthing cabin and another man began the wake-up call, walking along the berths yelling, "Early to bed, early to rise, makes a sailor healthy, wealthy, and wise; or so I hear!" He laughed heartily, knowing something that apparently the new recruits did not.

Seadon watched as the man carried a small belt, which he used on those who hadn't budged yet as he paced by the bunks, repeating his wake-up call until everyone was up.

Seadon looked over at Dowjun who seemed to have a little trouble pulling himself up. Seadon began to help him but then stopped. If he started helping him, then Dowjun would never toughen up.

Seadon leaned over toward him and said, "Get up, quickly!"

Seadon glanced down the berthing row and Dowjun followed his gaze to where a man with a leather strap was smacking people who were still in their berths. The realization of what was coming made him move quicker to stand.

Seadon nodded to him and Dowjun replied likewise. They did not need any more marks across their bodies. The whipping from two days ago was still quite fresh. Another slap from a belt would only exacerbate the slow healing process, and their attitudes. They quickly turned to freshen their bunks and then followed the others on deck as the new recruits lined up awaiting their daily orders. There were twelve in all, recently captured for servitude to the *Raik*. Seadon and Dowjun stood still, staring straight forward like the others, who already knew what was expected of them.

The man that Seadon identified as the first mate walked the line, staring them all down as he passed them.

"If you were assigned a position yesterday, get to it. It will be your station on ship until otherwise instructed."

The other boys all scampered away to tend to their duties while Seadon and Dowjun waited patiently for instruction. The first mate stopped in front of them. "We have yet to be introduced, boys. I'm First Mate Xavier Whiteclaw." His deep, raspy voice was a stark contrast to his appearance. His short, curly, red hair, freckled skin, and average height did little to give him a menacing appearance. However, his voice, demeanor, and the way he carried himself with assurance made him appear threatening. And Seadon noticed that when he looked at you it was like he could see through to your very soul. Seadon decided he would take this man very seriously. This well-spoken man posed a striking figure and made you believe he was not to be taken lightly.

The boys didn't move or speak. The first mate raised his eyebrows questioningly.

Seadon took that to mean he expected a response. "Seadon Brinley, sir."

Xavier nodded and then looked at Dowjun, asking in his native Chindarian tongue. "And you are…?"

Dowjun bowed slightly and answered, "Dowjun Munjinow."

"All right, boys, the two of you will help Cook for the rest of the week since manual labor and sweat may cause infection in your backs. After that week of healing, I fully expect hard work from you just as I do the others, or the next whipping will not be handled with such care, regardless of the outcome. Do you understand me?"

Seadon said, "Yes, sir, First Mate Whiteclaw."

"I see someone has some military training when it comes to addressing officers."

"Yes, sir, First Mate Whiteclaw."

"And where has someone so young received such training?"

"I was in flight school, sir. I flew airships back home, sir."

"Well, I'll be watching you with interest Mr. Brinley. Make sure that Dowjun here knows what I said. I refuse to repeat myself."

"Yes, sir, First Mate Whiteclaw."

Xavier turned to leave and Seadon pulled Dowjun along with him to the galley. Seadon was happy to help Cook again, at least until his back healed. He didn't like being stuck in doors below deck all day for the next five days, but at least the sun wouldn't beat down on his and Dowjun's backs until they had time to heal.

The salt spray would have been a problem too, sticking to their clothing, sinking into the still open wounds, burning like fire. No thanks. He would do his service in the galley very well. But by the end of the week, Seadon would make the best of a bad situation and learn all he could from his present incarceration aboard the *Raik*. He wasn't afraid of hard work or fighting.

He wasn't sure what the purpose of the *Raik* was yet, but he figured he would find out soon enough. He doubted it was honest work, especially since the newest members were stolen and forced into slavery, and he doubted the practice was a recent development. There had to be others on board who had come from similar circumstances.

He wondered about the loyalty of the crew and remembered his lashings for speaking out. He figured that whatever loyalty the *Raik* had in its crew was from sheer terror of being flogged.

Cook looked up when he and Dowjun passed through the doorway. "I see you've been given galley duty, likely just until your backside heals." Seadon figured he wasn't the first to have a similar situation.

"Yes sir," Seadon responded.

Cook laughed heartily. "There be no sirs here, boy. Only old Cook here. No formal greetin' needed."

Seadon nodded. "Sorry, it's just habit."

"No harm, no foul. Grab a sack of wheat there, boys. We're making flapjacks fer breakfast today."

Seadon pointed at the other end of the sack and Dowjun helped him lift it and carry it to the table. He asked Cook to explain to Dowjun what Whiteclaw had instructed Seadon and him to do. Seadon decided that, as they worked in the kitchen, he would try to teach Dowjun English, and Seadon would try to learn Chindarian. They would both be better off for it. Not understanding what others say, especially when those others hold your very life in their hands would be frightening and dangerous, to say the least. The upper crew of the *Raik* obviously spoke Chindarian, but they expected the stolen to learn English.

"Cook, can I ask a question?"

"Sure, not fer certain I can answer it, but I'll do so if I can."

"Are there stolen boys on board the *Raik* from other places other than Chindaria?"

"Fer certain."

"Is the whole crew made up of stolen boys?"

"Why are you askin' such questions? The answers won't do you no good."

"I'm just curious is all. I like to know who it is I work and live alongside."

Cook eyed Seadon with suspicion. "I think the powers that be on this vessel had best watch out fer you, boy."

Seadon just smirked. "Me? I'm not a threat. I just figured I'd turn a bad situation into a learning opportunity."

"Well, just be careful what it is ya learn."

Seadon nodded. "You still haven't answered my question."

Cook grinned at the sly, outspoken boy. "Yeah, the whole crew from the first mate down is made up of stolen boys. Seventy in all. That number changes from time to time due to battles with other vessels, boys being lost to sea, or captain makin' 'em walk the plank fer whatever offense they did against him. We even had a few runaways who were never found, but not many manage that. If Bosun Kaliel or First Mate Whiteclaw even think your tryin' to make a run fer it they'll shoot you dead in the back fer the trouble." Cook eyed Seadon curiously. "I wouldn't try a move like that if I were you."

"I have no plans to do so." Seadon never said he wouldn't make plans in the future, only that he didn't currently have any.

"Aye, well, mind ya don't, boy."

"So, does that mean you are a stolen boy too?" Seadon asked, seeing a small flash of regret in Cook's eyes.

"Aye, that's fer certain. But that was a long time ago, boy. No need in dredgin' up old haunts."

"Seadon. My name is Seadon."

"I know yer name. Heard you tell Dowjun there yesterday. I'll call ya whatever I see fit ta callin' ya."

"Fair enough." Seadon nodded and gave Cook a crooked grin.

Cook grinned back in the same manner. "I have a feelin' yer gonna' be trouble, *boy*." Cook accentuated the last word for emphasis.

Seadon motioned to his backside and said, "After day one, I don't plan on giving anyone any trouble."

Cook stared at Seadon long and hard, then just chuckled a nervous, uncertain type of laugh that said he figured Seadon would definitely be a problem at some point, whether he meant to be or not. Cook could see the intelligence in the boy's eyes and the way he spoke.

Yep, he was gonna' stir things up fer certain. One way or another.

Chapter 4

Months passed on board the *Raik* with Seadon and Dowjun being assigned to the ropes, rigging, and swabbing the deck like the rest of the new boys. Their travels were mostly uneventful as the *Raik* pulled into strange and foreign ports to load and unload cargo. Most of which none of them had any clue what it was they transported or for whom they transported it. Seadon didn't really care anyway. He just kept his head down, did his work, and tried not to anger those in charge.

At night during downtime and after meals, Seadon and the other recently stolen sat around deck and schooled each other in their languages, often using drawn or roughly sketched images to help them learn more quickly. Many nights would end in fits of laughter as they often tried to figure out what the other person drew. Not many of the boys were artistically gifted, except for Dowjun, who had an amazing ability to draw whatever they could think up. During these times Seadon learned that Dowjun and Jonquin were cousins; which explained why Jonquin treated Seadon with great respect.

One afternoon when a strong beam wind blew across the sails, and waves began to slam the side of the ship, Seadon heard Captain Iramor yell orders to First Mate Whiteclaw.

"Here it is, Whiteclaw, the wind we've been waiting for! Take the Helm and keep her steady!" Captain Iramor then yelled over the Poop deck railing. "Bosun Kaliel, lift the sails and start the engines!"

"Aye, Captain," both men yelled, carrying out their orders.

Bosun Kaliel yelled, "All hands on deck! Batten down the hatches, men. Prepare for heavy seas and to catch the updraft for lift!"

Kaliel looked to the boy seamen. "Loose the rigging and set the pulleys to low mast."

Seadon didn't understand why but the energy on the ship was one of anxiousness. He and the other boy seamen were terrified that the ship might capsize with the quickly growing wind and waves crashing against the boat's hull.

He also didn't understand why they weren't dropping the sails but instead releasing the lower ropes and attaching them to the pulleys along the main mast. Then, connecting them to large planks that stuck out along the outside of the ship just over the bulwark's top edge. Seadon had often wondered what those planks were for, and he watched in amazement as the older sailors quickly attached the ship's pulleys and the sail ropes to each section of planks; three to be exact; all the way across the ship's upper deck Bulwark.

When a strong wind caught the sails, they opened up to their full capacity, filling and creating a balloon shape above the ship's highest mast. Soon the ship began to lift up and out of the rough seas.

Bosun Kaliel barked another order. "Start the engines! For better or worse, boys!" Bosun Kaliel gave a laugh charged with excitement!

Several men ran below deck and minutes later Seadon could hear the roar of several motors, a few loud bangs, and the smell of fuel that filled the air, partially masked by the heavy winds and rains that began to pound the deck.

All the boy seamen ran to the Bulwark and leaned out to peer over the edge to see what was happening. As Seadon and the others watched in amazement, the *Raik* began to lift high into the sky as several of the crew pulled large, fire-belching guns, like the ones aboard the airships back home in Zanchier, to the deck just below each sail, securing each of them to the deck with large hooks and ropes.

They then pointed the guns upward at the sails and pulled the triggers, causing small blasts of fire as the heat rose upward to be trapped inside the sail's balloon shape. This created even more lift as the ship rose higher up into the sky above, while the motors whirred below deck causing large propellers at the aft of the ship to push the ship forward.

First Mate Whiteclaw pulled a lever on deck which sat next to the ship's wheel. This action caused metal cogs to whir and clank beneath their feet, engaging the large propellers and connecting them to the ship's wheel, allowing the helmsmen to steer the ship in the air giving him control like it was still on the water.

Seadon was amazed. He was used to flying but not in an open-aired vessel. The airships back home were closed in, and the captain's seat was surrounded by glass.

This was a whole new feeling. Seadon stood, his arms wide open, reveling in the wind on his skin as it tousled his hair about. They were still below the storm clouds, but they climbed higher and higher until they broke through the ceiling of the dark clouds. The sun burst forth, enveloping everything and instantly warming their soaked skin and clothing. As the *Raik* pushed forward, cheers and whoops rang throughout the ship as excited sailors all took a moment to take in the beauty of the clearing clouds around them.

As the *Raik* broke through the final vestiges of the misty white cloud cover, it immediately flew into the middle of a pirate ship battle amongst the heavens. Cannon and gunfire exploded on both sides of them as First Mate Xavier Whiteclaw quickly tried to maneuver the ship out of the direct line of fire streaming from both ships. The *Raik* took some damage as she sailed past the two ships which hovered dead still in the air.

"To Arms!" yelled Bosun Kaliel, not waiting to hear orders from Captain Iramor.

Every man scrambled into position, quickly pulling holstered weapons, or taking their place at the cannons. Some of which were on deck and some of which were below deck. The boys all stood still in fear, unsure what to do. Seadon yelled and motioned for them to follow him, leading them to a secure place and making sure they each had a weapon of some sort.

"Here, take these," he said, passing out some firearms, swords, and bow and arrows he found in an armament barrel they had passed just moments before.

"Seadon," Dowjun said wearily, "I don't know how to fight."

"Then you'd best learn quickly, Dowjun. Just point the barrel of the gun at what you want to hit and pull the trigger. It's automatic so you won't need to reset it. When it's empty just drop the clip and add another one, like this." Seadon quickly showed him how to do as he was told.

The boys all looked at one another and then Seadon led the charge as they ran into the battle, firing at the other ships and the men who flew through the air from ship ropes, landing on their deck from both sides of the *Raik*. Seadon and a few of the other boy seamen ran amongst the fighting. Others hid behind ship masts or barrels to shoot from a protected area.

Seadon ran and jumped up on top of some barrels, aiming his weapon and firing with precision. His actions caught the attention of not only Captain Iramor, but Xavier Whiteclaw, and Bosun Kaliel as well.

Seadon was used to war. The Three-Army War over a three-year period back home during his formative years made Seadon brave and fearless. He could handle a ship, a weapon, or even a strange creature at command if needed. He had become a soldier at fifteen, like so many of his friends. He had also experienced great loss due to the wars of men; some he would never forget.

Xavier Whiteclaw snapped his attention away from the display of sheer bravery by young crew-member Brinley and back to where it should be, pulling on another lever and whipping the ships wheel sharply to the right as the *Raik* quickly lifted higher and sailed just above one of the other ships, evading the gun and cannon fire as the two ships fought against each other. The men who had landed on board the *Raik* fought against the crew until none of the uninvited guests were left. One of the ships began to closely pursue the *Raik* as the second ship pursued the first.

"Captain!" Xavier yelled. "What now, sir?"

"Keep her steady until we reach that cloud bank straight ahead. Once you enter, lift her up higher and turn into the thickness of them. We'll take cover until the Sailmen can let some of the heat out of the sails to drop us low and out of the other ship's line of fire."

"Aye, Captain."

Bosun Kaliel ordered the Sail-men to do as the captain said. Cannon and gun fire could be heard exploding all around them. As the Sail-men pulled on some of the ropes the heat slowly escaped the sails and the ship began to drop back toward the water below. Just as the ship slipped beneath the clouds and into open air, one of the other ships was falling, splintered and battered toward the open water below. The other ship had turned sharply and was headed directly for the *Raik*, cannons and harpoons firing as bullets and spears flew through the air toward them; one long-lined harpoon sticking fast into the bow deck.

Captain Iramor yelled, "Load the bow chase guns!"

Men scrambled to execute the captain's order as the captain watched and waited. When the first gun was loaded, he yelled, "Fire at will!"

The three cannons located on the bow of the ship fired on alternating patterns striking the rapidly approaching ship. The cannons reloaded quickly and fired again. Handgun fire was exchanged as the ships passed one another along the starboard side of the *Raik*. The harpoon which had found its mark earlier pulled loose and stripped the bow deck of several boards. Cannon fire exploded from both vessels as Captain Iramor yelled, "Load the aft chase guns, and fire at will, men! Blow the blaggard who dares fire unprovoked upon the *Raik* out of the sky!"

The *Raik*'s aft and starboard cannons returned fired in rapid secession upon the other ship, striking the vessel's main mast and splintering in, sending shards of wood in all directions. Something must have struck the ships engines because just as it passed the *Raik*'s aft, the tail end of the other ship exploded and it began to fall and list sideways, back toward the dark water below.

"Release sail-air and send us back to sea! We'll need to make repairs to the *Raik* before we can catch another updraft! Make ready the longboats to search for flotsam from both wreckages! They were likely transporting cargo of some sort!"

As the *Raik* sank to the ocean's surface not far from where the other two ships crashed, the men of the *Raik* took stock of the damage and piled the dead in a heap in the center of the deck. Some of the crew took to the boats while others made small repairs, cleaned up debris, and began wrapping the dead in burlap and rope for burial at sea. After several long hours, the crew was spent.

Seadon sat like the others, beaten, battered, and bruised. His thoughts returned to Dowjun and a few of the new boys who were lost during the fight. They never had a chance in a battle like that. Especially one where they were ill-prepared and taken completely off guard. It seemed the crew of the *Raik* were feeling the same way as several crew members had lost their lives fighting.

As they all sat, quiet and downtrodden in spirit and body, Seadon heard something strike the deck, slowly repeating over and over. He looked up to follow the sound, finding it to come from the poop deck where First Mate Whiteclaw stood, his rifle in hand as he stared off across the ocean. He was tapping the butt of his now empty rifle on the deck in a steady rhythm.

Soon, one by one, each crew member joined in; minus Captain Iramor and Bosun Kaliel; until the steady drumming rhythm grew intense and loud and could be felt coursing through Seadon's body as it rattled his very chest. Suddenly all the men began chanting 'go home' in a deep resonating pattern then stopped after four repetitions.

Go home, go home, go home, go home

Here one of the older men began to sing a sad joyless tune in a minor key.

When I was just a wee young lad upon my mother's knee
She sang a song to tell the tale of boys stolen to sea
Stay close my boy, please heed my words for now you are so young
But one-day too soon you'll come of age and my words will no longer be sung,

Seadon listened intently to the words. At the end of the verse the men would repeat the opening of the song, 'go home', singing it with gusto and intensity four times over again:

Go home, go home, go home, go home

Then one lone sailor with a deep resonating voice sang another verse:

As I grew older my spirit soared
And my will to see the world took hold
My father said to plant my feet
Upon the ground we seed
And to keep my wandering heart bound
Before to my ruin it leads

At the end of this verse, the entire ship erupted in song as they sang:

We rage against the men who come from far across the sea!
They'll watch for you at the edge of town and they'll steal you away from me!

Then the chanting of 'go home' for four more measures.

Go home, go home, go home, go home

Here began another two verses by another lone sailor that warned boys about heeding their parents, all the while the thumping on any available surface of the ship loudly continued.

My want is not to break you boy
But wanderlust often destroys
Please heed my words my son forewarned
These pirates they come with scorn

Leave not your parents to rage in tears
Hear our song, relinquish our fears
Our sons of old who heed not the song
They all were lost to sea
The pirates stole them from we

Again the chorus loudly and with feeling was sung at fullness of voice and spirit.

We rage against the men who come from far across the sea!
They'll watch for you at the edge of town and they'll steal you away from me!

The last verse was sung with gusto and power by all the men of the *Raik*:

Go home, go home, go home, go home

When I was just a wee young lad upon my mother's knee
She sang a song to tell the tale of boys stolen to sea
Her words we did not heed
We are those boys you see
The Raik, the stolen, we!

Go home, go home, go home, go home, go home...

And when the fifth and final 'go home' was heralded, and the last thump of the weapons hit the deck, all went silent. Only the lapping of the waves, the burning and gurgling of the other two sinking ships, and the cry of a lone gull somewhere in the distance could be heard. All the men and boys sat for a few unmoving seconds longer before Bosun Kaliel's voice rang out.

"All right, men, back to work. We have a lot of repairs to make and a few burials at sea to attend to."

With the Bosun's words the men separated and got to work repairing torn or burnt sails, removal of the splintered wood of the ship, and making note of what repairs could be made now and what would have to wait until they made port for supplies.

Seadon asked Cook, who was on deck helping with clean up, "What was that song called?"

"The Stolen We."

"Where did it come from?"

"It's an old song sung by mothers in ports far and wide, tweaked a bit by the men of the *Raik*. It originated in Chindaria because that is the place from where most of the new boys are stolen."

"Why Chindaria?"

"Because for whatever reason, they are easier marks. Maybe it has to do with their smaller stature, or their culture. The reason why don't really matter. Boys are taken from all over. From sky villages to the ground. We're all pretty much the same on the *Raik* no matter where we hail from. We've all lost those who mattered most. If not when stolen, then on days much like this one."

Cook tossed a splintered piece of wood on a pile on the deck and turned to disappear below deck. Seadon could tell that he was remembering something, or someone, and that it bothered him. Seadon understood his feelings. At this moment he couldn't help but think about his parents and sisters, and the anxiousness about what they must be feeling. The words of the song rang in his ears. He had not heeded the warnings of his parents, and he wished he could go back and do things differently. He also thought of Bain and wondered if he was experiencing the same sort of life that Seadon now found himself living.

"Boy Seaman Brinley."

Seadon heard Bosun Kaliel's voice penetrate his thoughts.

"Yes, Bosun Kaliel?"

"Captain Iramor wants a word with you in his cabin."

Seadon nodded and headed for the captain's cabin located beneath the poop deck. He wondered what he might have done wrong for the captain himself to want to speak with him. The large oak and iron hewn door loomed in front of him. He raised his fist and hesitantly knocked, nervous about the impending conversation.

"Enter," he heard the gruff voice of the captain say from the other side.

Seadon opened the door and walked through, stopping just inside the door and closing it behind him. He wasn't sure why, but he was glad to see First Mate Whiteclaw in attendance as well.

"You wished to see me, Captain."

"Yes, Seaman Brinley, have a seat." Captain Iramor gestured to a chair in front of his desk.

Seadon approached and sat as the captain suggested.

Iramor began. "I happened to be fortunate enough, along with Xavier and Kaliel, to witness your actions in today's unexpected battle."

"Did I do something wrong, Captain Iramor?"

"On the contrary Seaman Brinley. We were all quite impressed by your bravery and how you handled yourself today. None of us have ever witnessed a boy seaman take to a battle so vigorously."

"I've been in war before, Captain. Three years' worth in my home country."

"How old are you exactly?"

"Seventeen, Captain."

"You're older than some, yet younger than most. Do you possess any further talents of which we should be aware?"

"Well, Captain, I'm unsure if this qualifies but I used to fly airships in those very same wars."

"That would put you around fourteen to your current age at the time of said wars."

"That's correct, Captain, sir."

"Your country allowed one so young to fight?"

"Many who fought in the Three Army Wars were my age and some even younger. Some of them were even more gifted than me."

"How so?"

"Certain children could speak to creatures telepathically, using those creatures in the wars. But I'm afraid that I do not have this gift. My gift was being a prodigy in flight academy." Seadon refrained from telling the man that his sisters did have the gift of telepathy. If Bosun Kaliel saw them in Chindaria, he may return for such gifted people. His sisters would not be safe on board a pirate ship. It may be a way to get himself returned to his family, but he would not risk their lives and futures for his own selfish needs and wants.

"Where exactly is your home and how did you get here?"

"I'm afraid you might not believe me, Captain, sir."

"Why is that, seaman?"

"Because my family and I came here through a portal from another time and place."

The captain and first mate exchanged looks, then they both looked at Seadon.

"Could you show us such a portal?"

"I'm not sure, Captain. I've only ever seen it once and that was back on Zanchier. I don't know how to find them, or if they even exist anywhere else."

"What about the one you came through?"

"As soon as we passed through to Chindaria, the portal disappeared."

The captain stood and Seadon took that to mean he should stand as well.

"Tomorrow morning I want you to report to the Poop Deck. You are to be trained by First-mate Whiteclaw as a future first mate. You're dismissed, Seaman Brinley."

"Thank you, Captain." Seadon left the cabin to return to his bunk.

As he left, Captain Iramor turned to address his first mate. "Xavier, I want you to keep a close eye on that one. His manner of speech shows he's more intelligent than many of the others, and his military training, and fearlessness makes him dangerous. We need to keep him on a short leash."

"Yes, Captain Iramor."

Seadon lay in his bunk, staring at the ceiling, tracing the slight curvature of the ship's hull. He thought about his conversation with the captain and how the other boy seamen would take the news that he was being promoted so to speak, hoping it wouldn't make him an outsider to them. He also thought about the telepaths he had mentioned and the time-portal.

Perhaps he had shared too much with Captain Iramor. He was beginning to get too comfortable with his new life. In the future, he needed to be more careful what he shared and with whom he shared it. He had a feeling this was the reason the captain now wanted to keep him close.

Chapter 5

Years passed with the crew of the *Raik* continuing on with their duties, and Captain Iramor and Bosun Kaliel still happily kidnapping unsuspecting boys. The *Raik* had a reputation of underhanded dealings, and the crew were feared far and wide.

Everyone had heard the stories of Captain Iramor's unfeeling character to kidnap those he wanted and make them crew. Also widely known, was Whiteclaw's gentlemanly manner, yet steady even temper. And, his quick and unflinching ability to slit your throat if you wronged him in any way. Bosun Kaliel was scary enough to look at much less his reputation as being cruel and hard, and enjoying it. Then there was Seadon, the bright new shining star of the *Raik*. He had a more playful personality, was known as a ladies' man at port, and a light-hearted banter often followed Seadon's conversations.

He was never one to get serious about anything or anyone, but wrong him and you'd find yourself on the ground, either at the point of a sword or staring down the barrel of a gun. He was patient in some respects, but his temperament could change quickly, at which point there was no going back.

Seadon had grown up and was now ten years older than when he was first brought aboard the *Raik*. First Mate Whiteclaw had trained Seadon in all things nautical over the years, Captain Iramor showed him how to navigate not only by charts, but by the stars as well, and Bosun Kaliel had trained him to fight like a man, and roughly so.

Seadon had never bested Kaliel, but he learned to hold his own. Seadon had become one of the most feared pirates on board the *Raik*, being known as the boy who looked danger in the face.

He was one to never give up and never conceded to lose a fight. He would win or die trying. His reputation as a skilled fighter followed him everywhere he went. He could handle a sword very well with either hand, shoot a pistol, or bow and arrow straight and true, and had even trained his body to be a weapon.

He was fast, strong, and often unforgiving. The other men who had been stolen with him as young men were still his friends, but they feared him more than they befriended him.

Seadon's position on board the *Raik* was just below the bosun, third in line to the Captaincy. This made the captain's cabin boy angry, and he and Seadon had words and even a few fights early on in Seadon's new training with Xavier Whiteclaw. But Bill Danport was no match for Seadon these days and hadn't been for the last five years.

Dan had picked a fight with Seadon when he had turned twenty. Seadon and his friends had been to port celebrating his birthday when Dan had walked up to him in a local pub. He started spouting off curses at Seadon and calling him the captain's favorite and accusing him of brown-nosing his way into Captain Iramor's and Whiteclaw's good graces. He jumped on Seadon, and a fight ensued; one where Seadon had held Dan's life in his very hands. He had spared his life, but Dan was worse for it. Seadon had broken one of his arms and dislocated one of his knees in the fight. Dan never bothered Seadon again, but the man certainly hated him.

As far as being on good terms with Bosun Kaliel, no one ever was in the Bosun's good graces. He performed his duties without forming any attachments. Seadon always figured he lost his heart and sense of fair-play the day he lost his arm. No one knew that story except Captain Iramor, and no one dared ask. Seadon had braved to ask the captain about it one day, and Iramor simply looked at him and said, "That is not a story to tell around the fire, Seadon. Best to let your curiosity pass on that one. It's no one's business but Kaliel's."

Xavier often handed the helm to Seadon on water and in air. Usually, once the right sort of storm rolled in and they took to the sky, Seadon was always at the helm. His gift for flight made smooth star-sailings and Seadon got them to the floating cities quicker and more uneventfully than even Whiteclaw. This, of course, didn't bother Whiteclaw in the least. His position as first mate was secure, and he knew he would be the next captain.

During storm uplifts while the *Raik* was lifting into the sky, and they were being beaten by the winds and rains, just before they broke through the ceiling of the storm, Seadon would often see glowing lights like the portal back home in Zanchier that he and his family had walked through, and that had brought him to this world. Seadon knew them to be portals to somewhere else, but he wasn't about to tell that to the captain.

Captain Iramor and the other men on board could see these glowing patches of light in the dark, lightning streaked sky, but they believed them to be pockets of gathered lightning that glowed brightly instead of streaking. No one ever even thought to go near them for fear of electrocution.

Seadon knew better but never said a word. He liked his life. He sailed this strange new world, was in a high position, basically did as he pleased on and off the *Raik* and was feared by most everyone. He had no desire to tell Captain Iramor that those lights were portals to other places. He had only traveled one once, and he knew he was being called to travel them again, but he refused to heed it.

He often still had the dream about the girl in the purple dress with the painted face and dark eyes. She called to him in his dreams, and in several, her extended hand reached out to him to pull him through a portal after her. This was where Seadon woke each time, just before he stepped through the portal. He knew 2

"I thought Captain Iramor said that the captain of the *Reaper* was not a trustworthy man. Why would a pirate known for his greed give up such valuable information."

"Your guess is as good as mine, Seadon."

Seadon was confused by the idea that Captain Iramor would take the word of a captain known as one of the most despised ships and crew around, even by pirate standards. The crew of the *Reaper* held no loyalty to anyone, not even their own crew if the rumors were true.

The *Raik* sailed straight for the remainder of the night and soon came upon a fortified city sitting upon the highest mountain. It looked as though it floated on the clouds as the mountain top was surrounded by white misty fluff. This supposed, wealthy, Eastern city looked more like an abandoned forgotten place. The walls were high and the tops of the buildings pointed like the spires of a castle. It was more castle-like than any other city he had seen over the last ten years. It gave Seadon a sense of foreboding, one he couldn't quite shake.

As Seadon steered the *Raik* up to the long mooring dock, they men anxiously prepared to disembark for an evening of revelry at a seedy pub somewhere in the city. Jonquin Manshaw, one of Seadon's fellow, stolen boys who helped to teach him Chindarian called up to him. "Hurry up Seadon, we only have tonight!"

"I'll be there as soon as she's set to rights and moored tightly," Seadon called down to his friends. The men slapped each other on the shoulders and sent up playful salutes to him.

Captain Iramor quickly said, "Seadon, I wish you to stay on board. I have some things to discuss with you."

"Certainly Captain." Seadon was displeased with the fact that he couldn't take shore leave, but whatever Captain Iramor had to say must be important.

"Meet me in my cabin in half-an-hour."

"Aye, Captain Iramor." Seadon was a little worried about the Captain's demeanor. He seemed a little off-standish, more so than usual. Perhaps he wanted to discuss the stirrings of dissension on board over the last several weeks. The men were becoming restless and little reckless even; more daring with their tongues and attitudes.

Seadon puttered about the ship and visited with Cook who usually stayed on board, saying he was too old for shore leave festivities. After about thirty minutes, Seadon excused himself and headed for Iramor's cabin. He knocked before entering as was the custom.

"Enter," he heard Iramor say.

When Seadon entered the cabin, he noticed Xavier standing to one side, his hands clasped behind his back as he stared at the floor. He looked as though the weight of the world sat on his shoulders.

"Captain, you wished to discuss something with me?" Seadon walked toward the desk but was suddenly grabbed from behind by several men and restrained. He fought against his captors but noticed that Captain Iramor and First Mate Whiteclaw did not move. Seadon was pushed to his knees on the floor, just as the captain of the *Reaper* walked forward.

"What's happening?" Seadon questioned Iramor.

"Seadon, I'm sorry about this but you've become a liability. One I can't afford."

"What do you mean? Have I displeased you in some way?" Seadon asked, confused.

"Not in the least. You've far exceeded your teachings, and have become a formidable pirate, however, the men of the *Raik* have recently been acting out. They seem to think that they can take advantage of their situations because you were given a rare opportunity."

"Captain, they are just restless. We've been out to sea and wandering the heavens longer than our usual voyages."

"It's more than that. The crew doesn't fear you. Respect you yes, but it's not real fear; and I can't have dissension in the ranks."

"I would never cause that to happen, Captain. You know me."

"Yes, I do. And unfortunately for you, you have proven to be the favored amongst the crew. So, I've sold you to Captain Veramere of the *Reaper.*"

"Sold me!?" Seadon looked to Whiteclaw, who said nothing. His jaw clenched in disapproval of the situation, but Seadon knew he would do and say nothing to contradict Captain Iramor's decision.

"Yes. As your captain, it is my right to do with my slaves as I see fit. You see Seadon, your free-spirited thinking has become your undoing. Your timely purchase will certainly set the crew to rights. They'll learn to fear me more than ever before. Bosun's cat o' nine tails can only muster so much compliance. The idea of selling them off to men like Captain Veramere here should make them toe the line quite nicely. And if I'm willing to sell my favored, then they will be all the more worried to be next."

Veramere handed Iramor a pouch of coins.

Iramor commented, "He is well worth the price."

Veramere replied, "Oh, I know of his reputation. I promise, he will not overshadow my own ship like you have allowed to happen on the *Raik.*"

"Watch your tongue, Veramere, you're aboard my ship. I may be in a gracious mood at the moment, but that can change in an instant." As Iramor spoke the words, Kaliel stepped forward from the shadows.

Veramere smirked and bowed slightly to Iramor. He then turned and gave Seadon a look that told him he was in for some rough times. Veramere's men pulled Seadon to his feet and he struggled against the bondage. He looked at Iramor and Whiteclaw one last time.

"Captain, please don't do this. You have nothing to fear from me."

"What's done is done. And you are correct. I no longer have anything to fear from you."

Seadon fought his bonds even harder as anger boiled in his veins at the idea of being sold by the man he had given his allegiance to and had learned to respect over the years.

Veramere took the butt of his pistol and hit Seadon over the head, quietening his struggles for freedom.

As his men dragged Seadon off the *Raik*, Captain Iramor and Xavier Whiteclaw followed them to the gangway.

Whiteclaw dared to ask, "Captain, are you certain about this? Seadon posed no threat to you or the *Raik*."

"Careful, Xavier, about questioning my actions, lest you find yourself in a similar situation." Iramor turned and walked back to his cabin, securing the door behind him.

Xavier watched with distaste as the men of the *Reaper* threw Seadon's limp body into a horse drawn wagon and prepared to haul him across the city to another dock where the *Reaper* sat moored.

Cook had been standing on deck at the Bulwark looking out at the dimly lit, looming, castled city when he heard the commotion coming from Iramor's cabin. He also watched with angst at the scene before him. He and Whiteclaw exchanged looks of disdain and concern at the events that had taken place just moments before, but both were unable to do anything about it. They both watched as Seadon was hauled away, before turning and disappearing to their own berths.

Whiteclaw did not relish the uproar that would take place when the men realized what had taken place in their absence. Or the lashings they would face at Bosun Kaliel's hand for their anger and protests. Tomorrow would be a dreaded day on the *Raik,* but harder still was what Seadon would face at the hands of Captain Veramere and the men of the *Reaper.* Veramere's crew were hard men who agreeably signed on to sail under the *Reaper's* captain and his command, not forced and trained through fear and loathing as the men of the *Raik* had been. Whiteclaw would get little sleep tonight.

Seadon woke inside a cell in what he assumed to be the brig aboard the *Reaper.* How did he come to this? Nearly first mate upon the *Raik* to the lowest of lows on the *Reaper.* As he struggled to sit up, his head throbbing in pain, he heard someone yell for Veramere.

"Captain, the slave is awake!"

Seadon looked up as Veramere walked down the steps to the brig level of the ship.

"It's about time you woke. I guess maybe I hit you a little too hard. But, no matter, you'll get used to flogging on the *Reaper,* even if Bosun Kaliel was a little light-handed on you over the years."

"What do you want with me? Why pay good coin for me?"

"I've heard you're the best sailor around, on wave and wind. My first mate went and got himself killed last week. You're captain—"

"He's no longer my captain," Seadon seethed.

"No…I am. Now don't interrupt me again, boy." Veramere threatened. "As I was saying, Iramor, said he had a problem that he was willing to part with, which, of course, we know to be you. He already has a perfectly effective first mate in Whiteclaw and I needed a man who could handle the shifting from water to sky. Uplifts can be tricky if not handled correctly. So, your new job on the *Reaper* is the helm. Do it well and you'll avoid the cat o' nine tails. Damage my ship, and I'll damage you. Your loyalty is to the *Reaper* now. I own you."

"I'm owned by no man, least of all the likes of you."

"You see there, boy. That's exactly the attitude that put you here."

"I'm no boy. Let me out of here and I'll show you just how much of a man I am."

Veramere laughed heartily and motioned to the man who guarded Seadon's cell. The man stuck an electrical prod through the bars and into Seadon's side. Seadon shook violently at the charge and fell to his knees, grasping the bars of the cell to keep from hitting the floor.

"We'll not be havin' any talk like that aboard the *Reaper.* Now, after you're finished stewing over the betrayal you feel from Captain Iramor, we'll talk again. But remember this, the longer it takes for you to come to terms with your new position, the longer I lose money. And I don't like losing money, boy. The angrier I get, the more lashes added to your floggin'. And if you think Bosun Kaliel is bad, wait until you meet Mr. Dracmoor. He's a little man, with a very big complex." Veramere's laugh grew as he left the brig, followed by the other two men who had been waiting for Seadon to wake up.

Seadon's vision had gone blurry with the jolt of electricity that had flown through his body just minutes earlier. He lifted his shirt to reveal a small burn mark on his skin where the guard had struck him.

Seadon tried to process the betrayal and anger he felt for Iramor, Whiteclaw, and Kaliel as well. He figured he was going to hate Veramere even more, but if he had any chance at all of getting off this ship he would have to keep his wits about him. Seadon could play the deceit game as well as the next person, better even.

He supposed he couldn't be too angry at Iramor. He had been biding his time, winning the loyalty of the crew to further his own intentions. He had planned to stage a mutiny to gain control of the *Raik*, years from now. But he supposed that Iramor could sense Seadon's intentions and decided to deal with it before it became a problem. Seadon decided that the next time Veramere visited the brig, he would be ready and willing to do his part for the *Reaper*. At least it would get him out of the cell. However, he had a feeling this cell would become his home when not at the helm for the foreseeable future.

Chapter 6

It had only been about thirty minutes before Veramere's men returned and pushed a shackled Seadon to the upper deck toward the Poop Deck where Veramere waited. As Seadon climbed the steps, Veramere motioned to him. "The Helm is yours, Mr. Brinley,"

Seadon took his place in front of the wheel and lifted his hands.

"I can't exactly steer your ship if I'm shackled at the wrists."

Veramere smirked. "I suppose you're right there." Veramere motioned toward a crew member. "Unlock the manacles from his wrist and put them on his ankles."

Seadon looked at Veramere with a question.

Veramere smiled. "You don't need your feet to steer, and that will keep you from jumping ship. Those chains are heavy, and you'll sink to the ocean floor as soon as you hit the water, or quick enough thereafter."

When the man finished placing the shackles on Seadon's ankles, Veramere ordered, "Head due west, and keep her straight. The *Reaper* has a date with some ships sailing this way loaded with riches from the West, and I aim to lighten their loads." He smiled and laughed, and the crew laughed with him.

Seadon turned the *Reaper* west and the sails caught the wind, pushing the ship; the *Reaper* quickly slicing through the water. It was smooth sailing all the way when they saw the ship in question. They soon intercepted one of the loaded ships they were seeking, and with a fight sure to ensue, Seadon nervously stated to Veramere, "Captain, I need a weapon to defend myself."

"You'll receive no such weapon, Mr. Brinley."

"Well I can't exactly run and hide, and with no weapon to defend myself, where will you be with your newly purchased Helmsman dead?"

"First of all, this here ship we are about to overtake is no match for the gun power of the *Reaper.* Second, I've ordered some of my crew to stand guard and keep my '*investment*' safe." Veramere nodded to Seadon, making sure he understood he was that investment.

"And if you all get shot and I'm left undefended?"

Veramere smirked. "Then I guess you'll meet your maker today, for if I'm gone, then I have no further use for you."

Seadon's grip on the wheel tightened. He didn't like standing by in a fight, depending on others to watch his back. He was a man of action, and he liked being in the thick of the fight. Besides, being one man with a gun against Veramere's loyal crew would be suicide. Seadon was brave, not stupid.

As the *Reaper* pulled alongside the other ship, Veramere gave the order for the cannons to fire, loosing explosive iron upon the other ship. The ship returned fire, however, the smaller number of cannons on board were no match for a pirate ship like the *Reaper.* It's size alone was intimidating, giving it room for extra cannons and men. The crew of the *Reaper* boasted just over one-hundred souls, ready to fight, plunder, and destroy. And if rumors were true, even though Captain Veramere had a reputation as a hard, evil man, he shared any and all bounty fairly amongst the crew. Which was another reason his crew was loyal.

Seadon steered the ship amongst gun, cannon, and sword fighting, ducking on occasion as a bullet whizzed by his head, or he happened to catch someone pointing one at him. Fortunately the ship's wheel was very large and managed to shield most of his body from gunfire, the wheel taking a stray bullet and splintering, sending small shards of wood in all directions. The bloody battle only lasted about ten minutes from start to finish, and Veramere's crew was plundering the ship's cargo hold and transferring all the loot over to the *Reaper*. Seadon watched as Veramere's men left only a handful of the other ship's men alive; a small skeleton crew to sail her home to port, and to tell the tale of the deadliest ship on the seas.

After Seadon's first day at the helm was finished, he was fed with the crew, placed back in the brig—where they at least removed the shackles for the night—and left till the next morning. Each day this was Seadon's life over the next several months as he performed his duties, shackled at the ankles. His feet were sore from the constant rubbing of metal on his skin, his body tired of the limited movement he got, and he seriously needed a bath. When they made port, a man was left on board to guard him; a very unhappy man who was mad about not getting his own shore leave and glared at Seadon the whole time. It wasn't Seadon's fault that he had to be locked up and watched. He hadn't tried to escape once, at least not that the crew or captain knew of anyway. He tried to pick the lock on his manacles when no one was looking, but that was rare. And when they put him in the brig, they removed them so he couldn't practice in secret while locked in his cell. The only time he got any privacy was when he was allowed latrine time, and on a few occasions, he was able to practice on the lock of the manacles. He was successful in opening them, and now that he had figured it out, he would devise a plan of escape.

Seadon grew weary of his confinement and chains as more time passed, until one day when a storm approached. This storm was moving fast and with winds so strong it caused the ship to list so badly that Seadon thought they might capsize before they achieved uplift for sky-sailing. The crew of the *Reaper* scrambled to hold onto something while still trying to perform their required duties.

As the storm's full rage was upon them, and the ship began to gain air and lift, a light appeared glowing and pulsating brightly, just off the starboard side of the ship right next to where Seadon stood on the Poop Deck. Lightning struck and lit the sky, churning the water below creating an arc so bright it was nearly blinding.

Seadon took the opportunity. He pulled the small piece of metal from the small pocket inside his waistband and quickly squatted, unlocked the manacles, and ran to the Bulwark. As he was climbing up on the railing, he could barely hear Captain Veramere's warning. He looked to the captain, and saluted just as Veramere pulled the trigger on his gun. A shot rang out just as Seadon dove into the light of the portal, and Veramere watched as Seadon disappeared just before the glowing oval of light vanished.

Seadon awoke hours later, his head ached, and his side hurt badly. He realized he was lying on the ground. He tried to sit up and a pain shot through his side and radiated across his abdomen. He grasped it, bringing his blood covered hand into view. Veramere's aim was true, and Seadon now had a bullet lodged in his side, but there was no sign of the *Reaper* anywhere. He looked at his feet, and the manacles were gone. He had managed to escape, but to where? As he sat there, he inspected the damage done by the bullet. His shirt and the side of his pants were saturated with blood. He took a minute to just sit and assess his situation. There was nothing but desert and rocky mountains surrounding him. The dusty valley looked barren of life of any kind, and there didn't appear to be water anywhere.

Seadon snidely said to himself, "So, this is your idea of saving yourself is it? Getting yourself stranded in the middle of the desert, shot in the side for your efforts, with no food or water to be had." Seadon pushed himself up to stand, grabbing and holding his side as pain shot through it once again. Each step he took was agonizing, but he had to move. He couldn't just lie there and wait for someone to happen by, especially since there didn't appear to be anything for anyone to happen by for.

He picked a direction and began to move, the blazing sun hot on his head and shoulders. He had no idea how long it had been with him passed-out underneath that same sun, but his lips were dry, his throat dusty, and he felt as though there was no liquid left in him for his body to sweat out. It had been years since he had been anywhere near a place like this. Zanchier had been half surrounded by deserts, but he saw very little of them except in the wars and from flying overhead. Life at sea was nothing but water, and he much preferred that to this miserable existence. He was beginning to regret his decision to jump ship. Captivity, food, and water were much preferred to this. As Seadon walked, nearly dragging his injured side, his body growing weaker from loss of blood as well as exposure to the elements, he soon collapsed.

Looking through a high-powered spy-glass from his lookout post atop the highest tower, a young officer named Nuncio Agnusdei spoke through his headset to his commander,

"Commander Quimby, I see something lying on the desert floor a few miles South,"

Quintessa Quimby, known as Quinn to her friends and troops, was standing along the upper-most wall which surrounded the city of Montesario-Belarusel.

She replied, "Can you make out what it is, Officer Agnusdei?"

"It appears to be a person, Ma'am, though the gender is unrecognizable from here."

Quinn turned to her second in command. "Captain Trent, dispatch a rescue team and bring whoever that is to medical."

"Yes, Commander."

Captain Trent saluted and gathered a crew of men. They attached a float-cart to the back of one of their speeders, mounted the hover bikes, and took off out of the gate. They reached Seadon in just over five minutes and dismounted their bikes.

Captain Trent squatted to inspect the man's wounds as the other four men shadowed Seadon's sunburned body.

Seadon felt the cooler reprieve from the blazing rays of the sun on his face. His eyes slit open just barely and he realized he was surrounded by men in uniform. Seadon groaned in protest as they lifted his body off the hard ground and placed him on a stretcher.

Captain Trent said, "Turn the air supply to high. This man will need as much support as possible. His wound appears to be from some sort of rudimentary weapon. The hole in his side is quite large and round, not like from a flat blade or laser weapon. It appears that he's lost a lot of blood as well."

Seadon heard a hissing sound and felt himself lift up from the surface of the stretcher. His body felt as though it were cradled in a cloud. The pressure on his side from the hard surface was now gone, and as his rescuers moved quickly along, Seadon didn't feel a single bump or jar. He turned his head to watch the quickly passing landscape, curious how he didn't feel anything at all from the obvious quick motion of whatever they were riding.

Seadon strained his neck to look up at where they were taking him. They approached a large walled structure and passed beneath a massive arched portico into an open courtyard filled with people milling about. His rescuers turned and sped up an incline, giving Seadon a view of what he had just passed through. It appeared to be a massive city, built on the side of a mountain. He wasn't sure where they were taking him, but the ride was quite enjoyable as the coolness of the stone city and the shadow of the mountain, along with the quickly moving pace of the vehicles, cooled his sun-burned skin and refreshed his overheated body.

Along the way, they passed a large waterfall, and the over-spray from the clear, clean-tasting, mountain mist further cooled his skin, the dryness of it quickly absorbing the droplets that landed upon his flesh. It wasn't long after that when the vehicles pulled to a stop. The men unhooked his floating cloud-like bed and pushed it through another large archway to a room with medical equipment. Seadon listened as the man who did all the talking in the desert continued.

"Doctor Breighton, Commander Quinn ordered this man to be seen to. We found him in the desert not ten minutes ago."

An older man, distinguished looking with streaks of gray in his otherwise black hair, stood over Seadon looking down at his bruised and battered body. His kind eyes looked into Seadon's barely opened slits, obviously seeing pain. "Captain Trent, could you see an exit wound for whatever made this garish hole in his side?"

"Not when we picked him up off the ground. But there is so much blood all around that area, there could be an exit wound."

"His clothing is unlike anything I've ever seen before. Do you know where he came from?"

"No, he hasn't spoken."

"Well that is certainly no surprise in his condition. Move him over to the operating table. I need to get started immediately."

"Yes, Doctor."

Captain Trent motioned toward his officers who quickly did as ordered. Seadon lay there staring upward at some bright lights just above him. A young woman with black-rimmed glasses stood over him. She placed an oxygen mask over his nose and mouth, strapping it around his head.

She looked down into his eyes, and said, "Do you have a name?"

Seadon's whisper was barely audible. "Seadon Brinley."

She grinned sweetly. "Well, don't worry, Mr. Brinley, you're in excellent hands, and we'll have you fixed up good as new in no time." She then proceeded to remove his clothing and clean the area where the bullet entered his skin.

"Marlaya," Doctor Breighton instructed, "make sure to sterilize the area well. From what I'm told, he was laying in the desert at the base of the Jaraphite Mountains. He may have some contamination so use the tracer to find out before we start so we know exactly what we are dealing with here."

"Yes, Dr. Breighton."

Seadon's mind whirled with questions, though his mouth could not express them. He listened as intently as possible for as long as he could, before he slowly drifted off into a painless, deep sleep as they worked diligently on his damaged body.

Seadon awoke, realizing it had to be hours later as the sun outside the windows of the hospital room had already receded behind the distant mountains. He had an I.V. in his arm, and a bandage over the previous hole in his side wrapped tightly with a bandage around his waist. He lay there, wondering where he was and what sort of world he had landed in this time. It couldn't be all bad if they had patched him up and left him unattended in a rather comfortable, and quite tastefully decorated room with a view; one like he had never before seen.

As he lay peering out the concaved window with it's high, pointed top and decorative glass-work around the top edge, the door to his room opened. He turned to greet what he assumed would be the doctor or nurse, but instead the shadowy figure of a woman began toward him. When the dim moonlight from the window captured her appearance, Seadon was taken aback. She was beautiful, in a dangerous sort of way. She was dressed in the same military uniform as the men who had rescued him, but the patches along the left side of her chest and on each shoulder said she was likely a higher-ranking officer.

"Glad to see you're awake and doing well. We weren't sure at first if you would pull through from all the blood loss and sun exposure." She walked into the room and stood beside his bed. Her dark eyes peering down at him. Those eyes reminded him of something, but he couldn't remember what.

"I'm grateful to whoever brought me here and patched me up." Seadon grinned slightly and tried pushing himself further up in the bed to talk.

"I'm Quinn Quimby." She stuck out her hand to shake his. Seadon took her hand. It was soft, yet strong. "One of the guards saw you lying out in the desert. However did you end up there? You're certainly not from around here."

"I can't say that I remember," Seadon said with a shake of his head. There was no way he was going to tell her he had time-traveled.

She gave him a curious side-ways glance before continuing. "So do you know who you are?"

"Yeah, I'm pretty sure that's not something I'd forget." Seadon smiled cockily.

"Well, I just assumed you had amnesia since you don't know how you got to the desert." Quinn gave him one of her own cocky smiles right back.

"I guess I was too out of it from my injuries by the time I reached the desert."

"Perhaps." She grinned again. "So, you never told me your name."

"Seadon Brinley, ma'am." He smiled again.

"I have to say, you do look familiar to me. Where do you come from?" Quinn's mind searched for where she knew him from.

"Just some place you've likely never heard of," Seadon stated.

"Try me. I've traveled to a few places when I was younger."

"I doubt you've been to where I'm from." Seadon grinned.

Quinn just raised her eyebrows in question waiting for him to answer.

Seadon cleared his throat and sat up further in the bed, feeling quite dominated by this strong-willed woman.

"Zanchier. That's where I hail from."

Quinn grinned. "You're right. I've never heard of such a place."

Seadon asked, "What about you? Where are you from, Quinn?"

"What makes you think I'm not from here?"

"Just trying to get to know the locals." Seadon smiled. "Where is here anyway?"

"This city is known as Montesario-Belarusel."

"That's a mouthful," Seadon joked.

Quinn grinned at his humor. "Yes, it is. It is an old-family monarchy. Ruled by King Montesario himself."

"Where does the Belarusel come from?"

"From the first union of marriages that connected the two cities into one, hundreds of years ago. Belarusel was the surname of the princess that the prince of Montesario married to join the two kingdoms. So, in joining the two kingdoms, the names of both were changed to Montesario-Belarusel so that neither kingdom was overshadowed by the first."

"Well, you surely seem to know you're local history." Seadon grinned.

"As Commander of the guard it's my job to know a lot of things, Mr. Brinley." Quinn smirked and said, "Now, I suppose I'll leave you to your rest. I'll return tomorrow to see if you are well enough to walk, and then we'll see about getting you to your destination."

"Oh, I have no destination. Just a man traveling who ended up in a nice place. And you can call me Seadon."

Quinn nodded and smiled. "Good night, Seadon. I hope you sleep well."

"Goodnight, Quinn. And I'm sure that I will." Seadon smiled and lay back against the soft pillows as Quinn exited, pulling the door closed behind her.

He hadn't had a place so comfortable in which to sleep since he was living at home. Sure, the bunks at the Airship Academy weren't horrible, but it wasn't like home, and it sure wasn't like this place. Especially since he had just slept on the hard cot in a ship's brig for the last few months. This was luxury to him. He pushed back into the pillows as the moonlight filled his room. He had a feeling he was going to like Montesario-Belarusel.

Chapter 7

Seadon woke to a disturbance in his room. He looked up from his night of blissful slumber to Marlaya puttering about.

She smiled brightly as he sleepily looked at her. "Good morning, Mr. Brinley. How are you feeling today?"

Seadon gave a small smile in return. "Fine. I slept very well, and I'm not in much pain."

"That's very good to hear, sir. Dr. Breighton will be in soon to speak to you about your ongoing care, but you should be able to leave today as long as you follow the doctor's instructions."

"Thank you, Marlaya." Seadon smiled at her and he swore he saw her blush.

She asked, "Do you need anything else before I go?"

"Nothing at all darlin'."

Marlaya giggled at the endearment, blushing all the way up her neck into her face. She gave him a little nod and curtsied before she walked briskly out of the room, grinning from ear to ear.

Seadon sat up and swung his feet over the edge of the bed and smiled to himself. "I still got it."

"Still have what?" he heard someone say from behind him.

He jerked around to see Dr. Breighton walking into his room.

Seadon suddenly felt a bit foolish. "Nothing Doc. Just making an observation to myself," he said as he slid from the bed. The coolness of the floor felt wonderful on his bare feet.

"I expect you are referring to the blush and giggling nature of my nurse Marlaya," Dr. Breighton stated rather than questioned.

Seadon replied, "She seems like a sweet kid."

"She is both sweet, and a kid," Dr. Breighton warned.

"Don't worry, Doc. She's not my type. Too young and too easily swayed. Besides, I'm not looking for a relationship."

"Good to hear. Now, how are you feeling today, Mr. Brinley? I expect there isn't much pain as you seem to handle walking with ease."

"I feel fine. Just a little soreness in my side, but I figure I'll heal well enough."

Doctor Breighton walked over to the counter and lifted a ball from a tray. He carried it over to Seadon and asked, "What sort of ancient weapon fires something so large?"

"That would be from a handgun. A pistol I believe."

"I've never seen anything like it. Where exactly did you get shot with a weapon such as what you described, and what did you do to get shot in the first place?"

"Well as far as where, you wouldn't believe me if I told you, Doc. And for the why, let's just say someone thought they owned me and I felt otherwise."

"Well, on the where, try me. I've lived here my entire life, except for a few excursions in my younger days to train for the medical field. I've seen many strangers from other places but none quite like you, Mr. Brinley. As for the why, no one should be owned by another person. However, your clothing, mannerisms, and even the barbaric scars on your back tell me you have quite a story to tell."

Seadon looked at him abruptly at the mention of his scars. "Let's just say that in other places I've been, people have not behaved so kindly to me as you have here."

"I can't imagine what you could have done that was so horrific that someone whipped you across your back. But then again, I know so little of you. I hope we won't have any problems with you here in Montesario-Belarusel."

"Doc, I don't plan to cause problems for anyone. I just want to get on with my life and see where this new road will take me."

"Well, Mr. Brinley…"

"Seadon. Just call me Seadon, Doc."

"All right, Seadon. Your clothing has been laundered, although I'm not sure all the staining was removable. They are a bit tattered in some places, but we had them mended by a local seamstress; especially the hole in your shirt; until you can get something better to wear. You'll have to take it easy for a week or so until your side heals completely. Nothing too strenuous or adventurous." The Doctor handed Seadon his clothing which had been neatly folded and placed on the counter.

"You say that like you think I might go out and try to climb the nearby mountain, Doc." Seadon took his clothing and tossed them onto the bed.

"You seem to be an adventurous man, Seadon. I hope you heed my warnings and just give it some time."

"I'll certainly do what I can to keep myself calm and out of trouble."

Doctor Breighton gave a small, crooked smirk at Seadon's reply. "Seadon, I have a feeling that trouble follows you."

Seadon stood at the window, his back to the doctor, looking down over the beautiful city and landscape below. "Well, now that isn't my fault Doc. It's not like I called it to come."

Doctor Breighton chuckled. "Commander Quimby said she would be by to collect you when you are released, so you can expect her at any time."

Seadon turned to look at the Doctor. "Collect me? Where is she planning to take me?" He turned back to the window, his aggravation at the doctor's comment making his temper rise.

"Since you know no one else here in the city, she figured you could use some assistance. You'll have to ask her what her plans for you are."

"Yeah, well, we will see about her plans. I may have some plans of my own, and they aren't to let someone else tell me what to do. Especially not some high-ranking, military commander with control issues."

"Talking about me?" Seadon heard Quinn's voice. He quickly turned to see her standing in the room just inside the door.

He rolled his eyes, "Doesn't anybody around here ever knock?"

She gestured at the open door. "The door was open."

"Yeah, well, I could have been naked you know."

"Then I assume that in such a situation, that your door would have been closed."

The doctor cleared his throat and said, "If you two will excuse me, I have other patients to see to." He then nodded and left the room.

Seadon looked at Quinn and she him. He asked, "Is there something you need, Commander?"

"I was just coming to inquire about how you are doing today, and to see what your plans are while you're here in Montesario-Belarusel?"

"First, I'm doing just fine. Second, why do you care what my plans are? That's my business."

"Perhaps, Mr. Brinley, but you see, city security is my business. And from the looks of you," she nodded at his side, "you're trouble, or at least you seem to find it. So, what you plan to do while here is very much my business. We are a very accepting people, and kindness is something you will find in most everyone, but do not mistake kindness for weakness, for you will live to regret it."

"Yes, ma'am," Seadon said, nodding to her. "Now, am I free to go, or do I have to tag along with you all day until you determine that I'm not a threat?"

"You're free to go, Mr. Brinley, but be aware that I and my team will be watching you very carefully, for a while at least."

"Fine. Now, unless you plan to begin your surveillance now by staying to watch me get dressed, I'm afraid that I'll have to ask you to leave. Oh, and, close the door on your way out."

"I have no intention of watching you that closely Mr. Brinley. Besides, you have nothing to see that's any different than anything I haven't already seen. Good day, Mr. Brinley." Quinn nodded, grinned, and walked out the door, pulling it closed behind her.

Seadon mumbled disdainfully under his breath while pulling on his clothing. He finished and left the room to wander the beautiful city to which he had been fortunate enough to time-travel. He had to admit he was hungry. He had no idea how long it had been since he had something to eat. He supposed he should have waited until they fed him breakfast in his hospital room, but it was too late for that.

As he walked the paved road from the hospital's high place on the mountain side, down toward the bustling markets and businesses he saw yesterday, he was fortunate to pass a tree that seemed to bear some sort of fruit. The pinkish-purple flesh with its bumpy, berry-like surface was larger than his hand and oval in shape. He noticed that the birds and animals seemed to eat of it by the scattered, half-eaten, fallen fruit.

Thinking it safe to eat he plucked one, smelled it, and took a cautious bite. The juicy sweet and spicy flavor of the fruit made his taste-buds sing. He hadn't had anything that tasted this good in a long time. He quickly stuffed a few more of the fruits into his pant-pockets and continued his walk. One side of the road was flanked by towering mountainsides, waterfalls, and upward growing trees and bushes with buildings tucked in between. The opposite side of the road was graced with a steep hillside that sank to the open courtyard below with much the same scenery as the other side.

He soon reached the level part of the road where it fully opened up onto a large courtyard area with moving vendors walking back and forth. Some of their carts were parked in what appeared to be a temporary spot. This market reminded him of Praxtingen Market back home. The difference was that the streets in Praxtingen had been packed on both sides with vendors tucked neatly in and around other businesses, such as hotels, animal auction areas, and eateries.

Here, there was no street, just a large, open area paved with cobblestone. Seadon walked past the vendors, chatting with them and checking out their wares. He was unable to purchase anything due to the lack of usable currency. He would need to find a way to quickly make some money.

As he walked he noticed that the open square did indeed lead to small streets that twisted and turned in different directions. Along those streets sat small businesses, one in particular caught his sailor-weathered eye. A brothel, one where men stumbled into and out of an ever-swinging door. He smiled to himself. Some things never changed, no matter where in the world you went. If man could figure out a way to make mead, he would. And someone apparently had here in Montesario-Belarusel.

"Now, time to figure out the local gaming situation, and to have a little fun."

What he didn't notice was Quinn Quimby and Captain Trent following behind him, far enough away to not be seen, but close enough to not lose him in the crowd of people who mingled and walked the streets nearly every night. Quinn watched Seadon enter the tavern and she sighed heavily.

"And so it begins. I had a feeling it wouldn't take that man long to find the seediest part of town."

Trent replied, "What now Commander?"

"We wait," she replied. "I have a feeling that within a few hours' time, Seadon Brinley will make an appearance. Either through a brawl with the local riff-raff, or all on his own with a full purse and a fuller belly. Hopefully, it's the latter so I won't have to arrest him for drunk and disorderly conduct."

Several hours later, to Quinn's chagrin, Seadon still had not exited the tavern. She and Trent decided to enter the establishment to find out what was going on. Once inside, they quickly spotted Seadon Brinley seated at a gaming table fully involved in a game of Shark. She had no idea how he had learned the difficult card game so quickly, which he obviously had based on the stack of local coins and bills he had in front of him. Seadon Brinley was proving to be a more complicated man than she expected.

One of the problems with Shark was that it was not only a card game, but a drinking game as well. The winner of each hand would have to drink a shot. The other players figured that this leveled the field. If one player wins too much, then after several shots of the strongest stuff behind the bar, they would begin to loosen up and lose their focus, giving the others a chance to win their money back. However Seadon Brinley didn't look drunk.

Quinn and Trent took a seat at the bar so they could see Seadon, but he couldn't see them. They sat watching the game ensue with Seadon losing a hand on occasion. Quinn figured that it was only so he wouldn't have to drink so much, since the hands he lost were small change compared to most of the hands that he played and won.

Several more hours went by and it seemed that the entire tavern was vested in the game which still included six men. Five had left just since Quinn had entered the establishment, many grumbling that they were broke, and others were too drunk to walk across the floor without bouncing off of everyone and everything they passed.

Quinn and Trent ordered dinner, and a few drinks. By the time they had finished eating their meal, and consuming their second glass of beverage each, the game of Shark was coming to a close as the men began to complain that they were busted. They fussed about Seadon being a newcomer and learning the game so quickly.

"Just good luck, boys. I've always been quick to learn such things. But I think it's time I retire. It's been a rather long day for me."

Curstel Borman, one of the local men who usually won at the tavern gaming tables, began to protest. "No, no, no. You can't just leave now. You have to give us a chance to win our earnings back. I can't go home flat busted. My wife will kill me!"

"Sorry, sir, but I'm done. Perhaps tomorrow night."

Curstel stood quickly, his chair falling over behind him from the force of his standing. He pointed a finger at Seadon and leaned over the table. "Now see here, fella. You're gonna' sit there and give me a chance to win my money back. I still have enough to put in for a few more hands."

Seadon stood, glaring at the man. "I said I'm done for the night."

The man's voice began to raise in agitation, "I said you're not!"

"Curstel Borman," Quinn's even tone broke the tension in the room, "the man said he's done."

"But, Commander Quimby, it ain't fair…"

Quinn moved quickly and stood in front of him. "Curstel, if you can't afford to lose, don't play the game. Now Mr. Brinley said he's done. And you are going to sit back down and enjoy the remainder of your evening, or I'll haul you home or to jail. Your choice."

Curstel sat back down. "I'll just sit here a while longer Commander Quimby. No need for either of those threats to take place."

"Glad to hear it."

Quinn turned to Seadon.

"Commander Quimby, how nice to see you again so soon," Seadon stated sarcastically.

"Mr. Brinley." She nodded. "I must say, I'm quite surprised to find you…still intact."

"I suppose you figured I'd be drunk by now and in a brawl with the local boys."

"Yes, that's exactly what I expected. And I was nearly correct."

Seadon tossed back another shot glass full of dark liquid and stuffed his winnings into his pockets. "Thanks for the coin boys. I hope to play you all again soon."

The grumbles and discontent around the table said that no one was in a hurry to do so. Seadon then turned toward Quinn and closed the short distance between them, stopping just in front of her, their faces just inches apart.

"I had everything under control, I assure you. And as far as being drunk, I hate to disappoint you, but I rarely get drunk, no matter how much I drink. And I don't really care for fighting. It's not sporting when you know you'll win. Have a good night, Commander." Seadon turned, took a few more steps toward the door, his pockets heaving with his winnings from the night, and then suddenly passed clean out, face planting on the floor. The entire place roared in laughter at his expense.

Quinn and Trent walked over to him and rolled him onto his back. Trent said, "Commander, I think we have a problem."

"What is it?" she asked.

"From the stains on his fingers and around the edges of his pant-pockets, it looks as though he consumed several of the Pepperberries from a Pepperbark tree."

Quinn sighed. "This is why I wanted to show the man around before turning him loose in the city. Call for a float-cart. He's much too big and heavy to carry. We need to get him up and to the hospital quickly."

"Yes, Commander." Captain Trent stood and went outside the noisy tavern to make the call.

Quinn leaned over Seadon's still body as she waited for the cart to arrive. "Well, I'm afraid it's back to the hospital with you, Mr. Brinley. And I don't see you leaving any time soon."

Captain Trent entered the establishment ten minutes later with the cart and lowered it to the floor. He and Quinn heaved Seadon's limp body onto it and then set the controls to raise up and float at waist level. They pushed him out of the door and connected the float-cart to a waiting speeder. Quinn hopped onto the speeder and took off toward the hospital once again with their unexpected guest.

Once she arrived, she unhooked the float-cart and pushed it into the hospital to find Marlaya at the receiving station. The look on Marlaya's face was one of concern. It was both touching and comical at the same time. The poor girl obviously had a crush on Seadon Brinley, although Quinn couldn't possibly understand why. The man was arrogant, rude, underhanded, sneaky, and conniving. An obvious rogue if she ever saw one. Still, she didn't want to see harm come to the man, no matter what her opinion of him was.

"What happened to him again, already?"

Quinn smiled. "He'll be fine if treatment is started soon enough, but I suspect that he has Pepperberry-alcohol poisoning."

"Oh my," the young woman said, concerned. "I'll page Doctor Breighton immediately."

As Marlaya rushed away, Seadon stirred a little, his eyes fluttering open as he peered into the face of Quinn.

Quinn leaned close to him and said, "It looks as though the fall you took when you passed out at the tavern has reopened your stitches. You're bleeding a little from your side. But that's not the worst of it. You've poisoned yourself by consuming Pepperberry and liquor together. Let's hope you have a strong constitution, Mr. Brinley, you're going to need it tonight, and maybe even into tomorrow depending on how much you've consumed. Before it's over, you may wish you were dead."

Marlaya returned and wheeled Seadon down the hall and back into the very room he left out of just six hours earlier. Seadon watched blurry eyed as Quinn turned and walked out of the hospital, her words bouncing around in his spinning head.

Chapter 8

Seadon woke several times during the night with horrible fits of retching and severe stomach pains. His entire body felt as though it were in shock. He hurt and ached all over with the contraction of his protesting muscles. His head felt as though it would explode. He had never experienced such illness in his entire life. With each episode he fully awoke to violent retching and then completely passed out again from exhaustion.

On one occasion he awoke enough to wonder where he was. He realized he was back in the hospital. He was aware of a nurse or someone in the room. Someone would occasionally wipe his perspiring brow and give him water to rinse his mouth, then cover him back up as he collapsed against the pillows. And he remembered Quinn bringing him back and saying something about Pepperberry and alcohol poisoning, and that he would wish he were dead before it were over. She was absolutely correct on that matter. Seadon didn't know how much more he could take. If he hadn't been hospitalized, he likely would have died. All because he couldn't handle the bossy Commander Quinn telling him what to do in this new city.

When morning's light broke through the window, and the landscape outside was bathed in shadowy light, Seadon wanted to crawl under the covers and block out the world. He threw the sheets over his head and sank further down into the bed, just before Dr. Breighton came into the room.

"Good morning, Seadon. How are you feeling today?"

Seadon exhaled heavily and pushed himself above the covers into a sitting position. "I'm better Doc, not great, but better."

"Good to hear. Marlaya and the other nurses weren't so certain you were going to pull through. You're a very blessed man."

Seadon ignored the man's reference to being blessed. "I'll admit, it was really rough for a while. I wanted to die and get it over with, but this morning I have a new perspective on death, and that blasted Pepperberry fruit."

Dr. Breighton grinned at him. "Technically, it's not the fruit, just the mixture of the fruit and alcohol, especially in the amount with which you drank last night. Your Blood-Alcohol-Level was very high. I don't know how you didn't pass out from that alone."

"It's a curse I guess, Doc. I can drink, but hardly ever get drunk. I just feel a little buzz on occasion."

"Well, then, may I suggest that you refrain from alcohol at all. Just because you can't feel the effects of something, does not mean it isn't doing damage to your body. And in the future, Pepperberries are quite delicious and healthy for you, just don't drink alcohol with them or within an eight-hour period."

"At the moment, I have no desire or taste for either of the aforementioned food groups."

"Well, that's quite understandable. However, you'll have to stay here for at least another few hours before we can release you. We want to make sure the poison is out of your system before we turn you loose again. And you'll need to take it easy for the remainder of the day, drink plenty of hydrating fluids, and eat light foods. Also, you should thank Commander Quimby for keeping such a close eye on you. If not for her diligence of duty, you, sir, would be dead right now."

"I'll try to remember that doc.."

Marlaya entered the room carrying Seadon's shirt in her hands. "I took the liberty of having your shirt laundered again

Mr. Brinley. The other nurse and I had to remove it last night. You had vomited on it from your horrible ordeal. Plus you reopened your wound and had bled some as well. You look better this morning."

"Thank you. Marlaya, I do feel better. And thank you, and the other nurse, for tending to me last night. I certainly would have had a much worse time of it."

"Yes, I believe Commander Quimby delivered you to us just in the nick of time."

"Yeah, I keep hearing that." Seadon felt that with each praise of Commander Quimby's diligence and foresight he was doomed to eat crow. As Seadon sat up and swung his legs over the edge of the bed to put on his shirt and take a trip to the bathroom, Quinn walked into the room. Her eyes caught sight of Seadon's back and she was slightly taken aback by the scars that marred his tanned, muscular flesh.

She cleared her throat to announce her arrival. Seadon turned to look at her as he slipped his shirt on.

"I see you made it through the night," Quinn stated.

"Yes. And apparently, I have you to thank for saving my life yet a second time, Commander Quimby." Seadon stood there waiting for the conversation to continue, his head still spinning a little.

"You're welcome."

Quinn smirked at his look of surprise at her reply.

"It must be exhausting saving everyone from their mistakes, Commander."

The look on Quinn's face was brief, but Seadon definitely saw something in it. Her demeanor changed as well, becoming colder toward him.

"Well, Mr. Brinley, I'm glad to see you're alive. I pray you get well soon and enjoy your time, however *short* that is, in

Montesario-Belarusel." Quinn turned and quickly left before Seadon even had a chance to reply.

He wasn't sure what had happened to cause her such a quick exit. He had somehow flustered her with his words. Quinn Quimby had something in her past that apparently bothered her to think of, and it had something to do with what he said about her saving people.

Marlaya came into his room with a plate of fruit and eggs. After a quick thank you to her and a trip to the bathroom he hungrily ate the plate of food, careful not to overstuff his still delicate stomach. After a few hours of rest and recuperation, Dr. Breighton signed his release orders.

Seadon had expected Commander Quinn to return at his release to show him the ropes, but she did not. So, Seadon stepped out of the hospital on his own once again. He would avoid eating from any fruit trees, and with his winnings in his pocket he had no need of tavern life, for a while that is.

As Seadon walked the now familiar road down to the square, he noticed, off in the distance, on the other side of the city, a rather impressive-looking castle. Even from a good distance it's walls appeared thick and strong, yet sleek with a structural design that stated elegance and wealth. Seadon was curious about the castle and decided to head in that direction. He did remember Quinn saying something about a king ruling over the region. He wondered how close he would be able to get to the castle before the castle guards escorted him away. There was only one way to find out, and that was to go exploring.

It took him a few hours to walk to the castle. He had to meander the city roads, cross a bridge over a river which flowed from a high mountain stream and waterfall, and trek the last few miles through a heavily wooded area. As he got closer to the castle's exterior walls that encircled the outer courtyards of the castle grounds, he walked through an ornately designed triple entryway. It looked like it had been abandoned for a few years. Vines and bushes threatened to overtake the structure and stone pathway which was barely visible beneath the forest debris and overgrowth that connected it to the castle.

Seadon stood beneath the old, yet still beautifully intricate entryway gazing up at the workmanship when he heard something behind him. He turned to see a beautiful woman watching him from the farthest end of the path which ended at an opened gate in the castle wall. She wore a blue dress that cinched tightly around a small waist. The skirt of the dress belled around her. Her puffed sleeves drooped slightly from the shoulders and fell to long sleeves that sat snuggly on her lower arms. She had a crown upon her head that sat encompassed by big, loose, brown curls cascading down toward her shoulders. Seadon's breath caught in his throat at the sight of her standing there just looking at him. The castle loomed behind her and the sunlight that streaked through the tree canopy danced around her in the slight breeze, creating enchanting shadows on the ground.

"What are you doing here?" the young woman asked.

For a moment Seadon wasn't certain she was speaking to him, lost in her beauty he was speechless, then he snapped out of the haze. "Just gazing upon the beauty that lay in this forest." Seadon could tell she understood his double meaning.

"That's not an actual answer to my question."

"I'm just a weary traveler, Miss, exploring this beautiful city."

"You need to be careful of where you explore, sir. And in the future, it will do you well to address me as Princess Willamina."

Seadon understood the power struggle happening at the moment, so he bowed slightly and nodded graciously to the princess. "My apologies, Princess Willamina. I had no idea I was speaking to a member of the royal family of Montesario-Belarusel."

"Now you do. Remember it to avoid future faux pas."

Seadon nodded and bowed slightly again.

"I've never seen you before. I thought I knew all the people of Montesario-Belarusel." Princess Willamina walked cautiously closer to Seadon.

"I've only just arrived here yesterday."

"And where exactly is it that you have come from?"

"No place that you'd know, Princess."

"Princess Willamina." She defiantly stood straighter as if trying to make herself taller.

"So sorry, my mistake, Princess Willamina."

"Since you refuse to tell me where it is you come from, I suppose I will have to find out for myself."

"Not refusing, I just truly doubt you've ever heard of my homeland, or the many places that I've traveled over the years."

She stared at him with uncertainty, unsure if he were sincere or teasing her.

"Well, perhaps you should tell me of these places. Life here at the castle can be rather dull most days. You appear as though you've had some excitement in your life." She pointed to Seadon's shabby, stained, and tattered clothing.

Seadon smiled and dared to step a little closer. Each of them inched their way toward each other as they spoke. "Oh, I've had many adventures, Princess Willamina. I've fought in wars at fourteen, rode on the backs of massive creatures which my sisters could communicate with, flown airships in peace and in battle. I've been kidnapped, forced into slavery and life on board a boat, sailing the seas and skies with pirates. Been beaten, shot, and feared for my abilities, and walked through time just to be here with you now."

Princess Willamina had never heard such a story. She grinned slightly. "I think, sir, that you are teasing me. And you have an unfair advantage. You know who I am, but I don't know your name."

"Seadon Brinley, at your service, my lady." Seadon knew how to speak to people, how to charm them. He was a pirate after all, and an educated one at that.

"Well, Mr. Brinley, I'd say it was nice to meet you, but I am wholly uncertain that it is just yet."

By the time they each stopped moving toward one another they were scarcely ten feet apart. Seadon could see the color of her eyes. They were blue like the sea he so loved to sail upon. Her skin was creamy and smooth, likely shaded most of her life from the sun's rays. Her hair was a soft yellow brown with large curls swept up into a messy bun that toppled around her shiny, silver crown. Her gown, although big, seemed lighter than air as it flowed in the slightest breeze. He was surprised to see that she was barefoot.

They both stood there, looking at each other, taking in the other's appearance. Seadon figured he looked quite shabby to her in all of her fine clothes.

She pointed to the recently mended hole in his shirt and the stain that accompanied it. "What is that on your shirt?"

Seadon looked down at the dull, now brown, stain. "Blood, my lady. You see, I was recently shot and although the doctors and nurses here are miracle workers and saved my life, they unfortunately could not get all of the stain from my clothing." Seadon's thoughts returned to Commander Quimby at the mention of his life being saved. He shook her from his thoughts and continued speaking to the beauty before him.

"Oh my. Perhaps your tales of pirates and time-walking are true. May I see the wound? For clarity's sake."

Seadon smirked a little. "I'm afraid it's not a pretty sight."

"I'll manage," Willamina said, anxious to see if he were telling the truth.

Seadon lifted the tail of his shirt to reveal the still red and slightly swollen area, especially after the night of retching which had reopened the wound.

Willamina stepped back, now a little unsure what to make of him, realizing that perhaps everything he told her was the truth. She began to speak as Seadon lowered his shirt but was cut off. A deep masculine voice called out from the other side of the large wall, interrupting their quiet meeting.

"Princess Willa?"

"I'm here, Captain."

Captain Trent appeared around the corner and stopped in his tracks when he spied the scene before him.

"Mr. Brinley, what are you doing out here?"

"Walking and exploring, Captain. As you know I've been rather infirmed on my first few days in town."

"Yes, I recall. But how did you find your way here to the castle?"

"This morning I spied this majestic structure from the city and just had to get a closer look. Then this magnificent creature stumbled upon me as I was admiring this wonderful structure that just sits out here in the woods."

Willamina blushed at his compliment, and Trent looked none too pleased. "Refrain from speaking of the princess in such a flippant manner, sir." Captain Trent stepped between him and Willamina, his defense of her quite telling.

"My manner was not flippant in any way, Captain, I assure you. Merely stating a fact in observation of stunning beauty."

Trent turned to Willamina. "Princess Willa, I think it is time to return to the safety of the castle gates and walls."

Willamina looked at the captain with a reprimanding gaze. "I assure you, Captain, I am quite safe. Please do not think that you may instruct my manner, or my day just because Commander Quimby assigned you to my security detail."

Trent looked contrite and bowed his head. "My apologies, Princess Willa, just doing my duty."

"Yes, well see that your duty does not overstep in the future, Captain."

Captain Trent only nodded, his jawline tightening in embarrassment.

Willamina turned to Seadon. "Mr. Brinley, I should like to speak with you further, to hear more about your life and adventures. I wish you to come to the castle later today, say twelve noon for lunch. And do see if you can find something more suitable to wear. And perhaps take a bath as well."

Willamina turned to walk back through the gate as a stunned Seadon stood there. Captain Trent smirked at the look on his face and said, "You'll find that Willamina Montesario has her own mind and is not afraid to speak it."

Seadon asked, "So I see. Do you know where I can find appropriate clothing and a place to take a bath?" Seadon said the last part with aggravation. He supposed he did look quite shabbily and likely smelled as well.

Trent pointed the way Seadon had come through the woods. "Across the river bridge to the left is a small square of shops that should be able to supply you with some new clothing. There is also a barber there who offers the works."

"Thank you, Captain. Good day." Seadon turned and walked away as Trent watched him go.

Trent wasn't too keen on Seadon Brinley getting to dine with Princess Willamina. Seadon seemed dangerous, but he supposed that was what made Willa curious about him. She spent way too much time in the castle and going to royal events. However, every day her driver would take her slowly through town in her open-air, horse-drawn carriage, and she would take in the city and its people, asking the driver questions as they went. Other than that, she never really got out of the castle much, which was surprising because she seemed to know about everyone in town. He figured she spent her days studying the people on her rides through the city streets. Trent turned and walked back inside the castle gate, pulling it securely closed.

Seadon crossed the river bridge and turned left. After a few hundred feet or so, he found a tailor's shop and walked inside. The man who greeted him looked him up and down. "Can I help you, sir?"

Seadon noticed that, sir, was said with disdain. He pulled the wad of cash from his pocket and wiggled it in front of the man's nose. "I need some clothing and something appropriate to wear to dine with Princess Willamina."

The man's eyebrows went up in surprise and then he smiled broadly. "This way, sir."

That time, sir, had some respect attached to it. It never failed, no matter where one went in the world money always talked. Seadon had the man find him something simple to change into after his barber visit, with a promise to return for a proper fitting of dress attire after a shave and bath. He walked the few hundred steps across the street to the barbershop with a cotton shirt, and a pair of slacks and new boots and, of course, the necessary undergarments.

The barber took him to a back room where a young boy attended to filling the tub with hot water and supplying Seadon with soap and shampoo. Seadon scrubbed well, brushed his teeth, and dressed; asking the boy for a fresh bandage for his side. He didn't want to chance ruining his new clothing. He was then led to a shop chair where the Barber cut his hair and shaved his thickly-stubbled face clean. After which, he splashed some aftershave on his face and neck, paid the barber for his services and left. As Seadon walked the street between the two shops he presented a striking figure. Women everywhere turned to watch him. Seadon grinned to himself. When he returned to the clothing shop to be fitted for his suit the shop tailer nearly dropped his pincushion.

"Well, you certainly clean up well, sir, if you don't mind my saying."

"Not at all." Seadon smiled.

He spent the next hour being properly fitted for his very first suit. Nothing too fancy, just a deep blue jacket and matching slacks to be worn over a pristinely white silk shirt. Seadon took his purchases and inquired about a hotel. The tailor directed him down a few blocks. Seadon found the hotel and checked into a room. He left his shirt and slacks on the bed, then went to ask the hotel clerk where he might find transportation.

After finding the shops he was instructed to, Seadon priced the speeders. Too rich for his pockets at the moment, so he walked down to the stables to inquire about renting a horse.

The stable keeper said, "To rent one, sir, is twenty dollars a day. I can make you a deal for purchasing one. Five-hundred outright and Old Buttercup here is yours. Then you can stable her for a hundred a week. We take care of food, grooming, and tacking for you; just let us know when you are on your way."

"Buttercup, huh." Seadon studied the old, tired-looking mare. "You don't have one that sounds more…masculine?"

"We have one we call killer, over in that stall there. But I don't recommend him for a gentleman such as yourself."

The man pointed to a stall where a magnificent-looking, large, black stallion pranced excitedly around his stall, tossing his head and mane about as though he were ready to run; like he was tired of being locked up in a small cell. Seadon understood this.

"I'll take Killer."

"Are…are you sure, sir?" the man asked nervously. "All sales are final, sir. And Killer there hasn't properly been broken yet, sir. The boys have had a hard time of it."

"I'm sure. And I'll buy him outright. Have him saddled and ready to go. I'll be back in thirty minutes."

Seadon left the stables and went in search of a shop where he could buy a small gift to present to his lovely lunch companion, hoping to gain another invite for another day.

Chapter 9

Seadon soon returned to the stable with his gift tucked neatly in a pocket. Killer was ready and pranced nervously in his stall.

The stable hand walked the horse outside, handed Seadon the reins, and he mounted the horse. Killer pranced nervously, though Seadon was unsure whether it was from excitement, or distaste for the man on his back. Seadon steadied the animal and then the two of them took off like a shot.

Seadon wasn't sure if Killer had pent up energy from being stabled for a long period of time, or if the horse just liked to run. Seadon gave him his head and just held on. He did manage to turn the horse in the direction of the river bridge, and when they reached the forest he let him run for as long as he liked. He did try to veer Killer toward the direction of the castle. He figured it would do him no good to keep Princess Willamina waiting. It would not bring him into her good graces; figuring it would have the opposite effect.

He managed to get Killer to slow his pace a bit and to head toward the castle grounds. When he arrived for his lunch engagement one of the castle's stable hands ran out and took the reins from him.

Seadon said, "Make sure he gets plenty of water. He's had quite a run."

"Yes sir," the young man assured him.

Seadon tugged at his jacket to straighten himself from the wild ride over. Perhaps buying the stallion had been a mistake. He certainly wouldn't be able to take anyone else on a ride with him until he managed to get the horse under control. He ran his fingers through his hair to make sure everything was in place and approached the massive double doors.

Before he could knock, one door swung open and he was ushered through the large foyer, then the receiving room, and out the back doors to a beautiful patio with a balcony that overlooked much of the city and lake. He was guided to a table where a display of food awaited him. The princess was nowhere to be seen yet. He supposed it was not customary for her to be waiting on her guests. She would likely make an entrance at any moment.

Seadon took a seat and sat looking out at the landscape. It was strangely divided. The portion to the right was another part of the bustling city, oddly divided by a wall running through the center, separating the two halves. One side must be Montesario and the other Belarusel. Past the lake a mountainous region sat just this side of the desolate, dry, desert. The climate of the surrounding mountains appeared just as dry.

As he sipped from the offered glass of water on the table, Princess Willamina made her appearance through the large doors of the patio. She was dressed differently than she had been this morning. Her gown now was one a bit understated and simpler than that of the earlier one. The color was a soft yellow with hints of colorful flowers that seemed to fall from her waist down along the length of her gown which brushed the ground as she walked.

"Mr. Brinley, I see you made it on time. And I dare say that you clean up very nicely."

"Thank you, Princess Willamina, and I certainly wouldn't want to keep you waiting on me."

"I hear you arrived on horseback."

"Is that unacceptable?"

"Not at all. I love horses and often travel that way myself."

"That's good to know since Killer will be my main means of transportation."

"Killer? He sounds rather dangerous in nature."

"Perhaps, but I think he just needs more time out of the stables."

"Well, see that he gets it. Now, Mr. Brinley, do you plan to stay here in Montesario-Belarusel?"

"I haven't yet decided, my lady. As I said this morning, I only just arrived here yesterday, and I am unsure what there is here to hold my interest enough to stay."

She grinned at his answer. "Well, you'll likely be needing a job, unless you are a man of certain means who doesn't need to make a living."

"I will be looking for employment of some kind. However, I'm afraid that my skills do not appear to be needed in a place such as this."

"Oh? And what are these skills of which you speak?"

"I'm a sailor, Your Highness, of both water and sky. And since I have been here, I have seen no signs of either a ship upon water or a ship in the air."

"I'm quite intrigued by what you describe. We have only the mountains streams and rivers, and a small lake. Nothing that would require a ship to sail across it. And as far as sky sailing, I've never heard of such a way to travel before."

"It's quite thrilling, I have to admit."

"And you did both of these before you walked through time to get here?"

Seadon smiled. "I did, my lady."

"Well, since there is nothing like that here, I should like for you to draw this ship for me. I should very much like to see it."

"I'm not much of an artist, but I'll do what I can."

"I can employ an artist, and you can describe these vessels of yours. We have some very talented people here, especially artistically."

"Good to know."

"Now, shall we eat our lunch before it grows cold?"

"Certainly, my lady, but I have a small gift for you first." Seadon removed the small, wrapped package from his pocket and handed it to her.

She carefully opened the package to reveal a small but beautiful set of silver and gem studded hair combs. "They are very beautiful, Mr. Brinley, thank you."

"You're quite welcome, Princess Willamina."

They spent the next thirty minutes eating the wonderful meal and talking lightly about themselves until Captain Trent made an appearance. And who should be with him but Commander Quimby.

"Good afternoon, Princess Willa." Trent stopped just at the table's edge, faltering for a minute until he recognized Seadon, addressing him. "Mr. Brinley."

Quinn seemed startled to know that the man seated at the table with Princess Willamina was none other than Seadon Brinley. He looked vastly different. And the last place she ever expected to see the man was at Montesario Castle. She nodded to him and then addressed the princess.

"Princess Willamina, I'm sorry to interrupt your lunch, but I'm afraid we have a bit of a dilemma. King Wilberforth has called an emergency meeting of the guard. I'm afraid he has also requested that you be placed into protective custody for a short time."

"Not again," the princess protested.

Seadon got the idea that this sort of thing happened often because of the nonchalant attitude of the princess. She stood and looked at him.

"I'm so sorry Mr. Brinley, but duty calls. There's no need in protesting; my guard is diligent in their duties. Father makes certain of it."

"Not a problem, Princess Willamina, I offer myself to your services if there is anything I can do to be of assistance."

Willamina's eyebrows raised high, and she pondered his offer. She turned to Quinn.

"Commander Quimby, see that Mr. Brinley here gets a position on the guard. He seems like he can handle the job well enough, and his other-worldly experiences and travels may lend to be beneficial."

"Yes, Princess Willa." Quinn looked skeptically at Seadon. Princess Willamina didn't know Seadon yet and had not yet seen the side of him the Quinn had. She didn't need a hard-headed, drunkard, on her team of highly trained, professional men and women. Least of all one like Seadon Brinley. True she had only known him for two days, but those two days had been enough to reveal some very disheartening qualities that she just didn't have the desire to deal with. His type of personality was one of a young man just out of school who thinks they know everything but actually know very little.

Seadon looked at her and bowed slightly. She had to admit he cleaned up very well. The man was devilishly handsome, but his trustworthiness was in question. She figured him for a player. He seemed the type of man who women often flung themselves at and who enjoyed it immensely.

She was not such a woman, and Seadon would find out Princess Willa was not such a woman either. Willamina was a force to be reckoned with, in both matters of the state, and of the heart. She was used to being the center of attention in every situation and commanded respect everywhere she went. Seadon and Willamina were two people who seemed to be very much alike, and not in a good way.

Quinn figured that watching these two getting to know one another was going to be fun. Her money was on the princess, and she figured she had better do Seadon Brinley a favor and warn him about matching wits and tempers with the princess.

As Captain Trent tended to Willamina's safety and whisked her away to an undisclosed location, Seadon waited just outside for Commander Quimby to make an appearance. The stable hand brought Killer to him and Seadon took the reins and petted the horse's nose and neck as he waited, cooing softly to the stallion.

It wasn't long before she appeared, and Seadon asked, "Well, Commander, it appears we are to be saddled with one another anyway."

"Yes, it does appear that way," she said, sighing in frustration.

"Don't look so down about the order to add me to the staff, Commander. I assure you I know my way around a battle, and weapons."

"Yes, I'm sure you do. But do you know how to take orders?"

"Yes, when need be." Seadon grinned at her.

"In my squadron, everyone needs to, at all times. Do I make myself clear, Mr. Brinley?"

"Quite, Commander. And understand that I am not some militaristic bonehead who knows only how to follow orders. I can think for myself and was quite sought after in my last profession."

"Is that the one where you were shot, or where you were flogged?"

The look on Seadon's face was pure anger. He walked over to her and stood nose to nose with her. She could tell he was trying to control his temper as his heavy breathing began to slow. Temporary confusion set in as Seadon looked deeply into her eyes.

"Do I know you from somewhere?"

"I don't see how that's possible," Quinn protested, but she sensed it as well.

Seadon shook off the feeling and returned to his earlier thoughts.

"Understand me Commander Quimby and believe me when I say that I will never take that sort of abuse ever again. And if I see anyone else doling out lashings from a cat o' nine, I will take it upon myself to turn it upon the one who wields it. No matter who that person is.

"As far as my being shot, it was while I was trying to escape my bonds of slavery to a man so cruel, the world I left had nothing but fear and angst for him and his crew. And yes, it was with those very people with whom I was so prized. Imagine being treated as the lowest of the low and sold as a slave because you were so good at something that people feared you."

Seadon did not wait for a reply. He climbed upon Killer's back and rode off so quickly that Quinn could only stand there and stare after him, her mouth slightly agape, the words of apology never able to form or be spoken. She knew she had gone too far, but his cockiness had made her want to smack him down a few notches.

Seadon rode Killer hard. The coolness of the afternoon air on his skin did wonders to ease his troubled mind and soul. He knew he made too much of what Quinn had said, but the woman had a way of getting under his skin. If she hadn't acted like him being a part of her squadron was the worst thing to happen to her as of late, perhaps he wouldn't have gotten so angry. He didn't understand why it had bothered him so much. But something about Commander Quimby had a way of irritating him.

Once he reached the stables where he had purchased Killer, he dismounted, asked the stable hand to keep killer saddled but give him water, then walked the distance back to his hotel. He changed out of the hot and cumbersome suit jacket and slacks into the regular everyday clothing he had purchased, then returned to the stables.

He asked the stable hand where to find the military headquarters where he hoped he would find Commander Quimby to see what he was supposed to do for his assignment by Princess Willamina. Seadon mounted Killer and took off in the direction the stable hand sent him.

Seadon's mind was a jumble of thoughts. He wasn't so sure that joining in with the military was such a good idea, but he supposed he didn't have much of a choice since Princess Willamina ordered it. If he were going to make a living here in this strange place, then he would have to bite the bullet and do as he was told once more.

Seadon was ready to be the master of his own destiny for a change. The last ten years had been a hardship at the hands of very cruel men, and he had been trained to do as instructed without question. But as he grew into his own, his mind followed. He supposed that was why Captain Iramor sold him. He had become a danger to the man.

Now, Seadon could do as he liked, but to win the favor of a woman, he was willing to conscript to the military. However, this woman was no ordinary woman. Not only was she beautiful, strong of mind and will, she was the reigning Princess of this society. He could do much worse. And with being in the military, he hoped it would give him the opportunity to see her more often.

Perhaps he could even be on the detail that protected her. He certainly wanted to spend more time with her, to get to know her. Knowing a princess would certainly be a good position to be in; a great connection in a new world.

Seadon approached the building that housed the local authorities, dismounted Killer, and threw the reigns around the handrails of the step railing. He entered the building and went straight for the front desk.

"I need to know where I can find Commander Quimby."

The woman looked up at the sound of Seadon's deep voice. She smiled at him and sat up straighter in her chair. Seadon smiled back.

"She's in her office. Just through those doors there, straight back to the end and turn right."

"Thank you…," Seadon's reply was open ended, waiting for her name.

"Oh…Milicent." The woman gestured to herself, smiling broadly.

"Thank you, Milicent." Seadon smiled at her again, making a giggle erupt from the woman's lips.

He strode through the building garnering looks from every direction. When he reached the last door to the right, he knocked.

"Enter," came a voice from inside.

Seadon opened the door and walked inside, catching Quinn standing in close proximity to a rather official looking man in uniform. They both turned to look at him. The man's expression was puzzled, Quinn's seemed more shadowed, like she was trying to hold her tongue.

"Colonel Manning, this is the man I was telling you about."

So she talks about me. Seadon thought,; his countenance bolstered by the knowledge.

"Ah, yes. The princesses latest stray project."

And then it dropped at the Colonel's words. But he stepped further into the room and offered the man his hand anyway. "Seadon Brinley, Colonel."

"Have you had any type of military training in your past?"

"I have sir. Many years ago I'm afraid, but I have been trained in military tactics, wars, and other forms of fighting."

"Perhaps Princess Willamina's newest project won't be so hard on us after all, Commander Quinn."

"Let's hope, sir."

Seadon just looked at her with frustration. She knew nothing about him. Not really. But he supposed he did seem like trouble since that was how things had appeared since he had arrived in the city.

The Colonel said, "Well, Commander Quimby, if you will excuse me. I believe you have duties to which to tend with training Mr. Brinley here."

"Yes, sir," Quinn stated, leaning her backside against her desk as the colonel left.

Seadon walked forward and looked down at her, their eyes locking for a moment. "Are you for certain that we've never met?"

"I believe so. Why do you ask?"

"It's your eyes. They remind me of someone I saw once when I was younger."

"Surely we've never met before, Sea…um Mr. Brinley."

Seadon shook off the feeling a second time that day and returned to their conversation.

"You know, Commander, I think you see me as useless, but I assure you I am definitely not useless."

"Being useful in the correct way is what I'm concerned with Mr. Brinley."

"How so?"

"Being a smooth talker and having a way with certain types of women, or being good at gambling and drinking is not a qualification for this job."

"Only certain women, you say."

Quinn rolled her eyes. Of course, he ignored the rest of what she had said. "Yes. And I'm not one of them." Quinn stood to her full height and crossed her arms over her chest.

Seadon backed up a step. "Trust me, Commander Quimby, I'm not interested. If I were, you'd know it."

"I would have to care, Mr. Brinley."

Seadon just looked at her, causing her to quickly look down at her desk before looking back at him and speaking. "A word to the wise, Mr. Brinley, Princess Willamina can be a very fickle woman. Take care that you mind your wits and heart."

"So, you're worried about my heart now, are you? You've helped to patch up my body, now my very soul is at the center of your concern?"

"You read too much into my words, sir. I figure your soul is too black for me to concern myself with, and I only say to be careful because when Princess Willamina is finished with you, she's finished. Nothing can sway her or change her mind."

Seadon looked at Quinn and nodded. "Thank you, Commander, note taken. But I grew up a long time ago. I'm a big boy. I can handle myself quite well in most any situation."

"We'll see about that, Mr. Brinley. Or I suppose I should call you Recruit Brinley."

"It appears so, Commander."

She walked past him and out the door as Seadon followed. "Let's get outside and see if you can handle yourself in combat and get you trained on our speeders. We have a horse brigade, but they service the mountainous regions mostly since speeders don't handle rocky terrain."

"Killer might be my current mode of transportation, but I'm game for learning a new one."

"Good." Quinn stepped outside the back door of the building onto a training field. They crossed the yard and walked into another building full of speeders, float-carts, and other types of supply vehicles.

Quinn walked over to a speeder and straddled the vehicle. She took a helmet and put it on, tossing another to Seadon and motioning for him to take the other speeder beside her.

"What? No instructions first?" Seadon asked, straddling the speeder and donning the helmet

"The best way to learn is to just jump in with both feet." Quinn pointed at things and spoke quickly, but Seadon, familiar with buttons, gadgets, and engines caught on quickly.

"This is the starter," she said, thumbing a button on the right handle. "This is the throttle," she said, twisting the handle on the right. "The left handle is for a boost of power, but careful with that. Make sure you're in a pretty level area before twisting it. The foot pedal is the brake if you push back and down. Since you know about ships and all, I figure you have steering figured out. Start it up and follow me."

Quinn's speeder charged up and she took off with Seadon following closely behind. They exited the city gates and traveled out into the desert beyond the walls of Montesario-Belarusel.

Chapter 10

Seadon was a quick study on the speeders. He liked speed and wasn't afraid of it, as Quinn soon discovered.

They stopped for a moment to gauge where they were in reference to the city. Fortunately the speeder helmets had on-board air circulation or the helmets would be very hot.

Quinn communicated to Seadon over the headset, "Do you see that mountain chain to the far right?"

He nodded.

"That's where we found you. It is known as the Jaraphite Mountains. Over exposure to its surroundings, like dirt getting on your skin for too long, or soaking into a wound can poison you slowly."

Seadon stated, "The Doc never said anything to me about that."

"He was certain the exposure you had was treatable. You must not have been lying there for very long before we found you. Can you show me where you entered this world from the portal you spoke of?"

Seadon looked around the area where they were. "I'm not sure. I was pretty out of it, but I think I came from that direction." Seadon pointed toward the open desert and the two of them took off.

As they rounded a small stack of rock and desert plants Seadon stopped and Quinn did also. He turned off the speeder and removed his helmet for a better, unblocked view of his surroundings. Quinn followed behind doing the same.

"I believe it was here where I came through."

Seadon turned to look at Quinn, and the expression on her face was one of surprise, or perhaps recognition, he wasn't certain.

"There's nothing here. No rocks, or plants, or distinguishing marks of any kind," Quinn stated.

"There never is," Seadon confirmed.

"What do you mean?" Quinn walked over and stopped just in front of him, her curiosity piqued.

Seadon looked at her. Those eyes were mesmerizing, if she weren't such a control freak they might actually get along better.

"This wasn't my first experience with time-walking. I've done it before. It's been a long time but it happened once about ten years ago." His statement seemed to pique Quinn's interest.

She asked, "Where was the first time?"

"A place I barely remember, called Chindaria. I was only there for a few hours before I was taken by Bosun Kaliel and forced into servitude on a ship called the *Raik*." He noticed Quinn's expression change and she turned her back to him for a few minutes while he talked.

She asked, "How were you taken?"

"My curiosity got me into trouble." His slight chuckle was laced with sarcasm. "There was a festival happening in the city where we happened to find ourselves. Father and I went out to search for food. The atmosphere just drew me in. Later that night I sneaked out of where we were hiding to watch a stage performance and enjoy the festivities. Someone stuck me in the arm with something, and the next thing I knew I woke up in the hold of the *Raik* with twelve other boys about my age."

Quinn turned to stare at him. He could see her mind working, as though she were trying to recall a memory.

She shook herself from her stupor and said, "That's quite a story, Seadon. I'm sorry that happened to you."

"Thanks, but it's all water under the bridge now."

"And you never traveled through time again, until recently?"

"Nope. I saw portals opening all the time when a strong storm would blow in, but I was content with my life. I had been trained well as a pirate. I had no desire to be anything else."

"But those men; pirates; they are so cruel."

"Because most are trained to be. You either learn to be the same, or you suffer greatly for your inability to be tough." They were standing in front of each other again, only a foot separated them. "The marks on my back that you obviously saw in the hospital; I received those the first day on the ship. All because I decided to stand up for another boy who was so frightened he was making himself ill and taking severe punishment for it. I got to share in his lashings."

Quinn looked at the ground and swallowed hard. She looked up at him and said, "This afternoon at Castle Montesario, I misspoke. I'm sorry I said what I did about you deserving what you got."

Seadon nodded. "Apology accepted, Commander."

Quinn's nerves were on end and she backed away from Seadon. The man was way too good looking and had a devilish charm about him that got under her skin, both irritatingly and attractively so; which irritated her even more. She didn't want to be attracted to the man, any man really; especially not one who had enjoyed his pirate lifestyle. Her experience aboard those same types of ships had been much like Seadon's. She wasn't ready to share that information yet. She had learned years ago not to over-share, for people, even the ones who said they were your friends, tended to use such things in their own favor.

"So, I think you've had enough training today, Recruit Brinley. You've proven that you can handle the speeders, and I already know you can handle a horse." She smiled at him at the remembrance of his riding Killer at full speed away from the castle. Seadon's dimpled crooked grin made her stomach do flip-flops.

He asked, "Back to headquarters then?"

"Yes. I think our day has been full enough."

They straddled the speeders once more and took off across the desert toward Montesario-Belarusel. Once they reached the city and the military headquarters, they put the speeders away. As they walked back into the building to have Seadon fitted for his uniform, he asked a question.

"Commander, may I ask why Princess Willamina was whisked away this morning and placed into hiding?"

Quinn thought of what to say and how much to reveal to a new recruit. "All I can say, as it is a matter of state security, is that there are people who would kidnap the princess and hold her for ransom, all in an effort to get King Montesario to comply more strongly with peace talks."

This surprised Seadon. "The city already seems to be a peaceful place. The only animosity toward others that I've experienced or seen as of yet was when I won all of Curstel Borman's money at Shark."

Quinn smiled and giggled at the memory. "Poor Curstel. He's not used to losing you know. He was top Shark before you came along. It was good for him to experience for a change what all the others that play him have to deal with. I doubt he'll be spending much time at the tavern for a while. Going home with an empty pocket after a full week of work likely put him in hot water with Maggie."

Seadon's brow creased in thought. "Are there others here in the city that would harm the princess?"

Quinn's demeanor turned serious. "I believe so. She is under constant watch. Poor thing never has a moment's peace."

Seadon noticed a fondness for the princess in the way Quinn spoke of her. "Do you not know who the danger is?"

"No. We have a constant detail with her at all times, even on her daily outings through the city. She doesn't always know we are following her, but we feel it necessary to keep her safe."

"Why do you think it is someone here in the city?"

"There have been too many attempts to kidnap her in the last year. It has to be someone from here. Our gate detail is too vigilant for someone to get into the city without us knowing about it."

"Perhaps if you put someone else on watch detail that no one from here is familiar with?"

"Like yourself?"

"Yes, exactly."

"I wouldn't say that no one is familiar with you. You've made quite a splash in some areas since you've arrived."

"Well, I doubt the kidnappers are anyone from the hospital, or the tavern. Besides, I did look a little different when I was at the tavern, and most of those fellows won't remember me anyway as they were all likely drunk."

"You have a point." Quinn looked at him with reservations.

Seadon added, "And, Princess Willamina has requested that I join her at the castle on a regular, daily basis."

"Whatever for?" Quinn's curiosity was piqued.

"She wishes to pick my brain concerning the airships I used to fly. I assume to build a fleet of them for Montesario-Belarusel."

"That would be something. It would certainly give Montesario-Belarusel an upper hand when dealing with heads of state of other governing countries."

"Doesn't the city have a nickname? Saying the full name all the time is quite a mouthful."

Quinn grinned at him. "No, it does not. And you had best not let King Montesario or Princess Willamina hear you shorten it. The family lineage is a very big deal, as is the name of the city."

"Note taken." Seadon smiled at her.

Quinn stopped beside a closed door. "Well, here we are. Just through this door is the uniform office. Mr. Norton will fit you with your uniform. You should be fitted and able to wear it tomorrow."

"Thank you, Commander. I'll see you tomorrow morning then. What time?"

"Be here by seven."

"Yes, ma'am." Seadon saluted and opened the door, closing it behind him.

Quinn exhaled slowly before turning to leave for the day. She didn't know if working with Seadon Brinley on a daily basis was going to work out. She would just have to keep her distance from the man and busy herself elsewhere.

After being fitted for a uniform, it was near dinnertime and Seadon decided to find a place to eat on his way home. Home; that was a strange term, especially since it was merely a rented room in a hotel, but it was all he had at the time. Seadon hadn't had a home for more than ten years. The Three Army Wars of Zanchier had chased nearly everyone from their homes. They had lived in tree-houses and hidden complexes beneath caves and waterfalls for a while, before taking to the outer edges of Zanchier where they discovered an abandoned city, only to learn the dangers of living there. That was all before time-walking happened.

He found himself often thinking of his parents and siblings, wondering how they were all doing. Was Bain safe and having adventures like he was? He missed them all terribly. Especially since he had been in this beautiful city, somewhere in the universe.

He shook his dreary thoughts from his head and spurred Killer on for a trot through the streets. After dinner, he took Killer to the stables for his dinner and stabling for the night. He really should give the spirited animal a new name. He was by no means a killer, regardless if someone died trying to break him in. He had to admit that at times the horse wanted his own head and Seadon was obliged to give it to him in the right circumstances. He then walked the short distance to his hotel where there was a letter waiting for him at the front desk.

"Mr. Brinley, a letter for you. It looks quite official." The desk clerk handed him the envelope and smiled in a way that made Seadon think the man had read the letter somehow, but it was still sealed; and with what appeared to be the royal family's crest. He only knew it to be because he had seen it this afternoon at lunch with Princess Willamina. Seadon took the letter to his room, sat upon his bed, and opened it.

It was a request for Seadon to be at the castle by ten in the morning for a meeting with Princess Willamina and her sketch artist and engineers. Seadon smiled, tossed the letter aside, and scooted back against his headboard, crossing his arms behind his head, and laying back into the soft pillows.

Seadon's day had been a very full one. As a matter of fact, the last few days had been a whirlwind. He had quite a bit of excitement since jumping ship. A very good decision if he did say so himself. How fortunate that storm appeared right at that moment, causing a portal just off the Poop Deck Bulwark, right next to him.

Seadon knew it was more than luck, but he wasn't speaking to the Creator. After what He had allowed to take place in Seadon's life he knew the Creator cared nothing for him, and frankly, he was just as disinterested in the Creator's will as He was in Seadon. No, Seadon had learned to make his own way, to be the master of his own destiny, or to laugh at it; either way. He would not be controlled by the Creator, destiny, or any other force of nature that chose to try and seal his fate. He would control his own life and choices from here on out. No man would ever control Seadon the way he had been controlled over the past ten years. He was finally free, and he had plans to make the most out of it. If he ended up marrying Princess Willamina, wouldn't that one day make him a king? And, to Seadon's knowledge, no one had more power than a king ruling over a kingdom of his own. Seadon would make the most out of the time he spent with Princess Willamina Montesario-Belarusel, and he was certain he would enjoy every minute of it.

The hum of city life in the streets below his window was a pleasant refrain from the rocking and creaking of a ship's brig and the miserable cot he had slept on over the last several months on board the *Reaper*. The *Raik* had been little better as well with the small built-in cots in the small section of the ship with other men, most of whom never bathed. Seadon smiled to himself and drifted off to sleep, sleeping more comfortably than he had in years, including his recent hospital stay.

The next morning Seadon reported to headquarters and was met by another man who said he was instructed by Commander Quimby to see to Seadon's further training. He was surprised by this, but figured someone in Quinn's position had no time to train new recruits. After a few hours in the sparring room, Seadon went in search of Quinn to give her the princesses' request of Seadon's presence at ten, which was half-an-hour away. Seadon headed to Quinn's office hoping she was there. He knocked on the door and heard "Enter" from within. Seadon opened the door and found Quinn in her office with Captain Trent. The two of them appeared to be locked in a compelling conversation; standing quite close to one another as they peered out a large picture window on one side of Quinn's office. Seadon cleared his throat.

Quinn and Trent both turned to look at who had entered her office. Quinn was not prepared to see Seadon.

Seadon came to a halt at her desk and said, "Commander, Princess Willamina has requested my presence at ten this morning."

Quinn said, "I've received no such request."

"She sent it to my hotel yesterday evening."

Quinn looked confused. "Who did she get to deliver such a letter? Was she not in protective custody yesterday?"

Captain Trent cleared his throat. "I had it delivered, Commander."

Quinn gave him a disapproving glare. "Have I not given explicit orders concerning communication during such circumstances. There is to be no communications sent or received when she is supposed to be in hiding."

"Yes, Commander. I understand, but Willa—"

"Princess."

"Yes, Ma'am. Princess Willa was determined I should have it delivered."

"Perhaps, but Princess Willamina also has no regard for her own safety. She takes her position too lightly as far as I'm concerned. You, Captain, should be more forceful with her as her main security or she will run right over you."

"I'm sorry, Commander, but I don't have the same relationship with her that you do."

Quinn looked at Captain Trent with irritation. They both turned to Seadon, who gazed questioningly back at them. He was about to ask what Captain Trent had meant when Quinn cut him short.

"Permission granted, Recruit Brinley. Captain Trent was just about to head to the castle to check on Princess Willamina. You two can ride over together. After your meeting with the princess, which will likely last until after lunch, you are to report back here for a briefing this evening in the meeting room. Captain Trent will show you where it is located since the two of you will likely be returning together as well. Good day, gentlemen."

Quinn quickly left her office, obviously irritated by whatever Captain Trent had meant. Whatever it was, Seadon was determined to find out. He wanted to know all about Quinn and Princess Willamina, and Captain Trent's relationship with both women.

The two men vacated her office with Captain Trent closing the door behind them.

"What was all that about?" Seadon asked.

"What do you mean, Recruit Brinley?"

"What kind of relationship does Commander Quimby have with the princess that you don't?"

Captain Trent looked regretful for his words earlier. "That's not my story to tell. If you wish to know about Commander Quimby and Princess Willamina you'll have to ask Quinn; not the princess; I highly advise against that. Not that it is any of your business anyway."

"Then why do you know about such secrets?"

Captain Trent stopped walking and turned to face Seadon. "Let's just say that Commander Quimby and I are closer than we appear. That's all you need to know."

Seadon felt a little pang in his heart at the Captain's words. Were he and Quinn in a relationship? That might explain why they were standing so close earlier. Come to think of it, just in the few short days he had been in Montesario-Belarusel nearly everywhere Quinn was Captain Trent appeared, and vice-versa. He was beginning to understand a little about the happenings around him. Eventually he would win the good-graces of Princess Willamina and he would know everything he needed or wanted to know. Seadon had a way of convincing the opposite sex to give up their most hidden secrets, and he figured that the princess was no different. And as far as Quinn went, she would succumb to his charms eventually if he chose it to be that way.

Chapter 11

Seadon and Captain Trent arrived at the castle just before ten a.m. and were shown to the reception room where Willamina was discussing plans with two other men. She turned to greet them as they entered.

"Here he is, gentlemen, the man I was speaking to you about, Seadon Brinley."

Seadon smiled. "So that's why my ears were burning."

Willamina smirked at his reply.

Seadon shook hands with both men as Willamina also introduced Captain Trent as head of security at the castle.

Seadon had no idea Trent held an official position at the castle. He assumed that the man was just acting on Quinn's orders as military Commander.

Princess Willamina said, "Mr. Brinley, please describe these airships that you flew for Mr. Taupas, our artist. And explain the engineering that made them fly for Mr. Andipols. He's the man who plans to build the engines to your specifications. We will likely need you to advise Mr. Andipols on a more permanent basis over the course of the next few months as these ships are being built."

"I'll be available at your need, as long as Commander Quimby isn't opposed to it. I am a new recruit after all."

"Yes, well, Captain Trent will see to it that Commander Quimby is in compliance with my wishes."

Trent nodded his agreement to the princess.

Seadon added, "And I must admit, Princess Willamina, even though I flew the ships and have a basic knowledge of their inner workings, I can't say that I can accurately describe them to Mr. Andipols satisfaction to make them airborne."

Willamina smiled at him. "Don't you worry about that. Mr. Andipols is quite brilliant, and I have no doubt that he will make flight possible. This endeavor is important for the protection and strength of Montesario-Belarusel. I'm determined that it will work." They all nodded and consented to do their best.

Seadon stepped close to the princess as he spoke about the airships of Zanchier; how they were laid out inside and out, where the engines were located, and what he knew about their construction as he watched some being built while at Praxtingen Airship Academy. By the time lunch rolled around, they had several sketches about each section that Seadon spoke on as the artist was quick and precise.

Lunch was delivered on the outside patio and they all sat and talked over the princess' plans to begin construction immediately. She hoped to have at least three ships built and airborne within the next few months.

Seadon didn't understand the rush, but he supposed people with indispensable incomes were always in a hurry to see what could be accomplished.

After lunch, Seadon and Trent were excused as Princess Willamina held a private audience with the engineer Mr. Andipols.

As Seadon and Captain Trent rode back to headquarters, Seadon stated, "She's certainly task minded, isn't she?"

Captain Trent smiled. "Yes. When Princess Willamina sets her mind to something, there's no changing it. She has spoken of little else since you mentioned the airships to her. Tell me, this isn't some fanciful notion of yours, is it?"

Seadon looked at him. "I assure you; the ships are very real. I flew them myself for years with LAPS."

"LAPS?" Captain Trent asked, confused.

"Sorry. It stands for Loradin Airship Patrol Services."

"Was Loradin the main city where you are from?"

"Yes. It was a fortified island city. Its government was kinder than most others to its citizens. It was one of the last strongholds against the corrupt organizations. Sadly, I believe they all fell after many in charge and whoever else wanted to go, sought sanctuary elsewhere, leaving Zanchier behind for a better life."

Captain Trent said, "It sounds like those in charge gave up and just handed the city over to those who wished it harm."

Seadon's jaw clenched. "You have no idea how wrong you are, Captain. Those people, me and my family, fought for years to save our world, only to lose many that we loved and respected to unnecessary wars. Sometimes, no matter how hard you fight, evil will win out. Sometimes, to save the ones you love, you have to find a better way when fighting is all the opposition seeks and care not for what is destroyed or lost along the way."

"It sounds like you've seen quite a bit of destruction in your lifetime, Brinley."

"You have no idea, Captain."

Seadon clicked the reins and gave Killer his head, allowing the horse to run. Seadon too needed to let some of the irritation from Captain Trent's comments to be swept from his mind and soul as killer flew across the land. The wind always seemed to clear Seadon's mind and calm his spirit, making him miss life at sea.

The ride to headquarters didn't take long at the speed in which the horse traveled. Seadon pulled Killer to a halt and jumped down, handing the reins to a stable boy that worked at headquarters. Captain Trent followed close behind.

Trent yelled to catch Seadon's attention. "Brinley," he said, trotting up to Seadon, "It seems I have upset you somehow. I apologize if I said something wrong."

"It's fine. I just have a hard time when people criticize things that they know nothing about."

Trent nodded. "I understand, and if I overstepped I apologize. I wasn't trying to criticize, just make conversation."

Seadon nodded. "Apology accepted. Now, where is this meeting to take place that we are supposed to attend later?"

Captain Trent grinned and slapped Seadon on the shoulder. "Follow me. The meeting room is on the second floor of the main building."

Seadon followed Trent while he showed him around the building and grounds more, explaining what everything was for and where to find offices he would need. After about an hour or two of touring the grounds, it was time for the meeting of all the officers and recruits. The men returned to the meeting room and found open chairs and sat down, waiting for it to start.

Seadon looked around the large room, and realized he knew very few of the other officers. Many he had never seen before, and a lot of them wore a different type of uniform.

Seadon asked Trent about it. "Captain, why do those men and women have different uniforms?"

"They are from other patrol stations."

"Is that right?" Seadon smiled at a particularly pretty officer who was looking at him and smiling brightly in his direction.

Trent grinned at the interaction. "Be careful with that one Brinley. She's pretty enough, but she has a temper that far outweighs her looks."

"How so?"

"I heard the last guy who went out with her ended up in the hospital with a few broken bones after he called off the relationship."

"Good to know." Seadon turned his attention away from the woman to take in the presence of another woman, Commander Quimby. Seadon had to admit, she made for a striking presence in the room of several hundred. The woman certainly carried herself with assurance and authority. He could tell that everyone in the room respected Quinn and her position.

"Let the meeting begin," Quinn said, and the room grew instantly quiet. "We've had reports from border patrol that someone has been attempting to break through the walls in a few areas on the northern borders of the Montesario side of the city. We believe these attempts are to distract us from someone inside the city. Several attempts to kidnap Princess Willamina have been thwarted and we've found no recent signs of anyone actually entering the city at these points. I want all eyes on this. The princess must be protected at all costs. She is the last of the royal line and the future of the city. King Montesario will be returning in the morning from peace talks with other regions of Vondresonta. We will make no mention of these attempts on his daughter's person. He has enough to worry about with trying to keep Montesario-Belarusel and its central location out of the arguments of other regions. Do I make myself clear?"

A roar went up around the room in unison. "Yes, Commander!"

Seadon was impressed that Quinn drew so much enthusiasm and obvious respect.

"Mountain riders, keep diligent watch. The higher ground gives you an advantage for clarity."

The mountain riders saluted their Commander.

"Desert crew, keep watch over the mountains of the north. Make certain there is no one using the terrain for cover."

One person asked, "Would they do that Commander? Given the health effects of exposure to the Jaraphite?"

Quinn stated, "The Jaraphite mountains may be the closest to the city, but it is not the only mountain range out there. Plus, if people believe their cause to be right and true, whether it is or not, they can be capable of great sacrifice, even to themselves. Be diligent and take nothing for granted."

"Yes, Commander!" Came the joined salute from another crew who were also dressed in a different uniform.

"All groups, be prepared for visitations starting today with the mountain crew. Meeting adjourned."

Seadon supposed the differences in uniforms was to help others gauge the area in which a person was stationed. Perhaps the colors of some helped with camouflage in their natural environments. He noticed that the western desert crew Quinn had just addressed had on sand-colored uniforms, and the mountain group's uniforms were brown and green patterned. The group he belonged to was more of a black breathable type of material. He supposed there was no need for camouflage in a city environment as the military was the governing presence here.

He noticed another crew who wore dark blue uniforms and asked Captain Trent, "Where does that group serve?"

"The lake on the other side of the castle. The mountain rivers empty into it. The lake isn't very large but does provide many types of fish and muscles as a food source. It is also one of our weakest borders. Because of its size, the lake gives access to possible enemy crossings and attacks. There's not much we can do to fortify it, and outsiders following the rivers upstream have been a problem in the past, though few and far between. Especially since it runs directly alongside part of the castle walls and property. Commander Quimby and I will be heading to all the outer regions over the next week or so to inspect the camps and see what measures they've taken for increased security."

"I'd love to tag along."

"You'd have to clear it with Commander Quimby."

Seadon nodded and stood to approach Quinn about the trip when the pretty woman from the lower mountain region crew stepped in front of him, cutting off his path.

"Hi," she quickly announced, offering her hand for a shake.

Seadon smiled and took the offered hand, replying, "Hello. I'm Seadon Brinley."

"I suspected as much."

"You've heard of me?

"Well, only a little." She grinned; her eyebrows raised as if she knew something he didn't.

"But you have me at a disadvantage. You know of me, but I don't even have your name."

She smiled brightly. "Rendel Sweetly."

Seadon returned her smile. "Well, Rendel Sweetly, nice to meet you, but you'll have to excuse me for now. You see I'm on a mission, and I need to speak to Commander Quimby before she gets away."

"Later then." Rendel smiled at him again, and turned to leave, throwing one last encouraging look his way.

Across the room, Quinn couldn't help but notice the interaction between Seadon and Officer Sweetly. For some reason it caused tension in her shoulders, and she didn't know why. She stretched her neck to release some of it and noticed Seadon making his way toward her.

"Commander," he said, stopping in front of her.

"Yes, Recruit Brinley."

"Captain Trent was telling me that you are headed out to all the regions for inspections. I was hoping to tag along."

"Why?"

Seadon shrugged. "I suppose to get to know the terrain and territories better. Would the knowledge not help with my training?"

She looked at him for a minute, hoping that his reasons for wanting to tag along had nothing to do with the fiery redhead, Rendel Sweetly. "I suppose it would do you good to get to know the territories and regions, so yes, you can come along."

"Great, thanks."

"Pack appropriately Recruit Brinley. The upper mountain regions tend to get cold, especially at night. We'll be up there for most of the week visiting the different outposts. Then, when we come back down, we will end our trip by the lake, and back to warmer climates."

"Thank you, Commander. When should I be ready?"

"Within the next several hours. You'll need a travel pack. Go by the uniforms department and ask for one and supplies to go along with it. Then, like I said, you'll need warmer clothing. Do you have a way to purchase them?"

"Yes. I still have the majority of my winnings from playing Shark." He grinned from the memory of those first few days here. He noticed that the thought made Quinn smile too, if only briefly.

"Good. I suggest you get started preparing. I want to be up the mountain and situated at the first outpost before dark. Meet me in my office in two hours."

"Yes ma'am, Commander."

Seadon smiled brightly as the excitement of an adventure lay ahead. He wasn't one to stay in one place for long. Life at sea and traveling to all the different ports and cities was in his blood. His wooing meetings with Princess Willamina would have to wait, but he would have to keep his plans at the forefront of his mind if he were to be successful.

A woman like Rendel Sweetly would certainly be a temporary distraction and lead him astray if he allowed it. He'd have to hold that one at arm's length; especially if what Captain Trent had told him about her temper held any truth.

After stopping by the Uniform office and getting a packed travel bag, he and Killer rushed to the stables where Seadon informed the stable manager of his plans and asked him to have Killer ready to go in an hour-and-a-half. He then walked to his hotel, stuffed what meager belongings he had and would need into the bag, then walked across the street to the shop to purchase some colder climate clothing. He put his purchases into the travel bag, grabbed a quick dinner from one of the local street-side restaurants, walked back to the stables, mounted Killer, and excitedly headed back to headquarters.

Seadon was fully enjoying his freedom from his bondage. Even when aboard the *Raik*, when he felt as though he were free, he truly wasn't. Captain Iramor had made it clear that he had owned Seadon. He had sold him to another man who then locked him in the brig below deck for months whenever he wasn't at the helm steering the ship.

Here in Montesario-Belarusel, even though he worked and was commanded by the military, he could make his own choices, deciding where to go and when, if not at work. It reminded him of when he was young and living and studying at Praxtingen Airship Academy.

This adventure through the majestic mountains of this beautiful city, which sat tucked neatly at the base of it, was charging his very soul. He hadn't felt this much excitement in nearly six months. Even before being sold and leaving the *Raik* Seadon's life had begun to feel a little of the doldrums.

He was thrilled to have found this gem of a place somewhere in the universe. He only hoped that he could find a normal life here, but one that wasn't too boring. His thoughts went to the headstrong Princess Willamina, and he wondered what it would be like being in a relationship with her. He could tell that she was young, but certainly old enough to make up her own mind.

Just as thoughts of Princess Willamina entered his mind he arrived at headquarters where Quinn was standing outside talking to Colonel Manning. It seemed like every time he thought of Willamina Quinn somehow showed up. If not to replace Willamina in his thoughts, then in person.

Seadon pulled Killer to a halt and dismounted, throwing the reins around the metal hitching post outside the main office. As Seadon approached, Colonel Manning began to walk away. Seadon greeted the man.

"Colonel Manning, how are you, sir?"

"Just fine young man. Recruit Brinley, correct?"

"Yes, sir."

"Well, enjoy your mountain trip. It's a beautiful view but gets quite cold at night."

"I'm prepared, sir."

"Yes, well, carry on, recruit."

"Thank you, sir."

Seadon continued toward Quinn and reached her about the same time that Captain Trent appeared beside her. Why is it Seadon can never seem to get a moment alone with Quinn? Not that he needed one or was looking to have alone time with her. The thought shocked him, and he wondered why it had even entered his head?

Quinn watched Seadon approach. The man certainly carried himself well. 'Stop it, Quinn,' she admonished herself. Having that man along with them for a week in the woods was going to be difficult. She found herself thinking about him way to often and it irritated her to no end. How was she supposed to keep her cool all week in his constant presence? She shook off thoughts, stood straight and mustered her best Commander voice.

"Recruit Brinley, are you ready to leave?"

"As ready as I can be, Commander."

"All right then." She turned to Captain Trent first and then Seadon. "Let's mount up, gentlemen. Time to hit the trail."

The three of them mounted their horses and set out for the trail into the upper mountains of Montesario-Belarusel. The outpost camp was a two-hour ride nearly straight up the mountainside. Captain Trent took point, Quinn rode center and Seadon brought up the rear.

As they rode up the mountain Seadon was amazed by the scenic views. He thought his view from the hospital room was special, but it was nothing compared to being out in nature, surrounded by massive trees and animals. The further up they went the cooler it got until suddenly it was bitterly cold. Likely due to the soon to be setting sun.

After a few hours, they came to a wood wall that wove between trees and bushes. Some parts of the wall were cleared more than other areas.

They rode around the perimeter until they came to a gate where Seadon heard someone yell, "Commander approaching!" and a large gate swung inward, allowing them to pass.

Seadon was surprised by what lay inside the fence. There was basically an entire town. Small huts encircled the center courtyard along with supply bunkers and water barrels. Barns for the horses were positioned at the back side of the layout near the back wall. In the center of the courtyard was a large bonfire which appeared to stay burning all the time. Stacks of logs lined the front interior walls of the permanent campsite, ready to feed the fire.

As they approached the center of the camp, officers approached taking their horses by the reins and off to the stable, while the three of them were fed dinner and shown a place to sit beside the fire to get warm after the last thirty-minutes of the bone-chilling ride. Seadon and Trent both sat on either side of Quinn, all with steaming bowls of stew and bread, each taking large mouthfuls until their insides began to warm.

Seadon sat looking up at the night sky through the small openings in the treetops that surrounded the outer walls of the camp.

"It's strange not seeing the fullness of the sky, but being this far up in the mountains sure feels like the stars are closer."

Quinn smiled at the awe in his voice. "Yeah, it's pretty spectacular up here. There is a lookout point a few hundred feet west that gives you unobstructed views of the sky and land."

"This reminds me so much of home; back when I was in airship academy."

"I'm guessing this academy was located in the mountains."

Seadon took another bite of the wonderful stew and smiled. "Yes, but not like this. The academy sat in an open area on the mountain top. So, a full view of the sky was visible. This small circle of open stars makes it feel sort of cut-off from the rest of the world."

Quinn grinned and inhaled deeply of the cool night air. "Yes, it does. I could live up here, of course, I could be content in almost any place."

Trent put in, "As seen from your ability to adjust to any situation."

Quinn and Trent smiled at each other, and Seadon felt like they had a secret that only they knew. It made him feel quite left out. He returned to his soup and finished the bowl, turning down a refill.

Seadon turned to Quinn and said, "I'd love to see that view you mentioned earlier."

"How about we meet just before sunrise, and I'll take you to see it," Quinn offered.

"That sounds promising. You want to meet here around the fire?" Seadon confirmed.

"That will work. Now, if you gentlemen will excuse me, I'm quite tired and sunrise comes early." Quinn stood and walked to a tent reserved for the commander.

Seadon asked Captain Trent, "Where do I sleep?"

"You and I will share a hut right next to Commander Quinn's. Come along, I'll show you."

The two men walked to the hut, placed their packs near their bunks and decided to retire for the night. Seadon especially didn't want to miss out on the promised view in the morning by oversleeping.

Chapter 12

Seadon awoke and met Quinn by the continually burning campfire. The morning air was cold and crisp; the woody smoke from the fire lent a sense of exhilaration to the air.

"Good morning," Seadon said as he stepped up beside Quinn who was already standing at the fireside with a cup of coffee warming her hands.

She turned and smiled at him. "Good morning, the coffee is right over there on a smaller fire-pit."

Seadon grinned and said, "Thanks, that smells great."

"It is. It's strange how the mountain air makes everything taste and smell better." She breathed deeply of the aroma as Seadon moved over to get himself a steaming cup.

Seadon returned to stand beside Quinn. "So, do we grab breakfast first or after we return?"

"We'll take a few protein bars with us just to be safe, but we'll eat when we return. We'll head out after we finish our coffee."

They stood before the warmth of the fire as it heated their front sides. The coolness of the morning air cooling their backsides was a stark contrast. Seadon and Quinn both rotated simultaneously to allow the radiating heat to warm their backs as well.

They finished their coffee quickly and set out on foot through a walk-through gate. They needed flashlights as it was still too early for sunlight, and the thick tree canopy made moonlight all but non-existent. Quinn expertly navigated the trees and shrubs, and half an hour later she came to a stop, just on the edge of the mountainside.

Seadon came to a stop just behind her as a slight breeze swirled the air sending a coconut and vanilla scent sailing past him. It had to be the shampoo or soap Quinn used. Seadon breathed deeply, the smell lingering in his mind. He had to admit, the scent mixed with the experience of where they were, being alone in the woods, was certainly giving him thoughts about Quinn he did not want.

He stepped up beside her. "What now?" he whispered, not wanting to ruin the moment by being too loud.

"Give it just a minute. It won't be long now," she nearly whispered.

As they stood there awaiting the approach of the morning sun, the forest around them began to awaken. An owl could be heard making its last calls of the night before tucking into its hollow somewhere in a tree to sleep the day away. Animals could be heard moving about in the underbrush in the forest that surrounded them. And as the first rays of the sun began to peak over the distant hills, birds began to chirp to welcome the arrival.

Seadon's senses were on high alert, taking in all the sounds as he watched in amazement as streaks of light began to spill over into the valleys, illuminating the homes, small lakes, and farms that dotted the valley far below, all nestled between rows of trees that separated them. Seadon could see for miles in nearly three directions, as shadowy light dappled through the landscape, creating long shadows over the ground.

They looked at each other and smiled at the experience of it all. The quiet morning in the woods, the crisp cool air, the sounds of nature all around, and the rising of the sun as it bathed the world in light. And with that burst of light across the ground came a rush of solar wind, which suddenly cooled the air around them even more.

Seadon noticed that Quinn was shivering slightly. "Are you cold?"

She grinned. "Just a little. The first solar wind of the morning always gives me chills. Rainy days do the same thing to me. I guess my body has trouble adjusting to the sudden drop or change in temperature."

Seadon opened his arms and offered, "I'll warm you up."

Quinn shook her head, a little too violently. "I'll be fine, really." Her body began to shake more. She wasn't sure if it was from the cold, or the idea of moving into Seadon's embrace for warmth.

Seadon protested, watching her shake a little more violently. "Quinn, come on. I won't bite; I promise. You're starting to shake so much that your teeth are beginning to chatter." He raised his eyebrows in question and opened his arms even wider.

Quinn thought better against the idea, but she was beginning to shiver so violently that her jaw was beginning to ache from clenching her teeth. "We should just go back to camp."

"And ruin this beautiful morning?" Seadon's gaze pleaded with her.

Quinn huffed out, "Fine." She reluctantly scooted closer to Seadon, and he pulled her into his arms and against his chest, wrapping her in his strong embrace.

She soon began to warm as Seadon's arms blocked the cold and wind from her chest. The heat radiating from his body behind her enveloped her like a blanket.

Seadon could definitely smell the scent of her hair as she reluctantly leaned against him. The feel of her in his arms felt right somehow. Seadon wasn't sure that offering to shield her from the cold had been such a good idea.

To break the nervous tension in the silence, she asked, "Why aren't you cold?"

Seadon was glad for the distraction and answered, "I've lived on the water most of my adult life. There is nothing colder than the wind off the ocean, and no way to escape it. I suppose my skin has been toughened by it. It's not an experience you'd ever forget."

"I remember," Quinn absent-mindedly stated.

"What do you mean?" Seadon asked, peering down into her dark eyes.

Quinn squirmed a bit under his searching gaze. "Just that, the lake in the city, it can get quite cold there during winter, so I do understand what you say about the wind off the water, being cold."

Seadon nodded, taking her answer as an honest one. He couldn't take his eyes off of her, and he felt a pull to kiss her.

Quinn shook herself from his arms. "I think I'm warmed enough now, thank you, Sea…Recruit Brinley."

Seadon felt the coldness creep into where she had been just moments before. "You can call me Seadon, you know."

"Perhaps, but it would be grossly inappropriate for me to do so as your Commander." Quinn noticed that Seadon simply nodded in reply, all the while looking at her in a way that sent chills up her spine again. She quickly added, "I think it's time we get back to camp."

"Certainly," Seadon answered. "Quinn, Commander I mean, thank you for this, it was quite something to experience," he said, motioning at the scenery behind them now. "All of it."

She did not miss the meaning in his words or his expression.

"You're quite welcome, Recruit Brinley." She grinned awkwardly at him before quickly turning and beginning the trek back to camp.

Seadon followed behind her and admonished himself for offering to warm her up. He had to get his head on straight. He had been worried about encountering Rendel Sweetly on this trip; he never expected to have his emotions in turmoil over Quinn. He knew he found her attractive, but he found most women attractive. He was beginning to have deeper feelings for the woman, and that just would not do. That would greatly interfere with his plans concerning Princess Willamina; whom he also happened to find very attractive; and the desire to control his future.

He had really stepped in it now. Why had he offered to warm her up? It wasn't like him to be chivalrous. He usually did all things with another purpose in mind, but with Quinn, it seemed that his desire to protect her overruled rational thought. Not like she needed it. She was obviously squadron commander for a reason.

They made the trip back to camp in total silence and found Captain Trent waiting by the fire for them to make an appearance. He seemed a bit surprised to find that they had gone off early together. Seadon noticed him watching them, his mind obviously spinning with questions that he dared not ask Commander Quimby or Seadon.

"Good morning, Commander. Brinley." Trent nodded curtly.

Seadon noticed that the man looked perturbed. So, he had stepped on Captain Trent's toes! If Quinn and Trent weren't in a relationship, it wasn't because Trent didn't want one.

Seadon watched as a man approached Quinn, "Commander, the post is ready for inspection. After which we will show you our other defenses in the outer perimeters and at the mountain's High Wall."

"Thank you, Lieutenant Commander Jorgenson. I'm ready to inspect the premises."

Captain Trent and Seadon followed behind the two Commanders. Seadon listened and learned all he could about what was expected from the outpost, and the things that Commander Quimby ordered them to work on. There wasn't much that needed tending to, so the inspection went quickly. Captain Trent advised Seadon to grab his pack, and they were mounted on their saddled steeds and off for a ride through the forest to inspect the boundaries of the camp's stronghold.

Throughout the course of the morning, they were shown the different snares and entanglements that were set up far from the camp's wall.

Seadon asked, "How do the forest creatures not trip them?"

"They do on occasion. Some we set free and some we use to feed the officers stationed here. We have yet to catch a human."

"Then what's the point of the snares if there's no one out here to catch?"

"They are just precautionary safety measures, especially with the kidnapping attempts on the princess. We're not leaving anything to chance. If anyone does use the lower valley wall and manages to get across the mountain without being seen or captured, then I'd say they would have had to fly over."

"Good to know, Lieutenant," Quinn praised. "Now, let's break for some lunch, and after, we can head down to the valley outpost and have our inspection there."

"Yes, Commander," Lieutenant Jorgenson replied. "I'll send word back that we will be staying there overnight."

After lunch they continued on to the next camp and the same type of activities took place. They stayed in the valley camp that night and the inspection continued the next morning, after which they moved on to the next station. Each night they traveled around the mountain or across it, staying the night at the next camp, then were up touring the outpost. This pattern continued for the next five days until they reached Castle Montesario and the lake, the last outpost to visit before returning home. This military camp was located on the northernmost edge of the lake opposite Castle Montesario.

Seadon had to admit, it had been interesting seeing the countryside and meeting others from the outpost stations, but he found it all to be overkill. The combined cities of Montesario and Belarusel were definitely fortified. He found no fault in their security, he just wondered why it was all necessary.

As they toured the outpost and the security measures they had in place, the area around the lake was found wanting. The lake was too large to secure the whole border, and it lay too close to the castle walls on the other. Past military heads always figured that since the lake was open they had a good view all the way around it, so security for the lake was put on hold for many years. Plus, the castle was double walled by both the city perimeter and the castle itself.

Seadon could see where problems could arise, and he brought his concerns to Quinn.

"Commander," Seadon announced as he approached, "Is there any sort of safety precautions set aside for entering the city by way of the river?"

"Not that I am aware of Recruit Brinley."

"You don't think anyone would attempt going upstream?"

"I don't see how anyone could swim, or paddle against the force of the current."

"What if they entered another way?"

"How would anyone do that?"

Seadon remembered something from the Three Army War back home. "The organization our cities fought against had a machine that navigated beneath the water's surface. Couldn't your enemies build the same sort of machine?"

Quinn's brows creased in contemplation. "I suppose they could, though I've never heard of anything like that."

"Just because you haven't doesn't mean someone else hasn't."

"You're right, Recruit Brinley. We need to fortify the water entrance somehow, but with the size of the lake, we would need many more recruits and officers just to patrol the outer borders." Quinn sighed at the monumental task which lay on her shoulders. "To live in peace once again would be wonderful."

Seadon looked at her. "When was the last time that Montesario-Belarusel lived in peace."

"It has been decades. Long before I came." She stumbled over her words, afraid she had revealed too much, especially with the quizzical look that was his expression. "Before I was in the military I mean."

Seadon seemed to accept her answer as he nodded.

She continued, "King Wilberforth Montesario is a good and kind king, but he doesn't take the threats by the other nations as very serious. He thinks that running all over the country and organizing peace talks will solve the problems. Even though Montesario—which you saw over the past week—combined with Belarusel—which has its own military, which we, of course, work with—are very large territories, however, neither are a match for other cities.

"When King Montesario inherited the throne, he was young and inexperienced, or so I'm told. He did not have the upbringing he should have had as far as war strategy or military training goes.

The beginning of his reign was overshadowed by a messy battle over the throne. Belarusel had royalty that they wished to see set upon the ruling seat of the cities, but it was the divine right as first-born son for King Wilberforth to have the throne.

"Relatives from Belarusel threatened to overtake him and so he built his own personal military for this city alone, which is our organization. During his first few years on the throne, there was a civil war that took place which caused many deaths and much destruction of parts of both cities, where they meet along the borders on the south side of the castle walls. King Wilberforth's wife and unborn child were killed in that war because he was ill-prepared for such a thing."

"Surely the king would have had an elite castle guard. Why didn't they protect them?" Seadon asked surprised.

"He did have a guard, much of which was made up of family from Belarusel seeking positions in the monarchy, many of whom which had no faith in Wilberforth's ability to rule and turned against him, leaving his family unguarded; I suspect to ruin his legacy and kill off his line of successors."

Seadon's brow creased. "So, Princess Willamina is his daughter by a second marriage?"

Quinn had to think quickly. "She was the product of a cesarean. Though the queen was dead, the child was close to term and delivered in secret, hidden away for years until the king felt she was strong enough and it was safe to reveal her to the world." Quinn hoped that her answer would placate his curiosity, for she could say no more.

"So, is this why there have been so many attempts to kidnap her?"

"Yes. Many do not believe the story that she is actually the daughter of King Wilberforth."

"Is there proof that she is?"

"Yes, the women who performed the cesarean on the queen, and who also cared for the baby for years until the king declared her existence. They know the truth of it."

"And where are these women?"

"Safely hidden until their services are needed, if that ever happens."

"If captured, would they not be tortured to say otherwise?"

"That is the fear. Yet these women were servants in the Belarusel kingdom during the beginning of King Wilberforth's Reign, and they were selected to become the king and queen's personal attendants. Their appointments to such a position were to spy on the Montesarios and report back to their Belarusel relations, but the servants found the king and queen to be good, admirable, and kind masters, very different from the Belarusel household, so their allegiance changed. They pledged they would protect Willamina's future and legacy with their dying breath, contesting the claim to the throne by the cruel and unjust Belarusel lineage."

"Whew..." Seadon processed the information. "That explains the force with which Princess Willamina lives her life, and the desire for the airships to be built."

Quinn said, "Yes, she is quite determined to fortify Montesario-Belarusel from outsiders, and from those within who would do her or her people harm."

"So, if the threat is mainly from Belarusel, why aren't your forces protecting the border between the two cities?"

"We do the best we can without alerting Belarusel that we are keen to their betrayal and plans. That is one of the reason's Captain Trent is head of castle security."

"But Captain Trent has been touring the outposts with us all week. How is that protecting the princess?"

Quinn became agitated by his question. "Recruit Brinley, believe me when I say, the protection of Princess Willamina is our utmost priority. So, you have no need to worry. We've been doing this for years, and we have things well in hand."

Seadon nodded to her, although he decided that he would take some precautionary measures of his own. Being a pirate half of his life had taught him some valuable tricks, and he would put them to good use.

Upon his return he would be expected at the castle for dinner today to meet with the engineer, Mr. Andipols, to go over some details. Seadon was anxious to see the progress that had been made in his absence, and even more eager to see the princess. He would begin courting her tonight, with or without her permission or anyone else's for that matter.

Inspection of the lake outpost was completed by noon with orders from Commander Quinn to check on ways to secure the mouth of the river. After which, their party of three returned to Montesario headquarters in the city's center. Quinn had to meet with the Colonel to discuss findings for the remainder of the evening while Captain Trent had to return to the castle for his own inspection and report of events in his absence.

Seadon took Killer to the stables and ordered them to treat him to a good rub down and a special treat with his dinner. He decided to give the animal a break after carrying him all over the country the last six days, so he walked to headquarters and took a speeder to the castle for dinner. It was good to be in regular clothing for a change. The uniforms were comfortable, but he wasn't used to wearing so much clothing. As a pirate, clothing had been minimal as their days aboard ship out on the water tended to be quite hot. He hadn't gone barefoot since he had been in this city. It was hard to believe it hadn't even been two weeks yet.

His side had healed well, even with all the jarring and moving about on the back of a horse. He attributed it to the advanced medical practices of Montesario-Belarusel, and Doctor Breighton's knowledge more than anything else. Seadon thought about his life over the past few months.

More times than not he had faced death, only to overcome it somehow. He wondered if the Creator was trying to tell him something. He shook his head at the thought. Surely not. He was positive that the Creator hadn't thought of him since his days in Zanchier, especially since Seadon hadn't led a very honorable life since then. Surely there was nothing the Creator wanted from a man like him.

Which was all well and good, because Seadon had no desire to work for some deity that allowed such horrors to take place in his family's life and the lives of so many others in Zanchier. He had seen so much pain, hostility, and cruelty in his twenty-seven years, and experienced a lot of that himself. He was perfectly fine taking care of and securing his own future without help from anyone else.

Chapter 13

Seadon's arrival at the castle that evening was met with a quick meal, and then they, along with Princess Willamina's driver and several guards, left the castle grounds in her personal carriage and was taken to an out-of-the-way location surrounded by trees. In the center of the mass of trees was an open field with a large, enclosed building. This building had no windows, one large bay door, and a small entry door. Beside the large bay door was a large grassy open field about twice the size of the building itself.

The carriage pulled to a halt, and the driver jumped down to open the carriage door. Seadon stepped down to assist Willamina out of the carriage by offering her his hand.

"Thank you, Mr. Brinley. You're quite gallant." They talked as they walked toward the building.

"Princess Willamina, please call me Seadon. We are going to be spending a lot of time together after all."

"True. All right, Seadon. And you must call me Willamina."

"I don't think that would be appropriate Princess Willamina. It might seem to be presumptuous on my part when we are around others."

"True, and I don't wish to encourage such informality in others. Perhaps reserve the name for when we are alone together."

"Of course, my lady, as you wish." Seadon wasn't sure what she had meant by the statement, but he was certainly okay with the idea that she expected them to be alone at times.

Seadon opened the small entry door and they stepped inside. He was struck by the number of people working in the building, and the progress that had already been made on the newly fashioned airships. There were three ships under construction all at once, and nearly the entire frame of the ships' structures were intact, and the engines were mostly formed and it appeared that testing would soon be underway to make sure they operated and fired.

Willamina smiled as she watched the expressions on Seadon's face. "You seem shocked by the amount of work already completed."

"I must say, I am quite shocked. You've achieved a great deal of work in less than a week."

"Well, I suppose having access to disposable cash flow and being princess of Montesario-Belarusel tends to get things done."

Seadon looked around the building. "I suppose you want to keep this a secret; hence the lack of windows."

"Indeed I do. I don't want prying eyes taking advantage of all of our hard work."

Seadon asked, "What about the workers? Will they all keep quiet about the build?"

"I had them all sign secrecy waivers, but with so many people needed for the work to progress so quickly, eventually someone will let slip the nature of our business out here in the forest. Hence the rush to complete them and get them into the air."

"Well, I'd say it won't be long. Perhaps a month or so from the looks of it."

"Yes, structurally they will be fine, I just hope they can figure out the engines and how to get them off the ground."

Seadon grinned. "Well, I can only hope that what I observed and know will transfer over to Mr. Andipols' brilliant mind and that the airships will work. I have to say, I can't wait to fly one again. I used to love the feeling of floating through the sky." He almost let slip that he also had information on making water-ships fly as well, but he figured that conversation would lead to details about his past he wasn't ready to share with the princess of Montesario-Belarusel. He figured pirate was a dirty word in any city, and if it weren't yet, the description of the life-style would make it so. He hadn't said he had been a pirate, only that he had sailed as a slave upon pirate ships.

"I would like you to spend some time here with Mr. Andipols while the ships are being built to make certain that no details are missed in the creation of them. And as you are the only one who knows how to make them fly, I would like you to take charge of creating a new flight team to handle them once they are ready for the air. You know how many people it takes to operate the ships; therefore I want you to train the crews."

"Certainly Princess Willamina, but what about my duties under Commander Quimby?"

"Don't worry about that. I'll see to it that Quinn knows where you are most needed. Besides, she will likely be around much of the time for the building of the ships. She is military Commander after all. I can't exactly hide this from her, nor do I wish too. But it is imperative that we keep anyone else from finding out about our plans, especially anyone from Belarusel."

Seadon was surprised by her statement. "Why Belarusel?"

"Because my cousins and family from the city's governing offices wish to overthrow me and deny me my birthright."

She looked at him as she said this and watched as his expression turned to one of understanding.

"I see you've heard the story already. Are you surprised that I know who the financiers of my kidnapping attempts are?"

Seadon answered, "I'm learning not to be surprised by much when it comes to you, Princess Willamina."

She smiled at him. "Good. Because I am no ordinary princess, sir. I will fight if I have to and have trained over the years to do just that. Though, I've told no one else this; except Quinn, of course. I refuse to be a useless, mindless, weak female. I may not be as strong as a man, but I promise you, I'm quick in both wit and movement, and I can defend myself."

"I have no doubt about that, my lady." Seadon bowed slightly as he said the words, bringing a slight, crooked grin to Willamina's lips.

"Now, Seadon, shall we get to work on our experiments?"

"Yes, ma'am. After you," he said, ushering her to lead the way toward Mr. Andipols.

As they approached the man, Seadon noticed that he appeared haggard.

"Are you all right, Mr. Andipols?"

Mr. Andipols answered with frustration. "This undertaking is quite a challenge if I may say so. I seem to spend my time running between all the different crews, trying to explain the many aspects of the building of the airships. I have several supervisors who try to keep everything running smoothly, but the airships are an entirely new concept, and getting people to understand my instructions is quite difficult at times."

Princess Willamina stated, "You're doing brilliantly Mr. Andipols. Don't stress over it so much. When we complete these projects and the world sees what we've created, you'll be remembered historically for your contributions to Montesario-Belarusel and the royal family."

Mr. Andipols gave an exhausted nod. "Thank you, Your highness."

Seadon felt sorry for the man. "When was the last time you had a break, Mr. Andipols?"

"I go home to dinner and bed every night, though very late indeed."

"If the princess doesn't object, perhaps I can take over tomorrow for you to have a day of rest?"

Princess Willamina looked a bit perturbed by the suggestion but agreed. "As long as the work continues forward and doesn't fall behind with the absence of Mr. Andipols' presence."

Seadon's grin was strained. "I'm sure we can continue forward. Besides, one day giving the man rest won't hurt anyone."

Princess Willamina's demeanor changed a little and her back stiffened, but she only said. "Work begins at sunup, Mr. Brinley. Don't be late." With that, she turned and went to inspect the other ships and their progress. Seadon was left with Mr. Andipols who looked at him with uncertainty.

Seadon hadn't missed the use of formality when she addressed him. "It appears I've angered the princess."

"It certainly does. You need to be careful when criticizing or admonishing her, especially in front of others." He pointed to himself.

"I didn't criticize or admonish her per say. I only made a suggestion."

"Yes, one opposite to her own desires." Mr. Andipols smiled. "You haven't spent much time around royalty have you. The respect and power they expect can in no way be frowned upon or admonished in such a manner. You may well do with a tongue lashing later."

"No, not royalty exactly. But I have experienced many admonishments and the retribution of many power-hungry men." Seadon's jaw tightened at the memories flooding his mind. He shook them off; his mood lightened a bit as he watched Willamina walk around. He added, "And as far as the princess giving me a verbal lashing later, I think I can handle it, especially from someone who looks like she does." Seadon and Mr. Andipols smiled at each other, and the two of them, along with the crew, got to work, hoping to make the engines roar to life.

Over the next month Seadon spent most of his days and free time at the building site helping to move the airships' progression along faster and more smoothly. If he wasn't there then he was at the castle grounds with Willamina working on building a more personal relationship with her. Their feelings for one another had indeed grown, but Seadon had to watch everything he said, or she would take it as him trying to manipulate or control her, the situation, or the crown.

Two opinionated people in a relationship were hard to navigate in a normal situation, but when one of those people was a princess who would one day be the ruler of a kingdom, walking on eggshells had become normal for him, and he didn't like it one bit. He was growing weary of the strain and missing his freedom a little as well.

One morning he decided he was going to take some time to unwind. He and Killer took to the woods surrounding the two cities and just rode. The deep rhythmic breathing of the stallion beneath him made Seadon realize how much he missed horseback riding, as the powerful horse ran at full speed through the open fields, dodging trees, and jumping fallen wood.

Seadon breathed deeply of the cool morning air, the scent of pine filling his nostrils. He and Killer took the long way around, passing by some of the outposts he had visited months back with Quinn and Trent.

One of the outposts he passed was where the attractive redhead, Rendel Sweetly, just happened to be stationed, and she just happened to be on guard duty that day. As Seadon rode passed, she waved excitedly, yelling "Hello gorgeous" as he rode by. He saluted but kept riding, knowing full well that if he stopped, he would never make it to his destination. He rode the short distance to the old wall which once separated the two cities, having been partially knocked down years ago. He and Killer jumped over the now low, crumbling, stone wall and cut through the city of Belarusel and headed toward the northern side of the lake. He wondered if the lake outpost had followed up with the protective measures they were supposed to implement with fortifying the river where it emptied into the lake. Perhaps he would stop by and see just where they were on that.

When Seadon turned onto the road that would take him to the outpost, he saw a few other men riding back from that direction. They weren't men he had ever seen before, and they certainly didn't work for the guard. Fortunately, he was wearing his guard uniform today so his presence in the area wouldn't cause questions. Seadon, however, wondered about the two men as they passed by on horseback. He nonchalantly nodded in a friendly manner at the two men. The men tipped their hats in greeting. Seadon tried to commit their faces to memory just in case he needed it for the future. He didn't think pedestrians visited the outposts. Maybe they were merchants of some sort?

Seadon arrived at the outpost and was greeted by the men on guard at the entry gates; several of whom he had met last time he was here. Some, however, were obviously new recruits.

"Hey, Brinley, what are you doing out this way?"

"Foster." Seadon nodded, staying on Killer's back, greeting the younger man. "Just out riding and decided to run by here and check to see if the new river fortification plans have been implemented yet."

"You'll have to check with Lieutenant Commander Roberts about that."

Seadon asked, "Where would he be exactly?"

"Out by the edge of the lake on the west side, last time I heard."

Seadon addressed Foster more quietly. "Who were the two men I passed back on the road?"

"Oh, they were traders, trying to sell some supplies to the fort."

"You spoke to them?"

"Nah, not me. It was the two new fellas over there." Foster nodded to the men Seadon didn't recognize, and Seadon committed their faces to memory as well.

"Thanks, Foster. And do me a favor, keep an eye on the two new guys."

"Sure thing, Brinley."

"If anything unusual takes place, contact me over my headpiece. If you can't reach me there, send word to the castle or Riverside Hotel."

"Will do. See you, Brinley."

Seadon nodded and rode back out of the gate taking a good look at the new guys, then headed toward the lake's western shore. As he approached, Lieutenant Commander Roberts walked over to greet him.

"Recruit Brinley, what are you doing out this way? Did Commander Quimby send you?"

Seadon dismounted and walked toward the man. "No, sir, I was out riding and was curious about the river fortification plans."

The Lieutenant looked quizzically at him. "Why the interest, Brinley?"

"Well, the suggestion was mine to fortify it in the first place. I was just wondering if the plans we came up with are going to work?"

Commander Roberts watched him for a second then decided he was being truthful. "Well, we had a stiff, non-corrosive metal grid system built that we stretched across the mouth of the river. The grids are big enough to allow fish to pass, but not big enough for a man's body to get through."

"Can it withstand cutting?"

"Yes. We tested it and it withstood everything we tried. The only way to get past it is to squeeze beneath it and risk getting stuck. It's too deep to free dive, shimmy underneath, then make it back up to the surface before running out of air, especially since you would have to fight the current at the same time."

Seadon smiled. "Great, I'll pass the information on to Commander Quimby."

Commander Roberts nodded, then said, "You look like you have another question on your mind Recruit."

"I was just curious about the two men standing guard at the gate. I've never seen either of them before."

"They're both new. Came in a few days ago."

"From headquarters?"

"That's what their paper's said. Why?"

"There's nothing strange about them?"

"Other than the fact that they like guard duty and requested it for the next week, nothing that I can think of."

"What about the two men who came by earlier trying to sell goods to the camp?" Seadon had a feeling that something wasn't quite right.

"I didn't see any men. When was that?"

"Just a little while ago. Foster said that was what the two new guards told him they wanted."

Lieutenant Commander Roberts nodded. "Good to know. Perhaps our two new recruits would serve us better in another position, at least until we can confirm that they are legitimate recruits assigned to this outpost. I'll have them watched as well. Thanks for the heads up, Recruit Brinley."

"Sure thing. I'll take my leave now and share the good news with Commander Quimby." Seadon mounted Killer and turned him toward the road which would lead him to the eastern city gates. The eastern gates stayed open as they linked the two cities; an ever-opened passage of trust between them. Seadon wondered how trustworthy the government of Belarusel was. He knew they had paid for the kidnapping of the princess on more than one occasion.

He wondered why King Wilberforth would leave this gate open. He would have to have a talk with Princess Willamina about the ease of passage between the two cities. Especially if they weren't sure how strict the government of Belarusel was about their own borders.

Seadon approached the secret building grounds for the airships, only to find that the princess had not been there that day. He then rode toward the castle, arriving mid-afternoon, concern for her safety on his mind. It wasn't like the princess to miss a day at the building grounds.

He knocked on the door of the castle and the butler ushered him into the receiving room. "I'll notify Princess Willamina that you've arrived, sir." The older man bowed and closed the door behind him.

Seadon wondered what was going on. Normally he would be brought straight to the princess, but today he was put aside. The butler brought him a beverage and explained that she would be with him shortly. He sat and waited for fifteen minutes before she made an appearance. He had been pacing the room and peering out the large picture windows that overlooked the immaculately manicured gardens below when the door to the receiving room opened.

Princess Willamina entered the room, closing the door behind her. She knew from the time they had been spending together lately that he didn't like being kept waiting. He figured she was angry with him for not showing up at the building grounds this morning. Most people wouldn't dare keep the Princess of Montesario waiting.

Seadon approached her quickly and stopped just steps from her. "Where have you been? I've been waiting for some time."

"Do not question your princess about my whereabouts," she sternly admonished. "Besides, I could ask you the same question. You didn't show up this morning nor send word where you were." Her back was stiff, and her chin defiantly raised as she crossed her hands below her waist clasping her fingers together, which was her royal way of crossing her arms.

"I was worried something happened to you, like getting kidnapped. And besides, I'm not a castle employee, Willa. I don't have to report my every move to you."

Her jaw was clenched in anger, and she seethed through clenched teeth. "You know I do not like that nickname. And you, sir, *are* an employee through the military which is governed by this family. When I expect you to be somewhere you should be there."

"I have other duties and interests. You might be content spending all day, every day in the building hanger, but I'm not. I needed a change for at least one day. You'd do well to do the same and give your employees a break too."

"You may be content to while away a day of progress for a day of roaming the countryside, free from your burdens, but I am not. And do not lecture me again on how I treat those I employ. And as far as my spending all my time at the hangar and working everyone tirelessly, it is because I am trying to save my people from those who would do them, and our city, great harm. So, yes, I am content to spend my days completing the strategies I have put forth to make that happen! I am trying to get the airships finished to present them to my father, who by the way knows nothing about this venture just yet. So, please, keep quiet about it until I can reveal working flying machines, and my plans for the future of Montesario."

"Willa, pushing everyone to the point of exhaustion may get it done quickly but it could also cause expensive mistakes."

"Stop calling me Willa!"

Seadon got angry. "Why? Captain Trent calls you Willa all the time."

She flung her hands down beside her legs, her fists clenched tightly. "He calls me Princess Willa, which is different!"

"How? Why? Just so your spoiled self can hear the title Princess every time someone addresses you?" Seadon stood in front of her, both of them nose to nose, neither of them willing to give an inch.

"How dare you! That is not the reason. It is my business, and it does not concern you."

"It does concern me, especially since you and I have gotten close. I thought we had an understanding?"

"Just because we like each other doesn't give you the right to interfere in affairs of state, or my personal relationships."

Seadon just stared at her. He couldn't believe that she didn't understand how that statement would make him feel. Or perhaps she did and just didn't care?

"Fine. I can see that this conversation is going nowhere. When you calm down enough to talk, let me know."

Seadon stalked from the room, wishing the large doors he threw open would slam, but unfortunately they were on slow-release hinges for safety because of their size and weight.

"I did not dismiss you, Seadon!" he heard Willamina yell behind him.

Seadon ignored her outburst and marched right out the door, mounted Killer, and took off for headquarters to tell Commander Quinn about the fortified river. He hoped that his anger would subside before he arrived. Quinn had a way of telling when he was irritated or upset, and he had no desire to discuss his and Willamina's argument with anyone.

Chapter 14

By the time Seadon found Quinn outside in the training yard supervising new recruits, his temper was under control though not yet cooled enough to be good company for anyone, not even his horse Killer.

Quinn noticed his stiff stance instantly.

"Recruit Brinley, is something bothering you?"

"No, Commander. I was only coming by to tell you about the border fortification taking place at the river."

"All right, I'm listening."

"They have the plans we discussed in place. Nothing should be able to get through the new gate."

"That's reassuring news. Anything else to report?" Quinn watched his mannerisms closely.

"Did you send out two new recruits to the lake outpost?"

"I did not. Why do you ask?"

"It seems they have two new recruits, and a few men traveling on horseback who said they were wanting to sell provisions to the fort."

"Hmm, that sounds awfully peculiar. I'll make sure Colonel Manning knows about it."

"Good. I informed Lieutenant Commander Roberts of my suspicions."

"Sounds like things are being handled then."

"Yes, Commander."

Seadon's body language still spoke of agitation to her. "Recruit Brinley, is there something bothering you?"

Seadon looked at her, not really wanting to say, but knowing she would likely understand his meaning. "Just personal problems between Princess Willamina and myself."

Quinn's eyebrows raised in understanding. "Ah. I see you've seen her stubborn side, likely to its fullest."

"It appears that way." Seadon didn't want to say more for fear of disrespecting royalty.

"Well, I did try to warn you about Princess Willamina."

"Yes, I recall," Seadon said, his jawline twitching.

Quinn tried to stop the small grin that threatened to form on her lips, but she was too slow.

Seadon saw the look on her face and grew more agitated. "I'm glad my misery gives you such pleasure, Commander."

Quinn got her expressions under control. "Sorry, Brinley. It's just that I've known Willa for a very long time."

"I believe that's the first time I've heard you refer to her in such a personal manner, Commander."

Quinn cleared her throat, quietly admonishing herself for the slip up. "Well, like I said, I've known her a long time. I do try not to refer to her by her childhood nickname. It is much too impersonal and the princess should be held to a higher regard. If we as her security do not uphold such manners, the people will not either."

"I see," Seadon said, wondering just how far back Quinn and Willamina's relationship went. "So, the two of you grew up together."

Quinn thought of how to answer. "Somewhat. We've known each other since she was ten."

"So, I'm guessing you met about the time that King Wilberforth revealed her existence to the cities."

"Yes, something like that." Quinn was growing nervous. She wasn't lying exactly, but she was leaving out a lot of truth, so she decided to steer the conversation back to Seadon's irritability. "So what exactly are you and Princess Willamina arguing about now?"

Seadon looked perturbed by her statement. "You say that like we argue frequently."

"Don't you?" Quinn grinned slightly at his look of discomfort.

"I suppose we do argue more than most couples."

"Oh, I hadn't realized that you two had made the relationship official."

Seadon felt a little uncomfortable telling Quinn such personal things, especially since it seemed to bother her a little. He wondered if it was because of him or her concern for her childhood friend.

"We've been getting closer lately, especially with being together nearly all day, every day with all the work on the airships."

"So have you met King Wilberforth yet?"

"No," Seadon was puzzled by her question. "I can't meet a man who is never here."

"But he is here. He arrived this morning. That could be why Princess Willamina is ill tempered today. She struggles with pleasing the king; often to the point of making herself ill."

Seadon was surprised she had not told him her father was back. Now that he thought about it, he never gave her a chance. She asked him not to mention the airships to her father until she finished them. At the time, the statement went over his head because he had never met him, and didn't expect to anytime soon.

He asked, "Is the king a hard man?"

"Not exactly," Quinn stated, searching for the right words. "He's protective of Willa. With their history and her having to be hidden for the first ten years of her life, he just fears for her. He's never really stopped long enough to take a good hard look at the strong, independent woman she has become. Willa is a fierce being, with a decided future. She will get her way even if she dies trying. However, convincing the king of these attributes will be more difficult."

Seadon could hear the respect for the young woman in Quinn's voice. He had no idea they were so close.

He said, "Perhaps I can assist with that?"

"I caution you against interfering in their relationship, Seadon. Especially being new to Montesario-Belarusel. They will not take the interference lightly."

Quinn never used his given name, and he liked hearing her call him by it. Her voice had real concern for him that time.

"Perhaps the situation calls for a new perspective."

"Don't count on that," she warned. "Just be careful and tread lightly. Don't try to push your thoughts or ideas on either of them. They are very used to getting their own way. They are royals after all."

"I'll be careful. I do know how to handle people, regardless of their station."

Quinn looked at him more sternly. "I'm serious, Seadon. King Wilberforth will have you jailed if you overstep your station. And that's only if you're lucky enough to not get an order for execution."

"Execution?" he exclaimed. "You can't be serious? People actually still do that sort of thing; even here in this civilized world?"

"It is a monarchy after all, Seadon. People do what they must to keep control, especially from an outsider who challenges their authority."

Seadon couldn't believe that she was serious, but the look on her face said she was. "Thank you for the warning. I'll proceed with caution." He wasn't sure how to approach the subject and stumbled over his next question. "What do you suppose the king's thoughts will be on Princess Willamina and myself being in a relationship? One that might lead us to marry?"

Quinn's expression was one of surprise at his declaration. "I'm not sure he'll like that at all, honestly. You are not of noble birth, you can offer nothing to the union, and as a recruit in the military you hold the lowest position on the force. If you plan to propose marriage to the princess, you'll really have to sell yourself to the king, and Willa."

Seadon grinned slightly. "After today, I don't think I've endeared myself to Princess Willamina. I'll probably have to eat crow for quite some time, begging her forgiveness in the process."

Quinn looked at him with a questioning stare. "Whatever did you do, Recruit Brinley?"

"Let's just say I said some things I'll likely regret, and I walked out without being excused."

Quinn's expression was one of pain. "Goodness, you are in trouble."

"Yes, and I'm afraid I left her screaming at me." Seadon was very uncomfortable admitting that part to Quinn.

Quinn grinned slightly. "I have to say, I would have loved to have been a fly on the wall for that conversation."

"You laugh at my pain," Seadon said, grinning slightly at her.

"No. It's just that Willa takes her role very seriously, and few people can advise her otherwise without receiving a tongue lashing. With you just walking out like that, she is going to make you miserable for a while."

Seadon sighed. "I was afraid of that."

"I took you for a man who enjoyed a good fight, Recruit Brinley."

Seadon smiled and turned to face her, stopping their motion. "I do, when facing an admirable foe, but when facing a woman, especially one that I'm attracted to, I'd rather be known as a lover instead of a fighter."

Quinn's eyebrows rose and her cheeks flushed slightly as she stepped back and quickly said, "Well, if that's what you want then you best change your tactics when it comes to Princess Willamina. Now, if you'll excuse me, Recruit Brinley, I need to see to the training of the recent arrivals."

Quinn turned and quickly walked away, leaving Seadon standing there watching her go, and wondering if that was a blush he saw creeping into her cheeks. Seadon smiled to himself and turned to head home for the rest of the afternoon. He was ready for some quiet time alone. He would think about how to approach Willamina in the morning, and what he would say to King Wilberforth should he meet him soon.

Seadon rode Killer to the stables, grabbed himself some take-out, and headed for the quiet solitude of his hotel room. The only problem with solitude was that his thoughts kept returning to the mild-tempered Quinn Quimby instead of his current relationship with the princess. He had to admit, the princess was beautiful and offered a comfortable future should they become betrothed, but a woman like Quinn was quite enticing.

She was beautiful, strong, even-tempered, and easy to talk to. Seadon found himself thinking more about Quinn lately than he did Willamina, and that could definitely cause problems, especially if that blush he caused earlier meant that she had feelings for him as well. Yes, this could definitely cause some problems.

Early the next morning, Seadon got dressed and headed out on Killer. He hoped that Willamina had cooled off since yesterday afternoon's argument. They certainly did not need a replay of yesterday. His first stop was to go by the airship hanger to check on the progress of the ships. He tied Killer's reins to a pole and walked inside the building. He was very happy to see they were coming along quickly.

"Mr. Andipols, good morning," Seadon said, approaching the man.

"Mr. Brinley, good morning to you."

"The ships look wonderful."

"Yes," Mr. Andipols smiled brightly. "I'm quite happy with them. This one here—" He pointed to the first one they started. "—is ready for testing."

"That's wonderful. I'm going to the castle to find Princess Willamina, and when we return, we'll take this one out for a test flight."

"Wonderful news," Mr. Andipols beamed. "I'll be waiting anxiously. I'll have it moved to the open lot outside."

"Great. I'll see you again in a few hours then." Seadon smiled, ready to take the airship for a flight as well. "Princess Willamina hasn't been here yet has she?"

"I'm afraid not, but then with her father here, I assumed it would be hard for her to get away."

Seadon nodded his thanks and left to find Willamina. Mr. Andipols suggestion about her father being here and her not able to just disappear in the early morning hours, sounded plausible. He headed for the castle, arriving shortly thereafter, where he discovered a harried staff and king, all frantically searching for Willamina.

Seadon found Commander Quinn and Captain Trent inside the receiving room. Trent was reassuring the troubled king.

"King Wilberforth, we have all available guards out searching for Princess Willamina. I'm sure she will be returned safely, very soon."

"And don't worry, Your Majesty," Quinn added. "I'm sure we all know where she went."

Seadon stepped further into the room and the king looked quizzically at him.

"Who are you, sir?" King Wilberforth asked of Seadon.

"I'm sorry to intrude, Your Majesty, but Princess Willamina and I are good friends."

"Friends? I've never seen you before in my life."

"No, sir, I only arrived here a few months back."

"How do I know you are not the reason my daughter is missing." He looked to Captain Trent and Quinn.

Quinn said, "Your Highness, Seadon is a recruit in your military,"

Seadon bowed slightly. "Recruit Seadon Brinley, sir, at your service."

"Good. Now you three had best find my daughter, quickly."

The three of them bowed before leaving the room, quickly walking outside to mount their horses; the necessary mode of transportation for searching the mountainside.

Seadon asked Quinn, "What did you mean when you said you're sure you know where she went?"

Quinn sighed. "Willamina has a favored spot in the mountains that overlooks the lake. The problem is that it is very near the Belarusel border. With all the attempts to kidnap her lately, I fear for her safety. She knows that her family is trying to overthrow their claim, but she just doesn't fully understand the dangers of the situation, or how far they might go to achieve that goal."

"Does she take off like this often?" Seadon asked, now worried for her safety.

Captain Trent answered, "Not often, but on occasion she will."

"What's so special about this place where she goes?"

Trent said, "It's close to where we all grew up."

Seadon was surprised to hear him say that. He had no idea they had all grown up together. All the twists and turns to the royal family and all of their protectorates was beginning to give Seadon a headache trying to keep it all straight. The more he learned of these people, the more complicated it seemed to get. With every answered question, he found three more new mysteries. They reached their animals and before mounting up Seadon suddenly stopped.

"So you were all childhood friends?" Seadon asked, puzzled, and he didn't miss the exchanged look between Trent and Quinn. He asked more questions. "What exactly is you two's relationship anyhow?"

Quinn's hand lingered on the horn of her saddle and she turned to look at him.

"Yes, we all grew up together, and as far as mine and Captain Trent's relationship, that's really not important at the moment, Seadon. We have a princess to find who may be in great danger."

Seadon was taken aback by her answer. He watched them mount up and he quickly followed suit. He figured her answer meant that they were definitely in a relationship.

The three of them flew across the open courtyard of the palace and out the gate as it was flung open by the garden staff. They headed south toward the looming mountain before them, taking a small worn path upward and East. The terrain wasn't the easiest to climb, but the horses managed with little effort. About thirty minutes later they arrived at a small clearing where a little house sat tucked away against the mountainside. A view of the lake appeared just over the lower trees of the mountain. They turned a bend in the road and came upon three large trees with gracefully swooping, long, tendril-style branches standing along a stone fence. The fence was barely visible behind the trees, thick shrubs, and years of aging moss which covered it; all of which hid a little stone house from view.

Quinn quickly dismounted and ran inside the building. "Willa!"

Silence followed.

Seadon watched as Trent rode around the house, calling for Willa as well.

Quinn ran outside. "She's been here. Her provisions are still on the table."

Seadon asked, "Where now?"

Quinn said, "There is a flat, thickly forested area just West of here where we used to ride horses as kids."

She mounted her horse, and they all took off in that direction. As they got closer, they could hear several noises moving quickly through the underbrush in the distance. They all took off, pushing the horses as quickly as they could through the thinly marked pathway. No one called out for fear of alerting someone to their presence. As they rode, they caught a glimpse of Willamina riding through the trees at a fast pace, with two other riders hot on her heels.

The three of them spurred their steeds faster, Seadon's stallion easily taking the lead. He could hear gunshots echo in the forest, catching an occasional glimpse of the two men's outstretched arms pointed toward Willamina's retreating back. The fear in him escalated and he rode even faster, hoping Killer wouldn't turn an ankle in an unforeseen hole, or trip over a hidden fallen log.

As Seadon got close to the rider in the back of the line, he rode up beside him, knocked the gun from his hand, slid his foot from his stirrup and quickly kicked his leg out, knocking the man from the horses back. The man tumbled and rolled along the ground, stopping as he bounced off a nearby tree. Captain Trent stopped to lash the unconscious man to the tree, then remounted his horse and continued in the pursuit.

The second rider, hearing the commotion behind him, turned to fire at them. Seadon and Quinn both split from the trail in opposite directions to avoid the shots. As Killer got closer, Seadon quickly turned back onto the trail. It was harder for the man to aim behind himself than out to the side.

As Seadon kept the man's attention, Quinn approached from the opposite side, gaining ground on the rider. She pulled her weapon from her holster and fired at the man, striking him in the shoulder, causing him to fall forward on his horse and drop the gun. His horse slowed enough for them to overtake the man, who still fought to escape. Seadon reared back with his fist and struck the man across the cheek, knocking him backward as his feet flew over his head and he flipped over off his horse, hitting the ground hard on his stomach. The man gasped for air as he groped the wounded shoulder with his other hand.

Quinn continued after Willamina to assure her she was safe. She yelled after the woman, trying to get her attention.

Willa turned in her saddle to see why the gunfire had stopped and she saw Quinn behind her. She slowed her steed and came to a stop, happy to see her friend and Commander. She figured that Captain Trent was close as well. She took deep steadying breaths to slow her heart rate from the intensity of the situation and the crazy ride through the forest.

Quinn stopped beside her, slightly out of breath as well. "Willa, are you all right?"

She nodded, and said between breaths, "I think so."

"Are you injured or hit by any bullets?"

"I don't feel anything. I think I'm fine, Quinn."

Quinn slumped forward in her saddle a little, the release of anxiety over the situation leaving her body. She also felt a sting in her arm and turned to see that one of the bullets had indeed found a mark. Fortunately it was in the top of her right bicep.

"Quinn, you've been shot!" Willamina exclaimed, riding over next to the woman.

"I'm fine, Willa. Let's get you and the prisoners home before your father goes to war over this."

The two women rode back to find the others. Willa was surprised to find Seadon with them.

"What is he doing here?" she asked Quinn.

Quinn turned a confused expression toward Willa. "First, aren't you two in a relationship?"

Willa shrugged nonchalantly. "I'm not sure. I haven't made up my mind."

Quinn rolled her eyes at the young woman. "Willa, you need to stop stringing men along. Seadon Brinley isn't the type to stand for that."

Willa straightened in the saddle. "Yes, I'm quite aware of his...nature."

Quinn wasn't sure what she meant by that but continued to berate the young woman. "What has gotten into you lately, Willa. You know it's dangerous for you to go off alone."

"Nothing too dangerous has transpired lately so I figured things had cooled down a bit."

Quinn's demeanor was one of disbelief. "Willa, your indifferent attitude is going to be the death of me." She winced at the pain in her shoulder. "The reason things have cooled, as you put it, is because your guard has diligently and steadfastly worked around the clock on all sides of the border to set precautions in motion to protect you."

Quinn slowed her berating of the princess as they approach closer to the other men. Captain Trent and Seadon had picked up the second man, cuffed him at his back, and had him back in his saddle.

As they approached, Captain Trent rode up to Willamina, worry evident in his voice and expression. "Willa, are you all right?"

"Yes, Trent, I'm fine."

Seadon noticed the informality of the names this far from the castle and others.

Willa and Seadon's gaze locked for a moment. Seadon didn't know what to say and he noticed that she looked rather contrite for the trouble she had caused.

Willa then said, "Quinn however has been shot."

Both men's heads snapped around toward Quinn, noticing blood oozing down her black uniform sleeve. Trent ran over to her. Seadon badly wanted to be the one who did so but overcrowding her would do no one any good. Besides, she wasn't one to enjoy hovering and fussing.

"I'm fine," Quinn stated. "It's only a flesh wound."

Trent said, "Perhaps, but it still needs tending to."

Quinn allowed Trent to quickly wrap her arm as tension filled the air with all the unsaid things between them all.

"All good," Quinn said, remounting her horse. "Let's get back. We have a long ride, and we still need to pick up the other man Trent tied to the tree."

"Perhaps a wild animal has taken care of the brute for us." Willa said unfeeling, her agitation, anger, and embarrassment all marring her good senses.

Everyone stared at her. Quinn smirked at her words, the handcuffed man on horseback appeared horrified, and as Willa rode past him, she glared hard at him, kicked him in the thigh, and sat straighter in her saddle.

The man yelled in pain, glaring at her back.

Seadon shot him a look that said he had best leave all thoughts of revenge in the past. The man sat up, adjusting himself in the saddle, preparing for the long, slow ride to jail.

He dared say, "I can't exactly hold onto my horse without my hands."

Seadon said, "You'll figure it out, or you'll walk."

The man glared at him. "What about my wound?"

"What about it?"

"Aren't you going to bandage it?"

"What for? The king will likely have you executed anyway for the attempted murder of the Princess of Montesario-Belarusel."

The man's eyes grew wide. "We weren't trying to kill her. Just catch her."

"Do you often use bullets to catch your prey unharmed?"

The man fell silent.

Quinn rode up to him for questioning while Trent and Seadon caught the other man's horse and threw the still unconscious man over the saddle on his stomach.

"Who are you working for?"

The man said nothing.

"If you give up your financier the king may be lenient," she prodded.

The man still said nothing.

"Last chance to help yourselves."

The man just looked at her and smirked.

Quinn shrugged and said, "It's your funeral." She then turned and rode away.

Chapter 15

An hour later they rode up to the castle where the men were taken into custody and shipped to headquarters by guards stationed at the castle. Quinn, Trent, and Seadon escorted Willa inside.

Willa turned to Quinn. "There's no need for you to stay Commander. I'm fine now and you need to be taken to the hospital to mend your arm before you lose too much blood. You're looking a little pale."

Seadon noticed the concern for Quinn in Willa's voice.

Quinn said, "I'm fine Princess Willamina; besides I dare not leave before reporting to the king."

Willamina sighed heavily. "Well, let's get this over with." She marched up the steps and through the castle doors which swung open wide. King Wilberforth stood in the foyer waiting on them, alerted instantly by one of the servants the minute they appeared across the castle grounds.

He looked at Willamina's bedraggled appearance. His voice was harsh and demanding. "Willamina Revellia Montesario, I want a word with you in my private quarters."

Willa nodded and slightly bowed, "Yes, Father." She contritely followed behind the king as the rest of them stood waiting in the foyer, knowing they would be summoned to speak with him when he was finished with Willa.

Seadon turned to Quinn. "How's your arm? Willa's right, you look a bit pale. Your bandage is soaked."

"It's because the bullet is still in my arm. I think it hit the bone."

"You said it was only a flesh wound," Trent stated, concerned. "I'm going to find some fresh bandages to wrap that arm." He went in search of the housekeeper, leaving the two of them standing there alone.

Seadon said, "Let's go have a seat over there." He nodded toward one of the large floor to ceiling windows that graced each side of the massive entry doors. Each had an ornate, long, settee which sat in front of them.

Seadon unwrapped Quinn's bandaged arm to inspect the wound. It was small in size compared to the bullet hole he had in his side month's back, but it still bled profusely. It looked as though she had lost quite a bit of blood on the hour-long ride here, and now she sat waiting to give her report to the king who obviously had no concern for his Commander over the security of Montesario-Belarusel.

"Quinn, we need to get this seen immediately. You'll bleed out waiting on the king."

"I'll be fine. Just try to bind it tighter to help stop the bleeding."

"Much tighter and you'll lose feeling in your arm."

"I don't think that would be a bad thing," Quinn stated.

Her and Seadon's eyes met in close proximity again.

"I swear I know those eyes," Seadon said, mesmerized.

Quinn opened her mouth to speak but was soon interrupted by the servant's return, announcing, "King Wilberforth will see you now."

Seadon quickly and tightly rebound her arm using the same blood-soaked bandages, wiping the excess on his hands down the front of his pants. As they stood to enter the king's private quarters Trent was returning with some bandages and what looked to Seadon like tools of some sort.

They all followed the servant down a long, wide hallway and entered a large receiving room at the end of it. The king was seated on a small throne of sorts, peering out of the large windows that gave him a view of the beautifully manicured grounds. They all stopped just before him and stood waiting.

He peered down at them and waved his hand dismissing the servant. Willa was nowhere to be seen.

The king noticed the bandage on Quinn's arm and said, "Commander Quimby, I had no idea you had been injured in this morning's altercations."

"I'm fine, Your Majesty. I'll see to the wound when we are done."

The king sighed heavily. "I must apologize for my daughter's head-strong ways. You both know how she is," he said to Trent and Quinn.

They both nodded.

Quinn said, "I'm sorry for this, Your Majesty. I promise you we'll try to keep better tabs on Princess Willamina in the future."

The king chuckled. "Short of chaining her to her bedpost I feel you have your work cut out for you, Commander."

Quinn winced at his reference knowing he wasn't thinking about what he was saying.

Seadon too, noticed her expression, and how Trent looked at her when the king said what he did.

The king's gaze turned to Seadon. "As for you, Recruit Brinley, my daughter tells me you two have grown close over the last few months. What sort of position are you in, sir, to handle my rebellious daughter? You are a recruit after all, correct? Meaning you have nothing to offer the crown of Montesario-Belarusel other than your charms and good-looks, and perhaps some bravery as well."

Seadon was struck by the king's forthright observation and chose his words carefully. "True I am no noble, Your Highness, but I believe that I can bring much in the way of skill, experience, and ideas to help secure the borders of Montesario-Belarusel. And though Princess Willamina and I have not entered into any sort of understanding, rest assured, I have her best interests at heart. I should say that we are simply very good friends who are exploring the possibility of a deeper relationship, Your Highness."

The king looked at him admirably. "Well said, Recruit." He then turned his attention to them all. "Now, I have some things to take care of concerning the two men you brought in that attacked my daughter. And I know that you all have things to attend as well." He turned to Quinn. "Commander, I hope you heal quickly. Thank you for your service to my daughter."

"Of course, Your Highness. You know I will always protect her."

Seadon noticed a look passed between the two, some unspoken knowledge they both shared.

The king then addressed Seadon. "Recruit Brinley, you may be excused. I should like a word alone with Commander Quimby and Captain Trent."

Seadon bowed. "Certainly, Your Highness." He turned and left the room, going in search of Willamina. He found her on the second-floor terrace overlooking the lake and gardens.

As he walked out onto the balcony, he asked, "Do you really think you should be out in the open like this after this morning's attempt on your life?"

Willamina's back stiffened. "I need the fresh air after the verbal lashing I've just received."

Seadon asked, "Don't you understand why, Willa?"

She began to grow agitated. "I have asked you not to call me that."

"Oh, for goodness' sake, Willa, are we back to foolish arguments again?"

"If you think me so foolish, Seadon, then why are you here?"

"I never said you were foolish, only that some of the things that upset you are of a childish nature."

"Meaning that I am childish!"

"Your actions today certainly were and put you and others in danger. You know that you shouldn't disappear like that by yourself. You should think of the people who risk their lives daily to protect you, people like Quinn. A few more inches to the right and that bullet would have entered her chest."

Willamina spun around to face him, her temper at its highest, evidenced by her body language.

"I've had a sufficient enough tongue lashing from the king, and I do not need another from you on the matter! So, I ask you, who do you think you are, sir?"

"I am the man who cares for you, and one day might wish to be more; to stand by your side to help you rule Montesario-Belarusel?"

"I have given you no indication that I would accept a proposal from you, sir! The man I marry will allow me, the rightful heir and princess of Montesario-Belarusel, to rule the city as I see fit. He will not think that he can rule in my place or equally to me. Do you not think we are intelligent enough in our little corner of the world to know how to deal with our problems? My father, King Wilberforth, has been dealing with matters of state far longer than you've been alive. Our military is a strong and confident organization, as you saw today, and has been long before you arrived here. The city of Montesario-Belarusel has survived for hundreds of years before you and your ideas came into play. And as for myself, I do have a mind of my own, and I have been able to function and think long before our unexpected meeting in the outer garden. I might also mention your own mistakes and past life before coming here. Do you not realize that I know who you are; what you are by your own admission. It detests me to think that I even cared for you at all, knowing what I do now. Creator forbid, but a pirate should sit on the thrown of Montesario-Belarusel! Now, I would like it very much if you could leave me be." Willamina glared at him.

Seadon turned abruptly and stormed out of the room. He had stood there taking her ill-tempered ridicule, his jaw twitching with the words his tongue dared not speak. He knew he had pushed her too hard, thinking himself, and his opinion as the correct one. He supposed he saw this coming. His tactics at wooing Willamina and bending her will to his own was not only failing, but it had caused a major rift in their personal relationship. He wasn't even certain she would continue to want his help with the airship testing.

One day she would be queen, and she had no intention of handing over the reins of the monarchy to the man who would be her husband and king. Seadon had no problems with a strong female, but to sit back and have no say in any of the decisions related to the circumstances that would be and would govern their future lives, he simply couldn't do it. They both were too stubborn and too hardheaded to be a good fit. They would spend as much of their personal lives fighting amongst each other as they would fighting the world for the safety and security of the city. Not to mention, she had an obvious distaste for pirates. He was no longer a part of that lifestyle, but because he had once been one, whether he chose it or not, put them at irreconcilable odds. He wondered who had told her about his past and why. What had she meant when she said, 'knowing what she knew now'? The only person who could have said anything to Willa had to have been Quinn. Seadon decided that he would find Quinn and ask what it was she told Willamina, and why she desired to not only tear them apart but also ruin his reputation and standing with the royal family.

When he reached the courtyard, the stable boy was returning with his horse. He saw Quinn and Trent mounting their horses a little ways across the lawn. He knew Quinn was hurt, but this could not wait. He flicked the reins and steered his stallion toward them.

When he reached them he asked, "Commander, may I speak privately with you a moment."

Quinn nodded. "Certainly." She then turned to Trent. "Captain, you may go ahead, I'll catch up with you in a few minutes."

Captain Trent reluctantly nodded and turned his horse to leave, looking back at them curiously as he went.

Seadon wasted no time. "What did you tell Willamina about my past?"

Quinn looked taken aback by his accusation. "I have said nothing to her about you. What are you accusing me of?"

"Someone must have told her about pirates and the sort of life they lead. I only mentioned to her that I had sailed with pirates, not that I had lived as one for the last ten years."

Quinn adjusted her seat in the saddle before speaking. "I suppose she figured it out, Seadon. We're not uneducated people here. There is a whole other world out there other than Montesario-Belarusel, and we do know of it."

"Is there some reason you want to drive a wedge between us? Perhaps my past being too hard for you to think me good enough for your Princess?"

Quinn looked shocked, "I could care less about yours and Willamina's relationship. I do not look down on you Seadon for surviving being stolen and beaten by cruel men; forced at a young age to learn to survive. For your information, I happen to know a little about what that's like. Just imagine what it was like being a young girl in a similar situation."

Seadon looked at her, his eyes full of questions. He could tell she was not only growing more angry with him but also at herself for saying too much. "What do you mean?

Quinn was too angry and in too much pain to answer. "It doesn't matter. But, to answer your question, Seadon. I have said nothing about you to Willamina or the king. If you want answers, go back and ask her yourself."

Quinn turned and rode away, leaving Seadon sitting in his saddle watching her go. He felt bad for attacking her character so soon after their harrowing morning rescue, and he could tell she was in more pain than she let on and was growing paler by the minute. He decided to stay back a little to not cause her any more irritation with him being so close in proximity; following a good distance behind her but not too far as to keep an eye on her weakening body.

As he watched her carefully making her way through the forest he felt bad for accusing her. He also wondered what Quinn had meant by what she said about being a young girl in a similar situation.

Seadon noticed that Captain Trent waited on Commander Quinn just ahead, obviously worried about her; as they all should be. He watched as Trent escorted Quinn up the winding, steep, road to the hospital. Seadon decided that he would give her space and visit later. He was beginning to feel like a real jerk. And he was coming to the realization that his thoughts betrayed him much too often lately. Today when he realized that Quinn had been shot, his concern for her far outweighed his concern for Willamina's safety. Willamina was a tough, headstrong, young woman, but he was realizing quickly that she was much too immature and spoiled for his liking.

Seadon rode to headquarters to check on the prisoners, report the day's happenings in full to Colonel Manning, and then tend to some job details. He would go to see Quinn in the hospital later. It would be a unique experience for him to be on the opposite side of the bed this time. But he would trade places with her in an instant if he could.

Hours later when the workday was over, Seadon headed to the hospital to see how Quinn was doing.

When he knocked on the door to her room, he heard her say, in a weak though amused voice, "Enter. Trent, you haven't returned already have you?"

Her smile slowly faded as she realized it was Seadon. "Oh, hello, Recruit Brinley. What are you doing here?"

Seadon chuckled in an unsure way. "Just checking on my Commander, and I hope, friend."

The look on her face was full of doubt, but it slowly turned to acceptance. "Thank you, but I assure you I am fine."

Seadon pointed to her bandaged arm, resting carefully in a sling as well. "I guess the bullet has been removed."

"Yes." She just looked at him.

"Well, how's the bone?"

"Oh, fine. It did hit it, splintering it a little and cracking it. Doctor Breighton says that I will have to keep it immobile for a while. He can't cast it because of the open wound so I will be on light duty for four weeks, after two weeks of time-off, and that's only if it heals well."

"Well Commander, you're just going to have to do as the doctor instructs." Seadon grinned.

She looked at him with amusement. "Like you did, you mean?"

Seadon laughed at her reply. He knew she was right. He never once took it easy. Getting shot, then poisoning himself, joining the military, riding speeders, training, and then riding a crazy horse all over the mountainside for a week.

"I guess you got me there."

There was an awkward silence for a moment before Seadon said, "Quinn, I'm sorry for what I said this morning. For accusing you of outing me."

"Apology accepted, Recruit Brinley."

Seadon walked over and sat on the edge of her bed, near her hips. "Aren't we passed all the formalities of titles by now?"

She looked at him, a little nervous about him being so close, and her being in such a vulnerable position. "Those titles keep order and structure."

"But we aren't on the job now are we?"

"No, I suppose we aren't. But getting used to calling each other by our given names may get us into trouble when we are on the job. It's just not done, Recruit Brinley."

Seadon scooted a little closer to her. "Would you please just call me Seadon?"

Quinn could feel heat rising from her chest, threatening to redden her face. Why did his proximity to her always cause her to blush? She had to get a handle on her emotions. They had to be all out of sorts due to the trauma to her body, and the pain medicine she was taking. She shook herself back to her senses and said, "All right, Seadon. I suppose I can do that when we are alone."

Seadon cracked a small grin, the dimples in his cheeks making her heart flutter. "I guess that will work. Especially the being alone part."

Quinn sat up a little straighter, wincing in pain.

Seadon quickly asked, "Are you all right? Can I do anything for you?"

"Yes, Seadon, you can. You can stop getting closer to me and saying things like you just said."

Seadon backed off a bit, then his look took on a more serious tone. "I'm sorry, Quinn. I forget that you and Captain Trent are involved."

The amused look on her face and the laughter that followed, surprised him. "Captain Trent and I are not involved in the least. We are close, yes, like a brother and sister. Besides, have you never noticed how he pines for Willamina? He's been in love with her since they were children. But now that you are in the picture, he has gracefully stepped aside, if only for Willamina's happiness."

Seadon was surprised by this. "Well, I have a little piece of information that may well make Captain Trent a very happy man."

She looked at him, still smiling from his mistake. "And that is?"

"Princess Willamina and I are no longer seeking to further our relationship."

Quinn stopped grinning. "Oh. And who's idea was that?"

"Both of ours I believe. She wants nothing to do with a once-pirate, and I cannot tolerate her immature, selfish, and often volatile nature."

Quinn tried not to grin at his last statement. "I did try to warn you, remember?"

"Yes, I do remember that you did." Seadon smiled at her.

They shared quiet amusement for a moment longer before Seadon's demeanor turned serious. "So Quinntessa Annalyse Quimby, surely there is a man somewhere who holds your beautiful heart in his caring hands?"

She was surprised by the mention of her full name. "How do you know my given name? I've certainly never shared it with you or heard anyone else say it."

"I've told you that I am a man of many talents. I can find out anything I want to know." He smiled, then went serious again. "You didn't answer my question."

Quinn's heart began to race a little under his scrutinizing, yet heated gaze. "I'm not in a relationship with any man. I haven't been in a very long time."

"Why not? You're a beautiful, capable woman. I can't imagine any man not finding you attractive."

"Seadon, you're getting a little too personal."

"I'm just trying to get to know more about a friend." He grinned mischievously.

She gave him a reprimanding look, but continued when she realized he wouldn't budge. "I rose to the position of commander rather quickly after joining the military. I was strong, determined, and confident. Those aren't qualities that most men want when looking for a woman with which to have a serious relationship. I quickly rose through the ranks, and the men ran the other way. Plus, I'm rather picky."

Seadon smiled at her. "Well, I happen to think that those qualities in a woman are quite attractive."

"Aren't those exact qualities why you and Willamina are calling it off?"

He laughed out loud. It was the first time he had done so in many years and it felt good. "Yes, well Willa is quite on another level in so many different ways."

Quinn liked the sound of his deep, chest-rattling laughter. It caused her to laugh as well. His face lit up in a way she hadn't seen in him before. Of course, she wasn't exactly one to have a good belly laugh lately either. She had to admit she liked laughing with him. She liked this side of him, and herself.

She added, "Well, Willa's story is a rather difficult one, like most everyone else. I have to say she has adapted well and takes her role as Princess very seriously; as she should."

Seadon's look changed to one of curiosity. "There is a great secret that you, Trent, and Willa are keeping from me, and I plan on figuring out what it is."

He noticed Quinn's once playful mannerisms suddenly changed back to the cool, expressionless, facade she often wore. "I'm sorry, Quinn, if I said something to make you uncomfortable. It was not my intention. Especially since I was truly enjoying laughing with you."

Quinn's heart began to melt a little more each time Seadon opened his mouth or looked at her with his piercing eyes. She felt like he could see into her very soul. "No, it's fine. There are just things that I can't discuss. It's nothing personal, just confidential. So, I'm afraid your curiosity will have to be put aside for good if you wish to continue our friendship."

Seadon looked at her with all seriousness and said, "I do." It was all he could do to keep from leaning over and kissing her right then, but he could tell she was not ready for that. Seadon reluctantly stood up from the bed and said, "Well, Quinntessa Annalyse, I guess I should let you get some rest, even though I really don't want to leave."

Quinn looked at him, her heart racing. "I think it best if you do; for both our sakes." The words that were coming out of her mouth belied the ones in her heart. She was really starting to have feelings for Seadon Brinley, and she wasn't sure she was at all happy about that. He seemed like a man who liked to play at life and relationships, she feared there was no real seriousness in him for any type of long-term relationship.

Seadon nodded and gave her one, last, long look before leaving the room.

He stopped just outside the hospital room door; leaning his forehead against the coolness of the metal. What was he doing? Did he really want to pursue a relationship with his commanding officer? He had to be crazy going from one powerful woman to another. But there was a vast difference between Willamina and Quinn. With Quinn, it seemed that his heart was pulling him along without him having any control whatsoever over the situation.

Chapter 16

The next morning, Seadon was summoned to the hangar for testing of the airship. He was surprised to receive the request from Princess Willamina, but he supposed that he was the only man qualified for the job as he was the only person here to ever fly one of them.

He arrived to find the airship was outside the building, fueled up, and ready for lift-off.

Seadon greeted the engineer. "Good morning Mr. Andipols. Are you ready to go up with me?"

Mr. Andipols stuttered, "I…I'm not sure I could handle it."

"Sure you can. You did build it after-all. You should certainly be entitled to take the first flight."

"I suppose I could, if you think it's safe."

"I have no idea until we test it, but we won't go too high, that way if the engines fail, we only have a short distance to fall."

Mr. Andipols' face went white. "I…I think I'll sit the first flight out. I'll leave the testing to the professionals."

Seadon laughed. "It's up to you." He looked around the hangar. "Where's Princess Willamina?"

Mr. Andipols shook his head. "She sent word early this morning that after the attack on her yesterday, King Wilberforth refused to let her leave the castle grounds. And, of course, the king knows nothing yet about what she has done here. But perhaps if the machines fly today, he will let her come out and perhaps visit the hangar with her."

Seadon felt bad for Willamina. To work so hard at something and not even get to enjoy the maiden voyage.

"All right, let's get this show on the road." Seadon entered the cockpit of the airship with a few of the other trainees, all of whom looked terrified. He smiled at them and said, "Relax people. It won't be that bad, even if it fails. We won't be that high in the air."

Seadon started the engines and the trainees scrambled for their seats, quickly buckling seat belts. He called for the preflight checklist that pertained to each department of the ship to be read by each team member that controlled that department. After the checklist was complete, Seadon turned on the boosters and the balloon above began to push against its bindings, lifting into the air. Seadon smiled from ear to ear, turning to look at the crew who were trepidatious, yet excited as well.

"Here we go people!"

The ship lifted off the ground and hovered twenty-foot above those who stood below, marveling at the fact that the airship was airborne. After a few minutes, however, the engines began to sputter a bit and the ship began to bounce and lose altitude. The crew held tightly onto their seats or the consoles in front of them as Seadon sat the failing ship back down; securely landing without injury.

Seadon smiled back at the crew, who in all fairness looked terrified.

"It worked. It needs a bit of tweaking with the air to fuel ratio, but it worked."

Seadon walked out to talk to Mr. Andipols and explain what took place. They both agreed on the adjustments to be made on the engines and decided to try again to test all three machines the next day. Seadon wished the others could have been here to witness the successful lift off. Willamina was on house arrest, Trent was likely right by her side, and Quinn was hospitalized.

Perhaps he could figure out a way to get them all to the hangars in the morning to witness history being made right here in Montesario-Belarusel.

Seadon decided to ride by the hospital before reporting for duty this morning. Gone were the days where he spent much of his time with Princess Willamina, but he had to say, he was glad of that. Now he could just focus on his future, and the mornings and days stationed here in the hangar training new pilots; which would likely become a daily thing. He could only fly one machine at a time, and if they were greatly successful, Princess Willamina, and likely King Wilberforth himself would commission more to be built. They would soon give the city a great military advantage with airships that have firing capabilities from the sky.

Before heading to headquarters to inform Colonel Hastings of the somewhat successful lift-off, Seadon and Killer rode to the hospital to see Quinn. As he entered the hospital, Marlaya smiled brightly.

"Good morning, Mr. Brinley. I hope you are well."

Seadon smiled back. "Thank you, Marlaya. I am excellent."

The girl smiled and blushed, giggling a little with the other attendant as Seadon continued on to Quinn's room. He had to admit, it was fun making the women that he crossed paths with smile. Now if he could just convince Quinn to smile more with him life would be great. He knocked on her door and heard Doctor Breighton call, "Enter."

Seadon walked in to find Quinn sitting up in bed and the doctor checking her wound. Quinn smiled as he entered. He liked that look on her. "Good morning, Doc."

"Good morning, Seadon. How are you feeling lately."

"I'm great. It's this lady right here we are all concerned about." He turned to look at Quinn. "Good morning, *Quinn.*"

Seadon purposefully said her name, emphasizing it to confirm the pact they made the night before about informality.

She smirked at him, returning the gesture. "Good morning, *Seadon.*"

The doctor noticed the light banter between them and smiled. He turned to Quinn and said, "Your arm looks good, no infection present. You can be released this afternoon, but no work for at least two weeks, understand?"

"Yes, Dr. Breighton, I understand. Though I assume I will go absolutely crazy with nothing to do."

Seadon suggested, "You could always take a horse and come spend your days at the hangar watching and learning about the new technology successfully taking place."

Quinn's elation was soon deflated as Doctor Breighton said, "No horses for at least two weeks. Her arm won't heal with all that bouncing and use."

Seadon asked, "What about a speeder?"

"If she rides with someone and you're sure she doesn't take a tumble."

Quinn shook her head no. "The speeder won't work on the rocky, uneven terrain."

Seadon thought a minute. "Can a horse pull a float cart?"

Quinn slowly grinned. "We've never tried it, but I think so. We can certainly figure out how to rig a harness to work."

Seadon turned to the doctor. "Well, Doc, surely you can't contest her riding on a cloud of air in a float cart?"

Doctor Breighton said, "Well, a float cart should be safe enough. And if you can rig a harness that can be pulled behind a horse, that will greatly benefit the mountain regions to use the carts as well."

Seadon smiled at Quinn, her excitement evident at the prospect of not being stuck at home for two weeks.

Seadon said, "Well, now that I have a project, I'll head to work and see about fitting Killer with a float cart harness."

Doctor Breighton's eyebrows raised, "*Killer?* A horse like that sounds a bit too much for this job."

Seadon grinned. "He's not that bad Doc, just misunderstood."

"I certainly hope so, because her keeping that arm still is a must."

"Don't worry, Doc. I'll take good care of our patient."

The care in Seadon's voice and the way he looked at Quinn made her insides do flip-flops.

Seadon then turned to Quinn. "I'm going now but I will return in a few hours to take *you* off on an adventure."

Seadon adjusted his tone a bit when the doctor looked at him with warning. "But not too much of an adventure."

Seadon grinned at Quinn and winked at her before leaving.

Quinn leaned back against the pillows now that Doctor Breighton had her arm bandaged and slid back into its place in the sling.

Doctor Breighton smiled and said, "It appears that you have an admirer, Commander Quimby."

Quinn blushed a little. "We shall see, Doctor. I'm not sure that I completely trust a man like Seadon Brinley."

"Oh? And what makes you say that?"

"He's definitely a man who enjoys making women smile. I'm just not sure he's settled on making just *one* woman smile."

The doctor looked toward the door that Seadon had left through. "I don't know any more about Seadon Brinley than you do, but I'll venture to say that any man who looks at a woman the way Seadon Brinley looked at you, and is as attentive as he seems to want to be, is a safe bet."

Quinn grinned at the doctor. "Thanks…Shepherd," she said, using her old friend's given name.

"You're quite welcome…Quintessa." The doctor smiled at the accomplished woman who used to be the young girl he remembered running through the hills of Montesario, finally free and untangled from a past full of tragedy.

Seadon arrived at headquarters and went to Colonel Manning's office to update him on the progress of the airships. He knocked and was given permission to enter.

"Recruit Brinley, what can I help you with this morning?"

"I've come to inform you, Colonel, that the lift off was successful. There were just a few hiccups, but all should be right in the morning. We will try again just after dawn."

"Is that so? Good news indeed. I think I should like to attend the event in the morning," the Colonel stated.

"I'm sure you won't be disappointed, sir. I do have to state that I will likely be called to train future pilots for the foreseeable future."

"It's not my duty to give you station, Brinley. Whatever King Wilberforth or Princess Willamina says, goes."

"Thank you, sir. I'll see you in the morning."

Colonel Manning smiled and said, "You're dismissed, Recruit Brinley."

Seadon left his office, then went by the supply hangar and asked the technicians there if they could fit Killer's saddle or make a harness for a float cart to be pulled behind a horse. They assured him they could. After leaving Killer there with the technicians, Seadon took a speeder and headed for the castle to speak to Willamina and Trent. He also somehow hoped to convince King Wilberforth about the work that Willamina had undertaken for the benefit of the city.

He parked the speeder in front of the castle and walked up to the door. As usual, the castle servants were on point. The doors swung open before he even had a chance to knock.

Seadon told the butler, "I need to speak with Princess Willamina and Captain Trent."

The butler ushered him into the receiving room and closed the door. Seadon grinned, remembering the last time he was left alone in this room for too long. He and Willamina had a massive fight. However, this time it wasn't more than five minutes before the doors opened and Willamina and Trent entered the room.

Seadon and Willamina hadn't spoken since their fight yesterday morning, and he was quite over it. He certainly hoped that Willamina was too.

"Mr. Brinley," Willamina nodded in greeting, cool and collected as ever.

"Princess Willamina." Seadon nodded. He then turned to Trent in greeting. "Captain Trent."

Seadon turned to the princess. "I've come about the airships."

Princess Willamina's eyes grew large with excitement. "Do they work?"

Seadon smiled. "Yes, although there was a small hiccup with the fueling system, it did lift off the ground twenty feet into the air and hovered for a few minutes."

"That's all, just a few minutes?" The princess sounded deflated.

"Not to worry, my lady. Mr. Andipols is making adjustments which should allow the airships to glide effortlessly and work perfectly well."

She looked anxiously at him. "Are you certain of this?"

"I'm not one hundred percent, but I'm fairly sure they will work just fine. We plan on testing again in the morning. We were hoping that you two would be there. And perhaps even the king."

The princess clasped her hands together in excitement and sat on the edge of a chair. "I so want to come, but I'm not sure the king is done being irritated with my callous behavior from yesterday." She then looked at Seadon and asked, "Is Quinn all right?"

Seadon nodded. "She's fine, just on sick leave for two weeks. Doc Breighton says no activity."

He could see the relief in Willamina's face and the small exchange between her and Trent.

Seadon quickly added, "But we are working on getting her to the hanger in the morning. Colonel Manning also expressed being there. I really think you should speak to your father about what you've accomplished, Willamina. It's no small feat."

At that moment, the doors to the room opened and King Wilberforth walked in, his facial expression laced with curiosity. "I don't mean to pry Willamina, but I did overhear something about Colonel Manning coming to some event and something about an accomplishment. What is Recruit Brinley speaking about?"

Willamina stood and walked over to her father. "While you were touring the country in peace talks, Mr. Brinley here suddenly appeared in Montesario. He spoke about airships which he once flew. He and I, along with Mr. Andipols, the engineer, have built three of these airships."

The king stopped her from speaking. "You did this without my permission?"

"You weren't exactly easy to contact, Father. Besides, you are always telling me to take initiative to do something great and glorify the family name. So, I did. I made the decision to have three ships built with the premise of protecting Montesario-Belarusel. Peace talks have been a hardship on you, father. Always bowing down to the stronger country. Well, now you have something to show that we will no longer beg for favor. We can defend and fight like no other country can."

The king looked at his daughter, unsure what to make of what she said. He then asked, "These airships are ready to fly?"

Seadon stated, "We are testing them in the morning, Your Highness."

The king looked at everyone in the room, stopping at Willamina. "Well then, I suppose that the Royal Family should be in attendance at such an event, especially since it was undertaken and sanctioned by Princess Willamina herself."

Willamina smiled and threw her arms around her father's shoulders, taking the king by surprise. "Thank you, Father. I promise, you won't be disappointed."

The king looked at her with endearment. "I'm sure I won't be, Sweetheart." The two of them lovingly smiled at each other.

"Wonderful!" Seadon exclaimed, smiling and chatting with everyone in the room about the progress this morning.

King Wilberforth had many questions for Willamina and Seadon, and his excitement over what they said seemed to grow.

The king asked, "Recruit Brinley, we are about to sit down for a late lunch. Will you join us?"

He respectfully declined. "I'm sorry, Your Highness, but I have a previous engagement."

"And what is more important than dining with the king?" Willamina asked.

"Picking up a heroine from the hospital. The very one who saved a very important relative of said king."

Willamina grinned at the reference. "Fine. Give Quinn my love and ask her to visit me here as soon as she gets the opportunity."

"I will, Princess. She'll be there in the morning, and she should have plenty of opportunity over the next several weeks to do just that."

Seadon was impressed at how easily the float cart rode behind Killer. No matter how much jostling was caused by the large stallion, the cart effortlessly glided behind. He smiled brightly, knowing that he would get to spend the next several weeks in the company of Quintessa Quimby; without the constant reminder of her being his commanding officer.

He dismounted Killer and entered the hospital, greeting Marlaya who sat at the desk.

"Good morning. How's my favorite nurse?"

Marlaya smiled brightly. "Fine, Mr. Brinley. I'm guessing you're here to pick up Commander Quimby?"

"I am. I suppose she is ready to go?"

Marlaya nodded. "I'll go get her."

Marlaya left and soon returned with Quinn. She was wearing the same uniform from yesterday; the blood now washed from the garments by the caring staff at the hospital.

Seadon grinned at her. "How are you feeling now that you're able to walk around?"

Quinn winced and nodded. "Okay. I'm a little stiff from lying in that hospital bed, and my arm is a little sore, but I'm good. Ready to get out of here."

The two of them fell into step as they exited the hospital. Once outside, Seadon bowed slightly and said, "Your carriage awaits, my lady."

Quinn smiled and inspected the makeshift harness. "They did a good job on such short notice."

"Yes. The head tech assures me that they will produce a better-looking system and send new float-carts and harnesses to the mountain crews as soon as they are ready."

Quinn smiled happily. "I have to say, Seadon, since your arrival, there are things being created that we didn't even know we needed."

"Necessity is the mother of invention." He smiled and asked, "Where to first?"

Quinn said, "Well, since I won't be needing my uniform for a few days, I'd like to change and take a shower. So, home it is."

Quinn sat in the float cart; another adjustment made to the cart by the techs, on Seadon's request. None of the carts had a seated position as most of the people that used them were ill and needed to lie down. The chair floated on the air system with the rider but was strapped to the inside of the cart by stretchable cords, allowing it to stay put, but still have the floating capability.

She smiled at the adaptation. "Clever."

He turned on the cart's air-system and said, "Now if this gets uncomfortable for any reason at all just let me know."

"I'm sure I will be just fine, Seadon," she said, with a look that said he was worrying too much. She then added, "Thank you for this. I would be stuck at home and on foot if not for your ingenuity."

"You are quite welcome. Besides, I get to spend more time with you this way." Seadon smiled at the uncomfortable look that briefly crossed her face. He turned and mounted Killer. "Now let's get you home and into something more comfortable. Then, your wish is my command; wherever you want to go next."

Quinn exhaled to steady her nerves. "Perhaps just home for today. I don't want to overdo my first day out of the hospital, like someone else I know."

Seadon understood her teasing words and turned in the saddle to peer down at her. "I was uneducated at the time on the local vegetation."

They shared a smile before Seadon and Killer slowly started walking. The float-cart hovered above the ground, pulled by a ten-foot-long strap attached to the large horse by a harness system connected to the rider's saddle, safely carrying Quinn.

Chapter 17

Seadon arrived at Quinn's place with no mishaps. He pulled the cart up to the riverside cottage in a quieter part of the city, tied Killer to an available branch from a tree in the front yard by the sidewalk, and turned the float-cart off, allowing the machine to slowly sink to the ground. He offered Quinn his hand to help her from the cart, which she gratefully accepted.

Seadon's hand warmed from her touch. He was reluctant to let it go once she was firmly standing on her own two feet.

"Thank you for your help today, Seadon." She smiled and gestured to the cart. "This was a great idea, and it made the ride home quite comfortable."

"I'm happy to oblige. I'll walk you to the door," Seadon offered.

"I think I can manage from here," Quinn stated.

"Is there anything else I can get you? Perhaps some dinner? We could go out somewhere, or I can bring back takeout."

Quinn wasn't so sure that it was a good idea, but she really didn't relish standing in the kitchen and cooking this evening. Of course, she could just order and have something delivered, but the hopeful look on his face made her cave.

"Sure," she said.

Seadon smiled brightly. "What shall it be? I can even cook if you like. Believe it or not, I learned on board ship."

Quinn was surprised by this. "Really? Somehow, I can't envision you standing over a cook pot in a ship's galley peeling potatoes and baking bread."

Seadon chuckled, though her description and use of terms were spot on. He brushed the coincidence off and said, "Well, my first duty for weeks was to help Cook. That was literally the man's name. After the lashings that Dowjun and I received we were graciously given time to heal by helping in the galley. I learned a lot during that week. And Cook and I became rather close. I would often visit with the lonely man, and he would teach me things. It's not a five-star education mind you, but I do all right."

She said, "I do have some things that need cooked before they go bad, so if you want to start dinner while I get cleaned up, that will be fine."

Seadon smiled. "How about I come back in an hour? I'm still in my uniform, and poor Killer is tied to the tree with the hover-cart still attached. That will give you time to relax a little."

"That will be great, Seadon, and thank you again."

The look he gave her made her insides feel like jelly. "I'm available anytime you need me." She nodded and quickly walked inside, shutting the door between them.

She said to herself, "I must be out of my mind." She decided that the two of them should not be alone inside, and figured they could have their meal on her small terrace on the back of her house. It gave a splendid view of the mountain and river anyway, and the cooler weather lately was perfect. Plus, she had a few neighbors not too far away and the lack of privacy might help block any intimacy that might occur.

Quinn showered and dressed, which was difficult seeing as how she couldn't use her arm or get the bandages wet. She decided that a button-up shirt was easier to put on, unable to raise her arm over her head. She then set the outside table with a service for two. By the time she finished, Seadon was knocking at the door. She opened the door to find him holding a small bouquet of wild Autumn flowers, and a favored dessert from one of the local restaurants; cinnamon and sugar hot buns drizzled with a thin layer of icing.

Quinn's eye's grew large, as she welcomed him inside. "Goodness, you certainly know how to impress a girl by appealing to all of her senses. Thank you Seadon."

Seadon smiled. "I've learned a few things growing up."

Quinn giggled as she took the flowers and put them in a vase with water. "I can't imagine pirates taught you this?"

Seadon grinned a little sadly as he sat the buns on the counter. "No. My father did. Even though we were separated so much. His and my mother's relationship was one that has stood the test of time, trials, separation, and the ultimate betrayal. Watching how they loved each other, and us, has stuck with me, even during my hard times on the *Raik*. I often wonder how they are doing, and where they are? I hope they aren't still spending their days and lives searching for me. It's been over ten years."

Quinn felt bad for not telling him about seeing his father frantically searching for him after his disappearance. Doing so now may injure him more than helping based on his last statement. She shook off the dark emotions remembering that night so long ago, and pasted on a smile.

"Well, what do you want to cook?" she asked, turning to the refrigerator. "I have some fish I took out yesterday, and some steaks that have been staring at me from the back of the refrigerator for days now."

Seadon said, "How about both. A surf and turf style meal."

"That sounds great."

Seadon smiled as she pulled the items out of the icebox and handed them to him. "I figure you need the extra protein sources to heal well, anyway."

Seadon took the food to the stove and began, having Quinn sit at the high bar and visit while she rested her arm.

After the meal was cooked, they took it outside on the patio to eat. Seadon, not allowing Quinn to carry anything with her injured arm, handled both plates and his beverage while Quinn carried her glass. She protested slightly.

"I can handle a glass, Seadon. I have to use my hand to do other things like getting dressed. I can manage a little glassware."

"Yes, but that is something you can't help. If I'm around, I plan to make sure you take care of that arm by insisting you let others help you."

Quinn gave him a disbelieving grin. "Like you took care of yourself?"

"That's different. I'm a guy. We don't care. As long as we can still function, we just keep going." Seadon smiled as they sat.

"Women have a way of continuing on too, you know," she said, a little indignantly.

Seadon held his hands up in defense. "I won't argue that. My mother is one of the strongest women I know. I've seen what she has overcome. When I was younger, I never understood it. But over the last few years, in my later life, I've undergone a greater understanding and appreciation for who my mother is. I just wish I could tell her that now." Seadon picked up his fork and realized that Quinn just looked at him and waited.

Seadon knew that look, it meant he should wait for prayer. He sat his fork down while Quinn prayed over their meal. He had seen that look many times over the years when he was young and living at home. He hadn't realized Quinn was a believer in the Creator. She thanked the Creator for her safety, quick healing, their meal, and Seadon's friendship. The last one surprised him.

When she was done praying, she grinned at him. Seadon grinned back, unsure why people prayed to a distant Creator.

Conversation during their meal was pleasant. They laughed, getting to know each other, listening to stories they each had to tell. That is, until Seadon asked the ultimate question about her relationship with Willamina and Trent.

Seadon could tell Quinn was a little reserved and her manner changed.

Quinn fidgeted a little in her seat, trying to figure out where to start and how much to say. She still couldn't tell Seadon everything without compromising Willamina's future. So, she took a deep breath and gave the spiel she had prepared and reiterated what she had told him before. "There isn't much to tell really. We're just childhood friends who all grew up in proximity to each other."

"I thought Willamina was shielded from view during her younger years."

"She was. But when her father, the king, decided to reveal her to the world, we often played while growing up close to one another."

Seadon asked, "So, you all lived close?"

Quinn squirmed a little, adjusting herself in her seat. "Sort of."

Seadon looked confused. "If Willamina lived in the castle after King Wilberforth revealed her existence to the world, then how did you grow up together? There are no dwellings remotely close to the castle, not that I've seen anyway."

"We all knew each other during her days in hiding." She didn't lie, they did know each other, however short her hiding days were.

Seadon seemed to accept that answer. "What about Trent, how does he play into all of this?"

"Growing up together and being around each other all the time just cemented our relationship as a brother and sister type bond."

"But you said he was in love with Willamina. That's not brotherly."

Quinn smiled at his expression. "No, but with Willa, it was different. Trent was always protecting her, we both were. With her history and past, we have always felt defensive when it comes to Willamina. I guess that protectorate attitude has turned into love for Trent. Even growing up, Trent never dated or liked any other girl."

"Wow, that's dedicated. Especially since his feelings aren't reciprocated."

Quinn nodded. "Willamina loves Trent, but I'm not sure it's in the way he wants."

As they finished dessert and a few glasses of wine, the sun began to dip behind the mountains and Quinn began to yawn. Seadon took notice. He stood up and began clearing the table.

Quinn protested. "Oh, no please, I'll do the dishes. You've already done enough."

"I believe that I've worn you out, and I will not leave you with all this to do with one arm." He took them to the kitchen to begin washing them.

Quinn sighed. "Fine. But at least let me help you."

"You can stand here and keep me company."

Quinn shot him a sideways look. "Right. I can rinse with one hand and leave them to air dry on the rack."

"Sounds good." Seadon gave her another of his dimpled grins.

Quinn sighed again. "You certainly know how to spoil a girl."

"Not just any girl. I wouldn't do this for just anyone."

"Seadon, you have to stop saying such things. We are coworkers. I'm your commanding officer.

Seadon turned to look down at her. "Not tonight you're not. Haven't you ever heard of leaving your work at the job?"

Quinn let out a deep breath. "You, sir, are a dangerous man."

"Yes, I am. In many ways. But when I am determined to go after something, I go all the way."

"Like with Willamina?"

Seadon turned back to the dishes. "Willamina is great, for someone like Trent. I prefer a woman who is willing to at least listen to me and include me in decisions that affect us both. Plus, she's just a tad too immature and demanding for my tastes. I now understand the term 'spoiled princess' all too well."

Quinn giggled a bit then turned serious. "Willamina may take her princess role very seriously, but she must. She has to be strong, defiant, decisive, cautious, stubborn, and yes, even play the spoiled princess role to the fullest. There are people who will destroy her if she is found lacking."

Seadon nodded, his demeanor taking on a more serious tone. "I understand that attitude. I had to learn to do that on board the *Raik*. I've done things, seen things, and allowed things that should never have been. Turning a blind eye is as bad as doing it yourself."

Quinn touched a reassuring hand to his arm. "Perhaps. We've all done things we wish we could change. But a child learning to survive harsh environments is just simply survival; especially after being beaten for trying to help on day one."

Seadon held her gaze for a few more minutes, trying hard not to kiss her. He didn't think this was the right time.

Quinn suddenly removed her hand and went back to rinsing dishes, finishing up the last few.

Seadon said, "Well, all done here. I suppose I should let you get some rest. Tomorrow promises to be an exciting day." Seadon dried his hands, passing her the towel to dry her hand as well.

"Yes, the airship launch. I have to say, I am excited to watch such a thing."

"Good." Seadon began walking toward the door and Quinn followed. "I promise you'll enjoy it. I'll be here by sun up to get you. Make sure you wear something comfortable as it will likely be a long day."

Quinn replied. "I'll be waiting. And thanks again for this, Seadon. You are a good cook, and I had a nice time."

He turned to face her. "You're welcome. Anytime you need a decent meal just let me know. And I had a nice time too." He leaned down and gave her a slightly lingering peck on the cheek. When he pulled back, he could tell by the look in her eyes that it gave her conflicting emotions.

She looked at him and said, "Goodnight, Seadon."

He replied with, "Goodnight, Quinntessa," and a look that made her knees want to go weak.

Seadon watched as Quinn shut the door. He had to take a deep steadying breath himself. He had no idea that she could affect him the way she did. None of his time spent with Willamina even came close to producing the feelings that Quinn stirred in him. His selfish superficial feelings for Willamina had been just that. Quinn touched something deep inside. Something he had never felt before, except once in a fleeting moment; the girl with dark eyes and the painted face all those years ago in Chindaria.

Seadon arrived at Quinn's by sunrise and knocked on the door. Quinn was ready and waiting with two cups of steaming coffee in to-go cups.

Seadon gratefully accepted the cup. "Thanks for this."

Quinn's nose wrinkled in forgiveness. "I wasn't sure how you took it, so I just made it like I do mine. I hope it's all right."

Seadon took a drink. "A little on the sweet side, but not bad. We never had access to extras like sugar in our coffee on the *Raik*, but I think it might grow on me."

"Sorry. I like it with a little sweetener. I can't tolerate black. It's just too bitter."

Seadon smiled and helped her into the float-cart. They chatted while drinking their coffee before Seadon handed the empty cup to Quinn and mounted Killer. They headed into the forest, across the hills, rocks, and unlevel terrain. The cart did wonderfully, and they were both happy and surprised.

Seadon said over his shoulder. "I don't understand why the speeders can't navigate this terrain if the float-carts can."

Quinn said, "I think it has something to do with the way the sensors read surface obstruction."

"Surely, if your techs can build a float-cart to traverse tree stumps and other things, they can enhance the speeders to do the same?"

"You have a point," Quinn stated. "Perhaps, after today, I can talk to them about reconfiguring the system to read the ground around them. Create a more diverse steering system working on surface tension as well. We've been wanting to test the speeders across the lake. They move pretty quickly, and we've often wondered if they could skid across the water. That ought to give me something to focus on for my six weeks of light duty."

Seadon nodded. "That sounds like it would be fun to test."

Quinn grinned. "Maybe not as fun as you think. Going that quickly across the water may hurt if the speeder's nose dips into the water and you get thrown. It would likely feel like hitting hard ground."

"I'm game for an adventure." Seadon smiled and wiggled his eyebrows.

Quinn shook her head. "Seadon Brinley, you are proving to be a dangerous man, in more ways than one."

Seadon just smiled at her and turned to guide the horse through the forest path, arriving at the hanger within an hour. Not many of the guests had arrived yet. Mr. Andipols and the other workers were there getting the ships out of the hangar and into the open field. Seadon dismounted Killer, tying him off to a hitching pole a little ways from the hanger so he wouldn't be frightened by being too close to the noise. He and Quinn walked over to the hanger sensing all the excited tension in the air.

Mr. Andipols said, "Good morning Seadon. Commander Quimby, a pleasure to see you, I didn't know you would be joining us this morning."

Quinn Smiled. "Thank you and you as well. I wouldn't want to miss history in the making, Mr. Andipols."

Mr. Andipols said, "Thank you for the warning that King Wilberforth and Princess Willamina will be attending. We've taken extra measures this morning to make this an official event."

Seadon replied, "Good thinking. Colonel Manning and perhaps some other high-ranking officials will be attending as well."

"Goodness, our little experiment seems to have turned into something newsworthy." Mr. Andipols nodded to a reporter who somehow had gotten word of the flight test of the newly designed airships and was there to document the event.

Quinn's eyes grew large in disbelief. "Mr. Andipols, how could you not think that such an undertaking isn't a newsworthy event. What you've accomplished here is no small feat. These ships are amazing to look at, much less to think that they can fly."

"Let's hope they are more than just eye-catching, Commander. If they don't fly, we will have failed, and I don't know how the princess or the king will take the news."

Seadon smiled, slapping the man on the shoulder. "Don't worry, Mr. Andipols, I'm sure everything will be just fine after yesterday's little test."

Mr. Andipols nervously stated, "I certainly hope you are right, Seadon; for all our sakes."

Seadon showed Quinn around the airships, opening one to show her the interior and explaining how it worked as they waited for all the dignitaries to arrive.

Half an hour later, the king and princess, along with the colonel and others had arrived. They were given a certain spot from which to view the lift off. Quinn, Colonel Manning, and a few other higher-ups, along with King Wilberforth, Princess Willamina, Captain Trent, and Mr. Andipols, all stood on the edge of the shadow of the hanger where they could see the ship rise but not have the morning sun in their eyes.

Seadon and the crew boarded the airship and started the engines. A murmur of excitement rumbled through the gathered crowd. The preflight checklist was read again, and Seadon began the lift. The airship rose high above the crowd below, as Seadon propelled it forward above the tree line surrounding the open field. Shouts of joy and excitement filled the cockpit and the airship as the crew celebrated their true maiden voyage. Seadon smiled, true joy at flying his beloved airships once again filled him. He stayed within a certain distance of the hanger so people could watch it fly.

On the ground the excitement and exclamations of joy from months of relentless work filled the air. Mr. Andipols nearly fainted from relief as the princess hugged him, thanking him for his hard work. The king congratulated Mr. Andipols and Princess

Willamina on a successful venture, and he and Colonel Manning and the other military dignitaries discussed the uses and applications for such a machine.

Thirty minutes later, Seadon was landing the airship. He and the crew exited to shouts of joy and slaps on the back for their flight success. Seadon explained that they needed to test the other two ships and did so, each one floating beautifully through the sky. Once back on the ground, everyone anxiously waited to hear from the royal family who had undertaken the building of the machines. Seadon stood beside Quinn and Mr. Andipols.

King Wilberforth said, "My dear, I am beyond proud of you and this amazing undertaking you've achieved. This is your venture so therefore you should be the one to decide where we go from here and address the people."

Princess Willamina smiled. "Thank you, Father." She kissed him on the cheek and stepped forth to speak to the crowd anxiously gathered there.

Chapter 18

Willamina waited for the excited murmur of the crowd to settle down before she began. Every eye was on her as the camera rolled to record the historic moment.

"I'm so happy to share such a monumental event with each of you. And to assure the people of Montesario-Belarusel that over time, you will begin to see airships in our skies. Rest assured it is your country's defense at work. The accomplishments of Mr. Andipols' genius in engineering these ships, just from the descriptions given to us by Mr. Brinley, was an enormous task. Which as you witnessed today, was also an historic success for Montesario-Belarusel.

"As you all know, Montesario-Belarusel has always been a peaceful city, and many other nations seem to think that being a city of peace also means we are a weak city. My father, King Wilberforth, has spent much of his recent years traveling for peace talks. Making certain other nations will come to our aid in time of need.

"Some will now say that the building of these machines means we are a war-making city. We are not. These airships were built with the sole purpose of protecting our fair cities from would be attacks. Let me assure you, there have been no rumors of any such attacks, but we—," she gestured to her father, "—believe in being prepared. We will no longer beg for protection from other nations. Montesario-Belarusel has the most complete and highly trained officers in our employ. These ships will only further our ability to defend ourselves. These three ships are only the beginning. We will continue to protect our city and its people by building a fleet of such ships to defend and protect our borders.

Thank you all for attending, for your support, and long-live Montesario-Belarusel."

The crowd erupted in applause as Willamina nodded to the reporter and the camera's turned off. She then added to the gathered crowd. "Ladies and Gentlemen, we have prepared a small celebration reception on the castle grounds immediately following today's testing, and we invite all of you in attendance to join us."

Applause rang out once again, and everyone passed by the royal family, Mr. Andipols, and Seadon to congratulate them on the successful test of the airships. Once everyone had the opportunity to thank the royal family, they moved to their vehicle to return to the castle to receive their guests for the celebration. Everyone hurriedly moved to their mode of transportation and got into the line forming behind the now moving royal vehicle.

Seadon and Quinn took a shortcut through the forest seeing as how he was riding Killer. They arrived just as the royal car was pulling up to the front of the castle. He handed Killer to one of the stable hands, and while Seadon instructed him on how to remove the float-cart, Quinn was snatched up by Willamina and pulled into the castle, following the king, and Captain Trent.

When Seadon entered the reception hall the king called him over.

Seadon stopped and bowed to the king. "Your Highness."

"Recruit Brinley," the king acknowledged. At that moment, entering the room behind Seadon was Colonel Manning and the other dignitaries; they all approached the king.

"Colonel," the king said to the man, "I believe that after today's expertise in flying the airships, and the knowledge with which it takes to build such a device, Recruit Brinley here needs to be promoted to Officer Brinley."

Colonel Manning nodded, "Of course, Your Majesty. You are absolutely correct. Recruit Brinley has proved to be a great asset to our forces, and from henceforth should be an officer in our ranks."

Willamina spoke up with her own idea and opinion on the matter. "I disagree with both of those statements."

"Oh?" the king said, both he and Colonel Manning looking at the princess, perplexed.

"No disrespect meant, Father, Colonel, only that with the creation of our new flight department, Officer Brinley should have the title Commander Brinley since he will be heading up the new flight school and airship training center. I plan on turning the hangar into a complete training and development center to teach the next generation how to build, operate, and innovate the airships, and perhaps even invent future devices to benefit the people of Montesario-Belarusel."

Seadon was shocked by her words, as was most everyone else.

The king agreed wholeheartedly. "Excellent idea, my dear. Congratulations Commander Brinley." The king vigorously shook his hand, as did the others gathering around them. Quinn smiled at him as everyone vied for his attention for the next five minutes, discussing details of the assignment. Quinn wandered away to the large spread of food the castle chefs had laid out for the reception, filling a small plate with whatever her heart desired. It wasn't long before Seadon made his way in her direction.

Quinn smiled as he approached.

"Congratulations Commander Brinley. That is quite a quick step up. You went from recruit to officer to commander all in a matter of seconds."

Seadon grinned nervously. "Yes, but I am unsure if I am deserving of the title. Having the knowledge to fly and teach others to do so seems like a small precursor for becoming a commanding officer."

"Well, no one else in Montesario-Belarusel has the knowledge that you do, making you the best candidate. Besides, you also instructed the engineer how to design the airships. You undersell yourself, Seadon. Without your knowledge, none of this would have taken place."

He looked at her and leaned in closer. "There is one thing that I can say that is of great benefit to my new position."

Quinn looked up at him. "Oh, and what would that be?"

"You can no longer protest going out with me based on the argument of being my commanding officer. It seems we are now equals." Seadon grinned slightly at her discomfort at the knowledge that he did in fact want to date her.

Quinn blushed and cleared her throat, grinning up at him. She then tried to gather her composure at the approach of Willamina and Trent.

"Commander Quimby," Willamina stated, "may I steal you away for a while? I would like to speak to you in private if I may."

"Certainly Princess Willamina." Quinn sat her plate on the table.

Willamina turned to the men and said, "Please excuse us gentlemen, we shouldn't be long." Willamina took Quinn by the arm and whisked her out of the room toward the main receiving room.

Captain Trent turned to Seadon. "Congratulations are in order, Commander. Nicely done."

"Thank you, Captain." Seadon grinned. He watched the two women disappear into the receiving room, and asked, "What do you think that's all about?"

Trent shrugged. "Who knows. Those two are as thick as thieves, always have been ever since I've known them."

"Really," Seadon turned his attention to Trent. "And how long has that been exactly?"

Trent shrugged. "Since we were kids and my parents took them in."

"What do you mean? I thought Willamina grew up in a little house on the Belarusel border?"

Trent stumbled over his words a little. "She did. What I meant to say is when we took in Quinn."

"I still don't understand?"

Trent's face went white. "You two have become so close that I assumed she told you. Perhaps you should ask Quintessa about all that. I'm afraid I've said too much."

Seadon looked at him, then toward the receiving room doors. "I'm going to do just that." Seadon walked toward the receiving room with Trent fast on his heels. Stumbling over his words, trying to determine Seadon's motives.

"Seadon, it really isn't a big deal. Quinn was orphaned and my parents took her in. We all met and grew very close."

"So that's all there is to the story?" Seadon asked, stopping just outside the receiving room doors, which weren't shut all the way.

"Yes, of course. What else could there be?"

Seadon was about to say something when he overheard voices in the receiving room speaking Chindarian. He questioningly turned to Trent who seemed to be oblivious to the other language. Seadon turned and opened the doors walking through them, surprised to find that Willamina and Quinn were the only two people in the room.

Both women turned to see who had disrupted their privacy. When they saw Seadon standing there, Willamina appeared confused, but Quinn was obviously concerned.

Seadon asked, "How do you both know Chindarian?"

Willamina, rather convincingly said, "What are you talking about Seadon?"

He gave her a look that said he knew what they were saying. "Again, how do you both speak Chindarian?"

Quinn placed a hand on Willamina's arm to stop her from browbeating Seadon into thinking he didn't hear what he did. She walked toward him. "Seadon, I am from Chindaria."

"Then why does Willamina also understand Chindarian?"

Quinn tried to think of a quick answer.

Willamina added, "She taught me, when we were young."

Seadon wasn't believing it. "Then why does Trent not know it as well? If you all spent as much time together as you say growing up, then Trent would have learned it as well."

Willamina looked at Trent for a minute. "He didn't want to learn."

"Stop, Willa," Quinn said, turning to her. "It's time Seadon knows the truth."

"But Quinn, you can't. What if he says something?

Seadon just stood there, confused by what they were saying.

"I believe that we can trust him, Willa."

Quinn turned back to look at Seadon. "You have to keep what I am about to tell you a complete secret. You cannot tell anyone, Seadon."

Seadon nodded, looking at her in confusion. Quinn looked at him for a moment, took a deep breath, and exhaled slowly before she continued.

"Willa and I are from Chindaria."

"I can understand *you* being from there, but how can the rightful Princess of Montesario-Belarusel be from Chindaria?"

"Sit down while I tell you a story." Quinn looked at Trent, who closed the doors and stood guard so that no one else could enter the room.

Seadon sat on the couch and Quinn sat opposite him. Willamina took a seat in a chair opposite the couch.

Quinn looked at him nervously. "Willa and I were taken, like you were, when we were just girls. I was sixteen and Willa was ten. Like you, pirates came to Chindaria a few months after you were taken and whisked away many young girls with the idea of selling us into the slave trade. One night, while on board the ship that took us, a strong storm arose and the ship began to list. At one point it listed so badly that Willa and I were washed overboard. When that happened, we were swept into a portal, like the one you passed through, and ended up here in Montesario-Belarusel."

"Why haven't you told me this before?" Seadon asked, feeling like she didn't trust him.

"There is a lot more to the story. Just let me finish." Quinn adjusted in her seat. "We were pulled into the same spot in the desert that you were, and we found our way here to the city; only we entered closer to Belarusel.

"We spent a few weeks sleeping wherever we could, and eating what we could find. Willa was so small and weak from the ordeal of mistreatment on board the ship, then the tumble in the ocean, and living on the streets that she came down with pneumonia.

"One day we were just sitting on the street, and Willa was coughing so badly that it captured the attention of a young boy and his mother. That was Trent and Mrs. Mardel. They took us home and his mother tended to our needs, even going so far as to send for the doctor for Willa, Doctor Breighton actually, and he checked us both out and treated Willa for her illness. Trent's family allowed us to live with them. His mother became like our own. She was also one of the servants who had been the personal care givers to the royal family. She was one of the women who helped to hide and raise the baby that survived the birth to the dead queen.

"Trent's mother and another woman took turns tending to the little princess. She was sick most of her young life, and when she reached the age of ten, she suddenly died. Trent's mother had the idea of passing Willa off as the little princess. She was the right age, build, and even resembled the real princess."

"Does the king know Willa isn't his real daughter?"

"Yes. He was told about everything. He was there when his daughter died and was buried. Her name was Amelia Revellia Montesario. The king was heartbroken and at the same time, also worried for the future of Montesario. If his only successor had died, the Belarusel family would eventually claim the throne, and they are cruel people and would have ruled with a heavy hand. The king could not let this happen. So, he adopted Willa as his daughter and asked the women who had tended to and raised his real daughter to train and school Willa in the family history and teach her to become the princess."

"Wow, okay I understand all the secrecy about all of that, but why didn't you just tell me that you were from Chindaria when I told you what had happened to me?" Seadon was still confused why she would keep it all a secret.

"There's more." Quinn scooted closer to him and took one of his hands in both of hers. "Seadon, I saw your father the night you went missing. He came looking for you right after you were snatched by the big man with the metal arm."

"What?"

"He was frantic. He tore through every docked boat, ran up and down the riverside, asking everyone if they had seen you. He ended up with the parents of the other taken boys and was told he would never see you again."

"How do you know all of this?"

"I watched it all from the riverside stadium stage. I felt so helpless. My heart ached for him, and for you."

"I still don't understand how you know all of this? How do you know who I am?"

"Because...I am the girl on stage. The dancer you saw that night."

Realization dawned on Seadon as he looked at Quinn. "The eyes. I knew that I recognized you, I just couldn't remember how." He pulled his hand from hers and stood, pacing the floor. "Why didn't you just tell me the truth when I asked you about it? Why did you lie to me and keep me in the dark for so long?"

"It was because we were sworn to secrecy, Seadon. I couldn't reveal something so personal without you finding out about Willa. You have to keep this quiet. It could ruin the family, and the king will have to hand the throne over to the wrong people to rule the cities."

"But why didn't you tell me about my father? I've spent so much time wondering how my family was, and if they even knew what had happened to me. How could you have kept this all from me for so long? Every time I talked about my past and the things I've been through; wondering about my parents, you had the opportunity to say something. Yesterday at dinner when I was telling you about it; you could have said something then!" Seadon was now angry, and he felt betrayed. He thought he could trust Quinn, but it was all a lie.

For months he had let her into his past, his hurt, his disappointments, and all that time she had been keeping information about him and his family a secret.

"I thought I knew you, Quinn. I thought we were getting to know one another, sharing our lives and our history. I guess I was wrong." He turned and stormed toward the doors.

Trent quickly side-stepped as Seadon threw them open, quickly crossing the foyer and heading toward the front doors and outside. He crossed the lawn, stalking toward the stables, finding Killer stalled there.

Fortunately, the stable hand had detached the float-cart. He mounted Killer and took off toward his place, putting as much distance between himself and Quinn as possible. Seadon rode Killer hard, but the horse didn't mind as Seadon gave him his head and he galloped at full speed across the expansive lawn.

Quinn sat there on the couch trying to steady her nerves. She had watched Seadon pace the room, the questions and hurt on his face. After he ran out she tried to gather her composure before deciding to stand up and run after him. She was nowhere close to catching up with him however, so she stood on the front stoop and watched as he and Killer sped out of the stables and across the lawn, disappearing into the forest surround.

She felt awful for keeping such things from him, but as commander of the military she had little choice. How could she have revealed to him who she was without telling him the full story? There would be too many holes, and he would have asked questions, like he always did. If only she and Willa hadn't been using Chindarian to speak to each other about personal things, this might have never happened. They had become too comfortable and careless with their conversations in their native tongue, thinking no one here could understand them. Now, because of it, she had hurt and angered Seadon. Just when she had reconciled herself to the thought of allowing a man to invade her life, she had simultaneously driven that very same man away.

If only Seadon could understand the extent of torment she and Willa had suffered at the hands of horrible men. The threats, the beatings, the mistreatment and starvation when they wouldn't comply with orders. Many young girls had suffered, and it caused most of them to mistrust men all together; Willa and Quinn included. It had taken them nearly a year to trust the people who crossed their paths, especially men.

Fortunately, King Wilberforth, Dr. Breighton, Trent, and Mr. Mardel were all kind and generous. Willa grew to love King Wilberforth as a real father and he felt the same for her as his real daughter, and Mr. Mardel was patient and kind to both the girls. Realizing that they had not only been mistreated but lost their own families, with no way to return to them.

Willa, of course, had no desire to be reunited with her past. She had been born to a poor family, who had often mistreated her anyway. The short time on board the ship that had stolen them was little different for Willa, and when she was given the opportunity for a privileged life, she took it and never looked back; assuming the identity of the princess. Since no one knew of the princess's existence or her name, the king let Willa keep her own since neither wanted to overshadow the life of the real princess by assuming her name. He then added the name of his dead wife, Revellia, queen of Belarusel, as her middle name.

Both girls from then on were raised in loving homes for the remainder of their younger lives, though Quinn was nearly seventeen at the time and basically an adult. She had a harder time overcoming the mistreatment as more had been placed on her since she had nearly been a fully grown woman at the time of their abduction. Quinn trusted very few people, least of all men. She was given many opportunities in Montesario-Belarusel concerning education, and excelled in her last few years of school, learning proper English quickly. Her desire to defend herself and other young girls was her driving force in her secondary choice of training which was military school. Again, she excelled and quickly climbed the ranks to the position of commander at a very young age.

If only she could convince Seadon to listen to the rest of her story, perhaps he might understand her distrust, and maybe understand her hesitation at telling him about her past.

Chapter 19

Daikinar—the world on the other side of the Montesario-Belarusel portal. Somewhere in the ocean.

The *Raik* was still up to its old tricks of kidnapping young men for crew. Unfortunately, they had taken a few young men that belonged to some very important families throughout Daikinar. High prices were paid for information concerning the ship or ships that had taken the boys, and those families had commissioned military crews and ships, sending them in all directions to search the high seas for the young men. Ten ships in all set out in search of the dreaded *Raik* to capture the feared crew, return the boys to their homelands, and bring to justice the men who had left families bereft for many years.

Another ship also sought the *Raik*, but not for the same reasons. Captain Veramere was angry about Seadon's escape and he felt tricked by Captain Iramor. How could the captain of the *Raik* have the boy on board his ship for so many years and not know what he was capable of? He had picked the lock to the shackles and jumped overboard in the midst of a storm. Veramere wasn't sure what the glowing light in the middle of the storm was, but Seadon had dove directly into it and was gone.

When the light disappeared, Seadon was nowhere to be seen. That light had to have something to do with him being able to just vanish. The only thing that gave Veramere hope was the knowledge that his shot had found its mark and the Seadon Brinley had perished shortly after his escape. If he landed in the water when he jumped, a wound like that would have attracted every shark in the sea for miles finishing him off.

If not, then wherever the man ended up, hopefully he bled to death. Either way, Veramere had paid good money for Seadon Brinley, and he had been cheated out of getting his money's worth. Captain Iramor and the *Raik* would pay dearly for the treachery and deceit with which they had entered the deal.

Captain Veramere had been fortunate enough to be sitting in the tavern when the first mate of the *Sea Palisade*, a newly sanctioned military ship, had inquired of the tavern workers and regular customers of the whereabouts of the *Raik*.

Veramere smiled at the information he had just received, and he and his crew hurriedly took to sea in pursuit of the *Raik*, hoping to reach them before the *Sea Palisade* got the chance. Veramere wanted revenge and his coin back, and the *Raik* and its crew would pay dearly.

The *Raik* sliced through the water, moving as quickly as she could, pursued by the *Reaper*.

Captain Iramor yelled, "Mr. Whiteclaw, a tempest is brewing off the port bow. It looks like it'll provide us lift."

"But Captain, if we cloud-sail, won't the *Reaper* have the advantage?" Whiteclaw asked.

"Nay. The *Reaper* is larger and heavier than the *Raik*. We'll be in the air and halfway across the ocean before the *Reaper* obtains her sky position."

"Why does the *Reaper* wish to engage us anyway, Captain?"

Iramor said, "I heard that Brinley jumped ship and disappeared in the water's somewhere out this way. Veramere seems to think that I knew something special about Brinley and didn't tell him. So now, I assume he blames me for the loss of his slave and he's wanting his money back."

"Captain, that was six months ago."

"A pirate doesn't care about time, Mr. Whiteclaw, only revenge and what he thinks is fair. And Veramere doesn't have a fair bone in his body, and revenge is what colors his eyes."

Captain Iramor watched the storm ahead and the ship closing in behind them. He yelled, "Prepare for lift Mr. Whiteclaw."

Xavier Whiteclaw yelled the order. "Prepare the ship for sky-sailing boys but leave the mainsails until the last to continue our run from the *Reaper*!"

The crew of the *Raik* prepared for lift as the storm approached.

Iramor watched as the *Reaper*'s heaviness in the water pushed faster under the speed of the wind and was quickly cutting the distance between the two ships.

The man standing watch in the crow's nest yelled down, "Captain Iramor, there's another ship, a large one on the starboard aft of the *Reaper*, making a quick approach!"

Captain Iramor pulled out his spyglass and viewed the direction the report specified. "Well gentlemen," he yelled, "it appears we have a military ship approaching. I can't yet read her name though. It matters not anyway. If we go down today, men, we'll take them both with us."

The crew of the *Raik* shouted in answer.

Whiteclaw asked, "Who do you think she's after, Captain?"

Iramor laughed, "Either of us she can catch, Xavier. She may even be feeling her sea oats thinking she can best us both. We'll give her and the *Reaper* a run for their money." Iramor stowed his spyglass back in his pocket and ordered, "Those of you who aren't working the rigging for up-lift man the guns above and below, the stern and aft chase guns, ready your weapons and prepare for an epic battle at sea boys; one for the books if anyone survives to tell the tale!" Iramor's raucous laughter filled the air.

The *Raik*'s crew scuttled about the deck performing the duties laid upon them. Men pulled the fire guns into position, locking them down as others stood by preparing to quickly lash the main sails to the side planks to prepare for lift, waiting anxiously on First Mate Whiteclaw's last minute order to do so.

If they moved too early under the threat of being overtaken by another ship, they risked stalling the *Raik* in the water and giving the attacking ship leverage. The fact that there were two ships quickly headed toward them made everyone nervous. The crew waited with trepidation at their positions, now split between duties.

Normally they were preparing to do battle or preparing for uplift and sky-sailing; they had never had to attempt both tasks simultaneously.

Captain Iramor yelled, "The Tempest appears to be heading away from us, Mr. Whiteclaw. Catch her up or the *Reaper* will overtake us for certain before we even have a chance. Our guns are half what the *Reaper* boasts. We're ready to fight, but if we can outrun them, it's all the better for the *Raik*!"

"Aye, Captain! Should we use the lift engines for a boost in the water sir."

"Nay, Whiteclaw. To do so may foul them both and prohibit lift at all. Just keep her steady and straight on course and use the wind to push her along."

"Aye aye, Captain!" Whiteclaw expertly steered the ship toward the storm, using the outer bands of the storms circulating winds to fill the sails and push the *Raik* toward the powerful storm forming just a few miles away.

Iramor pulled his spyglass out once more, finding the military ship nearly upon the *Reaper*, and the *Reaper* only a few hundred yards behind the *Raik*, nearly within firing distance of the aft chase guns.

Iramor yelled over the winds that now whipped across the ship's deck as waves began to swell and break against the ship's hull. "Make ready the aft guns! The *Reaper* is soon within range and may be letting loose their bow chase guns. Don't fire until fired upon or until given the order!"

The crew of the *Raik* yelled their understanding as they hunkered into their positions. The anxiousness from the threat of war with a ship having the reputation the *Reaper* had weighed heavily upon them.

The *Raik* sliced through the water, catching up to the tempest; as the ship entered the outer bands of the storm. Large, heavy drops of rain began to pelt the deck as lightning and thunder sliced through the air above. The dark heavy clouds circled above them causing small waterspouts to reach up to the swirling clouds not too far from the ship.

Whiteclaw yelled, "Loose the sails for lift boys!"

The crew bolted, quickly loosening the ropes and attaching them to their positions along the bulwark.

The sails of the *Raik* began to fill and the fire cannons sang as the heat tried to push the sails to fullness; fighting against the swirling winds and rain whipping about then crumbling the large sails. After a few minutes, the ship began to rise from the water as the raging sea and waves slammed the hull, rocking the ship as it rose higher, eventually clearing the ocean's surface.

Whiteclaw yelled, "Engines full!"

The ship's propulsion engines for sky-sailing roared to life, but before Whiteclaw could engage the rudder connection, the deep thumping succession of cannon fire was heard and cannon balls slammed into the ship, one of which took out the main mast and ripped the sail ropes from the cleats. The large sails lost their air and the *Raik* fell from the sky, slamming down into the rough water below, sending several crew members overboard. The fire guns lit one of the *Raik*'s falling sails on fire landing on the deck, but it was quickly doused with the waves that sloshed across the deck of the *Raik*, sweeping even more of her crew into the angry sea. Whiteclaw heaved to keep the helm straight and to keep the *Raik* from listing from the force of hitting the water unexpectedly.

Captain Iramor nodded and Bosun Kaliel yelled, "Fire at will boys. Send the *Reaper* to meet her maker, down to the depths of hell by way of Davy Jones' locker!"

The *Reaper* was nearly starboard side as cannon fire rang out. Both ships let loose their weapons upon each other. Wood splintered and flew in all directions as pieces of the Bulwark of both ships blew apart. Cannon fire blew large holes in the hull of the ships as the *Reaper* caught up to the *Raik*. Men attempted to board the *Raik* from the *Reaper*, some making it on board and some overtaken by the violent sea that raged around them. The waves rocked the ships, causing them to collide on more than one occasion, breaking off further pieces of the ships outer hull. The boards that lined the bulwark on both ships which the sails attached to for sky-sailing were sheared off with each collision of the ships. The holes from the cannon fire let large amounts of water into the ships' lower decks, as the storm continued to rage and the waves pulsed around them.

The Sea Palisade, the third ship in the chase, slid up beside the *Reaper*. It was a heavily fortified military ship which was commissioned to find the stolen children by the government of Chindaria, and the other city ports in the Daikinar territories where children went missing. It bared down hard on the pirate ships; its guns and weapons systems were unrivaled by any other military ship at sea.

Captain Stratford yelled, "Stall the ship's men and take prisoners. The *Reaper* stands between us and the *Raik*, which is our target. Many of the boys aboard the *Raik* are who we've been commissioned to bring back; especially the Governor's sons! The captain and crew of the *Reaper* are known for their cruelty and unwavering ability to make widows of the sailors who dare to sail the seas on any ship but their own! Let's put an end to their treachery today, men! However, I want prisoners with which to return home so that those who have been harmed can find justice for the wrongs done against them!"

The *Sea Palisade* loosed cannon and gunfire upon the *Reaper*, ripping holes in the ship's starboard side as the *Raik* splintered the port side. The three ships fought the battle, the *Reaper* now receiving the worst of it as it was pummeled from both sides. The ships were so close at times men could have jumped from one to the other if the water would have been calm enough.

The men below decks worked frantically to try and patch the holes in the ships' sides but it was impossible to do with the constant rocking of the waves and the occasional cannon fire still happening. Some of the holes created by earlier cannon-fire had loosed some of the cannons below the decks and the large, heavy iron guns rolled back and forth with the constantly crashing waves and the impact from the other ships.

Men ran to avoid getting crushed by the large cannons, all while trying to secure them from smashing into the ship's hull and busting another hole in its sides.

The battle seemed to go on forever, made more difficult by the tumultuous sea, heavy rain, lightning, and waterspouts the helmsmen tried to avoid. Unfortunately, with the three ships side by side, the *Reaper* was locked into position when a small waterspout dropped down in their direct path.

Both outside ships quickly steered away from the *Reaper* giving it little time to maneuver. The *Reaper's* helmsman whipped the wheel left, turning the ship enough that the spout wouldn't travel the full length of the deck. The spout cut across the bow of the boat, sucking up loose rigging, cannon balls, tools, and men. The damage from the spout was brief but violent, and as it made its way across the water the debris it had captured was thrown in every direction, some landing on the deck of the *Raik*.

A cannon ball thrown by the waterspout sliced through the stairway to the Poop deck, dismantling a portion of it.

The ships all shifted, trying to navigate the intense storm and the ever-growing height of the waves. The fighting had ceased as each ship focused on surviving the intense tempest that didn't seem as though it would let up anytime soon. The ships spread out enough to avoid slamming down on each other in the high waves. They fought the sea for another fifteen minutes, everyone simply trying to survive the intensity of it.

The *Sea Palisade* continued its pursuit of the vessels. Even though the ships were far apart by now, the damage sustained by the *Reaper* and the *Raik* was taking its toll on the ships. Both were setting lower in the water now, their hulls full of the water washed into them by the storm. Both crews frantically pumped water from the lower decks, trying to avoid the sinking of the ships in the middle of the ocean.

The *Reaper* tried to take an outside position but was unable to navigate it quickly enough because of the size, weight, and damage to the ship as both the *Raik* and the *Sea Palisade* closed in around the *Reaper* once again.

The *Raik* fired, but with the uptake of the wave beneath the ship, her cannon missed the *Reaper* and struck the bulwark of the *Sea Palisade,* taking a few of the ships' cannons and men with it. Just as the ships got closer again, a portal opened up in front of them and all three ships disappeared through it.

The *Reaper,* which was in the center of the other two, crashed onto the desert floor first, capsizing to the left. The *Raik* crashed onto the desert floor, landing on top of the *Reaper's* masts and sails as she listed toward the *Reaper,* landing her starboard side against the *Reaper's* bulwark. The *Sea Palisade* landed at the hull of the *Reaper,* listing port-side toward the *Reaper's* hull and Keel. All three ships sat unmoving on dry desert land, as the water that had filled their damaged hulls and had moments earlier threatened to sink them to the depths of the ocean floor, began to spill out in every direction, soaking the dry desert ground beneath them, all three ships sliding to a sudden halt.

The jarring of the landing from waves to hard dry ground threw all the crew of all three ships forward to the deck or ground, depending on where and how the ship landed. Many of the crew of the *Reaper* were thrown to the desert floor upon their ship's sails, entangled in the ropes and upper ladders or buried beneath the material of the sails; many of the men crushed by the hull of the *Raik's* landing.

The *Reaper's* masts snapped as the *Raik* hit the hard ground. Others of the *Reaper's* crew were crushed by the falling of the ship's port-side cannons as the ropes that held them in place groaned and snapped from the weight and sudden impact of the ship landing dead on its side.

Confusion ensued afterward as people scrambled to right themselves, dizzy, injured, uncertain what had happened. The few crew members of the *Reaper* who were unharmed unbound themselves from the rigging and sails. They tried to help those they could hear crying out for aid, digging through the rubble and ruin, searching for their crew.

Slowly, over the next half-hour, people from all three ships began to wake after being knocked out from the force of the landing. Many crawled out of the wreckage and stumbled out onto the sides of the *Reaper,* sliding down loose ropes or ripped sails to the now wet desert ground, trying to figure out where they were and how they got there; confused by the desert landscape that surrounded them with no ocean anywhere in sight.

Chapter 20

After some time had passed, and the confusion was replaced with anger in realizing that they were still alive along with the enemy, the fight between the three ships ensued once more; only now the aid of the ship's cannons was of no use to anyone.

Iramor and Veramere began an onslaught of gunfire against one another. What men remained of their crews joined in the fight as both pirate ships fired on each other and the *Sea Palisade*. The *Sea Palisade* returned fire, engaging both ships in the fight. This went on for approximately ten minutes until Veramere decided to call for a truce amongst both pirate ships.

"Captain Iramor," Veramere yelled, still stuck in the middle of the firing, now standing on the ground in the shadows of the listed ships. "I suggest a truce between the Raik and the *Reaper*, and that we join forces to better secure our futures against the power and crew of the *Sea Palisade*."

Iramor didn't trust Veramere, but he was right about joining forces to fight the military ship that would take them all into custody or shoot them dead.

"I accept the truce," Iramor yelled. He then turned to Whiteclaw and said, "Only until we secure our freedom, then take out the crew of the *Reaper*. Spread the word to the men."

"Aye, Captain," Whiteclaw replied, telling the men to pass the orders around the ship.

"Captain," Whiteclaw said, "We need to get to the ground. I think we would have a better chance beneath the ships instead of standing amongst the rubble of the decks and sails."

"Good idea. Pass the word on. We take to the desert to better fight." Men from every ship crawled to the desert floor, each captain likely having the same clarity of thought.

Captain Stratford asked his passengers who had begged passage on the ship, "Mr. Brinley, are you and your family all right?"

Wilkins Brinley answered, "Yes, I believe so, Captain. A little shaken and confused but I believe we are all fine."

"Good. Do you know how to use a weapon?"

"Yes, sir, we all do." Wilkins nodded at Harper, Wynne, and Adda; the girls now eleven years older, making Wynne twenty-five and Adda twenty.

"Take care. This battle on land will be different from one at sea."

"We can handle ourselves, Captain."

Captain Stratford's men rounded up extra guns that had been abandoned by the lost or dead sailors and gave each member of the Brinley family a weapon.

Captain Stratford then said, "Let's make our way to the ground for better visibility but watch your descent as you'll likely be fired upon."

Men scrambled from every ship, running through the sails, riggings, and cargo that was tossed about. Random shots rang out here and there as people appeared from a fallen sail or a ship's bulwark. The battle ensued with everyone trying to get to the ground through the chaos of entangled sails, masts, and rigging.

Wilkins, Harper, and the girls all stuck together, taking a set of toppled steps down to the sides of the *Reaper*, carefully climbing over and through debris. They found the edge of the ship and shimmied down an obliging rope to the ground, quickly taking shelter beneath the *Sea Palisade's* massive hull.

Wilkins said, "Stay hidden. Do not engage anyone in a fight. Only use your weapons as a defense. There are too many blood-thirsty pirates loose on the ground and if any of them should see you two it will cause more trouble."

"Yes sir," the girls answered simultaneously.

"That goes for you too, Harper," Wilkins stressed.

"But I can help fight, Wil," Harper protested.

"I know you can, but I need all of you safe. You three are the only females across three ships of men. Please, just stay here, stay hidden, and be safe."

"Fine." Harper understood his concerns, and, of course, he was right. Her daughters were beautiful young women. She would protect them with her life, even though her girls were skilled in using many weapons. She and Wilkins had made sure they were capable of defending themselves over the years. Harper watched as Wilkins sneaked out from the protection of the ship, ready to take on any stray pirates that wandered in their direction.

Seadon and Killer were just passing over the river bridge when he heard a massive crash of some sort echoing from the desert far across the city and the surrounding mountains. It sounded as if it came from the same direction where he had come through the portal six months back.

"Back to the castle Killer. We need the crew to man the airship."

Seadon and Killer rode fast, reaching the castle five minutes later. As he reigned in Killer, the castle doors opened and people began to run out. The crew of the new airships all ran to meet Seadon on the lawn.

One of the crew said, "Commander Brinley, we have reports from Officer Agnusdei at the watchtower that something really strange is taking place in the desert out past the Jaraphite Mountains."

Seadon commanded, "Meet me at the hanger as quickly as you can."

"Yes sir," the man saluted as the crew all ran for their vehicles.

Seadon locked eyes with a distant Quinn as she and Trent ran for Trent's transport. Seadon was concerned for Quinn with her arm in a sling, but he was also still very angry. He pulled the reins to turn the horse in the correct direction, and he and Killer took off for the hanger.

Seadon and the crew reached the hanger ten minutes later, boarded the airship that took its maiden voyage only an hour earlier and lifted into the air, headed north toward the desert.

He looked back at the crew and said, "This is the real deal people. Buckle up, and let's hope that all systems are operational and ready for battle. We don't get the luxury of a trial run on the weapons systems."

The crew nodded nervously at him, all turning to their stations to perform the duties for which they were newly trained.

Quinn, Trent, and all the other military officials headed for headquarters to arm themselves and mount the speeders and horses. All officers and outposts were on high alert as the cities alarms sounded, letting the citizens of Montesario-Belarusel know to take shelter indoors until given the all-clear. People ran in all directions, scrambling to their homes.

They arrived at headquarters, and amongst the many other officers all preparing themselves in the supply building, Trent turned to Quinn who was arming herself. "Quinn, you can't fight with one arm."

"Watch me, Captain."

"Sorry, Commander. But how are you to ride a speeder and shoot with one hand."

"I'm riding with you and fortunately I'm left-handed, so shooting won't be a problem. I have plenty of clips for the gun, which I can easily load with my right hand."

"I don't like this, Commander."

"It makes no difference what you like, Captain. As your commander, you'll do as I say."

Trent stiffened at the order. "Yes ma'am," he answered.

The two of them finished putting on their bullet proof vests and equipment, straddled a two seated speeder, and headed for the front of the line of men and women who waited on the word from command to pursue the invaders of the city. Quinn and Trent took off for the city gate, followed by sixty speeders and officers armed and ready to protect Montesario-Belarusel.

The wrecked ships were emptying of men as they fled the chaos of shooting, seeking refuge beneath the fallen ships or a grouping of rocks in the desert. Just as most of the men's feet touched down on the desert floor and the gunfire began heavily again, a shadow from above fell across the desert floor briefly blocking out the sun.

The gunfire stopped as all eyes looked up at the large airship sailing above them. Guns on the airship's sides pointed down at the people running across the desert.

Seadon and his crew were shocked at what they saw sprawled across the desert floor. Three large sailing ships lay entangled with one another. Two of which Seadon recognized. The *Reaper* was lying on the ground on its side and the *Raik* and another ship lay sideways against it. Water still dripped from the boards and stained the now wet desert floor beneath the ships.

Harper and Wilkins were shocked at the similarities of the airship above to the ones that used to fly over Zanchier. They looked at each other, now hopeful, thinking of Seadon.

On the airship, Seadon used the communication system to speak to the people on the ground, knowing many would know him.

"This is Commander Seadon Brinley of the royal military for the city of Montesario-Belarusel. Stand down and drop your weapons."

Everyone reacted differently to the announcement. The Brinley's all cheered in excitement from the shadows under the ships. The crew of the *Raik* cheered loudly, as those who had known Seadon were happy he was alive; including Cook and Xavier Whiteclaw. Bosun Kaliel and Captain Iramor sneered in distaste and the crew of the *Reaper*, the few who remained, shot at the airship, spurred by Captain Veramere's anger.

When people heard the shots, the shooting began again amongst the crew on the ground. Speeders soon appeared, surrounding the ships and the people firing at whoever dared fire at them. Trent and Quinn warned the guard to be careful where they shot, but Veramere trained his gun at them and began shooting at them. Quinn and Trent ran for the safety of the ships, sneaking between the still creaking and often falling debris.

Seadon grew worried, recognizing Trent and Quinn out front of the speeder brigade. He fussed underneath his breath, knowing that Quinn's injuries were too great and she had no business engaging in battle at the moment. He needed to be on the ground.

He turned in his seat. "Officer Ebner," he said to the gifted young woman. "Take the helm."

Officer Ebner's eyes grew wide with protest. "But sir, I don't know how to fly yet."

"You controlled the landing this morning. Up is just the same, only in the opposite direction."

"Why sir, where are you going to be?"

"On the ground. They need help down there, and I have some scores to settle."

"So are we landing sir?" Officer Ebner asked, taking the Captain's seat, awaiting orders.

"No."

Seadon grabbed a rope coiled in the corner. He tied it tightly to the inside of the ship's metal framing, opened the door and said, "Let the ship down slowly until the rope's end gets close to the ground. Once I've dropped off, pick her back up and prepare to fire if needed. Just make sure you have a clear shot. Don't hit any of our own people or the other people in uniform; they're likely the good guys."

Seadon saluted, opened the door to the cab, dropped the rope, grabbed it, and wrapped it around his waist, leg, and foot. He then jumped out, sliding down the rope. What he didn't expect was to recognize his father Wilkins Brinley ducking in and out of the debris on the ground. Seadon quickly continued down the rope until he reached the ground, heading in the direction he saw his father go.

Several people whose eyes were trained on the airship watched the scene unfold.

Quinn sucked in a breath as she slapped Trent to capture his attention, pointing toward the airship.

Trent said, "I figured the man was a little crazy but that's over the top."

Quinn relaxed when he landed safely on the ground.

Captain Iramor and Captain Veramere also noticed the daring display by the fearless young man, each moving from their place to confront him.

Iramor smirked recalling the years he had spent having Seadon trained by Whiteclaw, and the time he himself had put into the young man. He cautiously made his way toward the area where Seadon had climbed down the rope, hoping to catch him off guard.

Cook also watched the captain head toward Seadon, following closely so as not to lose the man.

Seadon's descent had attracted more attention than he had planned on as people approached from nearly every direction.

Seadon stepped out of the shadows directly behind Bosun Kaliel who was menacingly approaching two unsuspecting young women.

Seadon called to him, "Bosun Kaliel."

Kaliel spun to see Seadon standing there with a gun in his hand. Kaliel asked, "Why don't you shoot me, boy?"

"I'd rather beat you to death with my bare hands, you know, for old-time's sake."

The girls didn't recognize Seadon, but he knew who they were. He chose to wait to tell them until after he was done with the bosun.

Kaliel dropped his sword as Seadon dropped his gun. The two men circled one another as the two girls watched, unsure who to root for. They decided to back up and watch from a safer distance.

Wynne said to Adda, "That man, he seems familiar."

Adda said, "Perhaps it's Seadon. We know he's here."

"But he's in the airship, remember. He announced it from the cockpit."

"Oh, yeah. Okay, back to not knowing who to root for."

Wynne nodded toward Seadon. "I'd have to say that we are safer with him than the large man with the partial metal arm."

Seadon and Kaliel paced in front of each other for just a few seconds when they both stepped forward together. Kaliel swung his metal arm at Seadon's head. Seadon ducked, kicking his leg out and tripping the bosun, causing him to fall backwards.

Kaliel quickly got up but not before Seadon swung, punching the man in the jaw and ripping the two hoop rings in his lip from their place. Kaliel took the punch and grabbed Seadon around the waist, pushing him backward against some toppled cargo boxes, punching Seadon in the stomach. Seadon kneed Kaliel in the stomach then brought his two clasped hands down slamming them between his shoulder blades, sending him to his knees.

Seadon then lifted his foot, kicking the bosun in the face, sending him backward. Kaliel quickly stood up and ran at Seadon, swinging hard in a downward motion with his good hand, catching Seadon on the side of the face.

Kaliel then brought his metal hand upward toward Seadon's jaw, but Seadon saw it coming and dodged the punch which likely would have broken his jaw. Seadon punched Kaliel in the side that opened up to him after the swing. Kaliel's elbow came down hard on Seadon's back knocking him to the ground.

Seadon grabbed a broken piece of wood from the ship's side, and with two hands swung with all of his might, sending the board across Kaliel's face and sending him sailing backward, landing on a piece of broken wood that impaled his chest, ending the fight and Kaliel's life. After a moment of staring at Kaliel's now lifeless body, just to be certain that he was dead, Seadon turned to Wynne and Adda.

"Are you two all right?"

Wynne answered, "We're just fine. What about you? You're the one bleeding?"

Seadon laughed. "Just like you Wynne. Straight forward with no mushy stuff."

The girls both squealed and ran at him. "Seadon!" They threw their arms around him, hugging him tightly.

Adda asked, "But weren't you in the airship?"

Seadon smiled. "I was." He then added, "You two stay here. I have to go help someone." He picked up his gun and looked at them.

They nodded their understanding, deciding to move further outside away from the body of the man Seadon had just fought.

Seadon ran through the debris hugging the shadows of the ship, searching for Quinn. He noticed his mother Harper moving through some debris just a little way across the desert. Another man was approaching her from behind. Seadon stood, took aim at the man, and fired.

Harper was suddenly startled by a noise behind her and turned to see a man lying dead. She searched the area looking for who had shot him, her eyes stopping at a young man whose gun was aimed in her direction.

"Seadon?" She yelled, unsure if it was him.

Seadon smiled, saluted her like he used to when he was young, and disappeared amongst the ship rubble.

Harper's heart soared knowing her second son was safe, although barely recognizable from the boy who had disappeared nearly eleven years earlier. Happy tears streaked her cheeks as she quickly made her way back toward where the girls waited out the fighting.

Quinn and Trent made their way through the rubble, shooting back at anyone who shot in their direction.

Trent said, "I'm not even sure who we're fighting here."

"Me either, but it's safe to say that the uniformed men are likely military like us."

Trent nodded. "True, but if we were fighting another country, their officers would be uniformed."

"You make a very good point," Quinn stated.

At that moment, Captain Stratford appeared beside them, and Quinn instinctively raised her gun to fire. Captain Stratford raised his hands in peace.

"Sorry, I'm Captain Stratford of the *Sea Palisade*. I hope we fight for the same side."

"Depends on what you're fighting for," Quinn asked, her weapon still trained on the captain.

"We are commissioned to bring the stolen boy's home and capture the pirates to stand trial for their crimes."

Quinn and Trent nodded. She grinned and said, "Then we fight for the same side. I'm Commander Quinn Quimby and this is Captain Trent Mardel."

"I'd say pleased to meet you, but this is hardly the time for pleasantries," Captain Stratford stated. "I assume you know the commander who is flying the airship?"

"Yes," Quinn stated, confused.

"I believe he is the son of the people who begged passage on my vessel. They said he was taken ten years back. Has he been here this whole time?"

Quinn was shocked to think that Seadon's family was here in Montesario-Belarusel. "No, he only arrived a few months back."

"Well, I'd say we were very fortunate to find him then. Now, back to fighting." Captain Stratford left them, going in a different direction.

Quinn said, "This fight will take forever with all the places the pirates can hide. We don't even know how many we are fighting against."

"Hopefully our troops will round everyone up soon and it'll be over."

Quinn and Trent stepped out from behind the rock to make their way across an expanse of desert. When she ran across toward another group of rocks Seadon saw her, watching with concern.

Veramere watched Seadon from a distance and realized that the woman with the sling must be important to him. If Veramere couldn't get to Seadon personally, he'd hit him where it hurt most. Fortunately the woman with the sling was headed in his direction.

Chapter 21

Seadon made his way toward where Quinn had disappeared into the rocky desert terrain, dodging bullets as he went. He followed where he thought Trent and Quinn had passed, coming upon a scene he didn't want to see. Trent lay on the ground, shot in the shoulder and bleeding from his head as well. At first Seadon thought he was dead, but he soon realized that he must have stumbled and hit his head on a rock. No one else was around; which really bothered Seadon. Where was Quinn? Seadon sneaked over to check to make sure that Trent was alive. Seadon took off his flight jacket and then his t-shirt. He stuffed the shirt over Trent's wound and used his gun harness to keep pressure by tightening the strap. He then put his flight jacket back on as it had a bullet proof vest inside and went looking for Quinn. He came upon a trail of blood, dropped here and there that disturbed him. If it weren't for all the people out here right now trying to kill one another he'd yell for her.

Seadon sneaked along carefully trying to keep an eye on the blood trail. He stepped out between some very tall rocks and suddenly came upon a scene that made his heart lurch in his chest.

"It's about time you came looking for this one, boy." Veramere sneered, his gun pointed at Quinn's head who was kneeling with her hands tied behind her back with her own sling. Veramere was bleeding from his leg, shot by someone. Seadon could see the pain in Quinn's eyes from the position of her injured arm.

"This is between you and me, Veramere. Let the woman go."

"Well, you see, I figure this isn't any ordinary woman. I figure, just from watching you, that you have feelings for this one."

The look on Seadon's face as he looked at Quinn told Veramere he was right.

"It doesn't matter. Let her go, and I'll go with you."

Veramere laughed. "Go where? My ship's lying in the desert, broken and unrepairable. Most of my crew is dead, and it's all because of you."

"Me?" Seadon asked incredulously.

"You!" Veramere yelled. "You didn't keep your part of the bargain, boy. Jumping ship and escaping; making me chase you across worlds." Veramere motioned to the strange place where they stood.

"I had no bargain with you, Veramere," Seadon seethed. "Your deal was with Iramor. I had no choice in any of it."

Veramere nodded. "Well, that's true enough. But chasing down Iramor for selling me a trickster was bad on him, so I went after the *Raik*. You can see the results of that."

"Listen, Veramere, I had nothing to do with you ending up here. Just let her go and you and I can settle this between us, like men."

Veramere sneered at Seadon. "I think not." He pointed the gun at Quinn and a shot rang out.

Seadon ran forward, screaming, "No!" stopping briefly when Veramere fell over dead. He stood there, shocked by the switch in circumstances. He closed the small gap between them and grabbed Quinn, pulling her to her feet, and quickly untying her hands, trying to be careful with her arm. He turned her to face him.

"Are you all right?"

"Yes, Seadon, I'm fine, except for my arm."

Seadon grabbed her and hugged her fiercely. He leaned back, planting a kiss on her lips, then pulled her to him again, not daring to let her go. He then looked around for the person who had killed Veramere. Seadon shielded his eyes against the sun, peering up over the rocks when his eyes landed on someone.

Just a little way off, Seadon could see Xavier Whiteclaw standing on top of a rock behind a taller one. Xavier saluted him, and Seadon, smiling broadly, saluted back. He turned to Quinn, helping her put her injured arm back into the sling.

Seadon said, "I doubt this will do much good now, but until Doc can see you it'll have to wait. Now, stay with me, you hear?" he warned.

"Yes, I hear," Quinn said. "Actually, I'm going to stay with Trent and see if I can round up a speeder and a float-cart."

"Fine," Seadon said. "Just please be careful, Quinn. I can't lose you."

The look on her face was one of surprise and compassion. "You won't Seadon." She touched his face, just before he took off again to rejoin the fight, only to run into Iramor who had apparently been watching for him as well.

"Seadon my boy, so nice to see you again." Iramor's gun was pointed at his head. His cool demeanor always put Seadon on edge. You could never tell what the man was going to do or when.

"Iramor," Seadon replied.

"Captain Iramor, Seadon. You do know better than to address me any differently."

"That was when you were my captain. You sold me giving up that privilege."

"Regardless, I'm still a captain; or at least I was. Imagine my surprise at traveling through those lights you were always telling us were just heat and lightning pockets. And imagine my further surprise at finding you here, of all places."

"What do you want from me?" Seadon asked, tired and irritable.

"I want you to show me how to get out of this God-forsaken place. I'm meant for the sea, not this dry, dusty, hellhole."

"I have no clue," Seadon lied.

Iramor, cocked the lever of his pistol.

Seadon quickly raised his hands and said, "Okay, but the only way to leave is by a storm." Seadon motioned around at the intense sun and dry desert climate. "Unfortunately, this isn't portal weather."

Iramor looked around at the desert in distaste. "No, it's not. But now that I know what I have to wait for, I no longer need you."

Another shot rang out, and Seadon jumped. Iramor fell backward, with a bullet hole between his eyes.

Cook stepped out of the shadows. "I've been wantin' ta do that for years."

Seadon smiled at his old friend. "Cook." He pulled him into a hug.

Cook wiggled out of it. "Now none a' that mushy stuff, boy." The old man smiled.

Seadon grabbed his hand and shook it heartily. "You're a sight for sore eyes, old friend. Thank you."

"Well, we've all had enough of that blaggard anyhow. Besides, with no ship, we ain't got no captain."

Seadon smiled. "I'll see you later. I've got to find my father. Be careful, Cook."

"I'll be just fine, boy. Go do what you got to do." Cook grinned and added. "I always knew you'd be trouble, boy," he cackled as Seadon smiled and turned running off in the opposite direction.

As he walked from behind a desert rock toward the large flat area in front of the ships, he saw that the Montesario military had rounded up the pirates, with help from the *Sea Palisade* officers. It seemed that everyone was being held at gunpoint as Colonel Manning seemed to have appeared at some point and was giving orders to line the prisoners up and walk them back to headquarters and lock up. He had ordered float-carts to be brought out for transporting the injured as well.

Seadon searched the crowd of people for Wilkins. He told a passing officer about Trent needing a float-cart and where to find the other bodies. He had just finished talking to the man when he suddenly heard his mother's voice yelling his name. He turned to see his father, mother, and sisters headed his way. Seadon ran to greet them, throwing his arms around his father's shoulders as Wilkins wrapped him in a tight hug. Seadon could feel his mother and sisters all gather around them. They stood there for a minute just happy that they had found one another again. When they separated, Wilkins took in Seadon's appearance.

"I never would have recognized you, son. If your mother hadn't pointed you out, I would have thought you were a stranger. You're grown up."

"You and Mother haven't changed a bit, except for a little gray hair." Seadon looked down at his mother, tears streaking her face. He looked at his sisters. "Though, it took me a minute to recognize Wynne and Adda. If not for Wynne's blunt way of speaking, I might not have known it was them."

Everyone laughed. Seadon said, "I'm happy to see you, but I need to go see about someone. I'll be right back."

Seadon ran back to where he had left Quinn and Trent. Officers were loading him onto a float-cart and he was awake and alert. Seadon walked over to Quinn taking her hand in his.

Seadon smiled at the man and said, "Good to see that you'll be fine, Captain."

"Yes, I see I owe you a shirt, Commander." Trent chuckled, tapping the shirt now covered in blood, coughing with the effort.

Seadon smiled. "We can settle up later,"

He and Quinn waved as they pushed the cart away. He then turned to Quinn.

"I'm sorry for being so angry at you this morning."

"Seadon, I understand. It was a lot to suddenly discover."

"When I saw you and Trent running through the desert, I wanted to give you a tongue lashing. But when I saw Veramere's gun pointed at your head I felt as though my life had just stopped. For the first time in my adult life, I was at a loss for what to do. I could always think on my feet, but at that moment, all I could think about was never having you in my life. Never being able to look into your beautiful dark eyes ever again."

"I'll always be here, Seadon. I'll never leave you."

Seadon leaned his forehead against hers and they stood there for just a moment, holding one another, reveling in the momentary peace and silence.

Quinn leaned back, grinned, and asked, "Who was the man that shot Veramere?"

Seadon and Quinn started walking toward the gathering of people in the desert by the wrecked ships. "Xavier Whiteclaw. He's first mate on board the *Raik*."

"I suppose I should have taken the man's life when I had the chance, then none of that would have happened."

Seadon was confused. "What do you mean?"

"I had shot the man in the leg earlier."

"Why not just kill him and be done with it?"

Quinn turned to him, and they stopped walking. "Seadon, it isn't my job to take a life. Life is precious, we only get one. My duty to the people of Montesario is to protect them, but my duty to the Creator is to affect change. A man can't change if he isn't given the chance. And taking his life too soon, will send his soul to hell for eternity. Who am I to take the opportunity for change away?"

"I understand what you're saying, Quinn, but some men are just purely evil. Veramere was going to kill you, and had it not been for Xavier being in the right place at the right time, we wouldn't be here now."

"Xavier, being where he was is not a coincidence, Seadon. I believe in divine intervention. I've experienced it too many times in my life."

Seadon grinned. "We can discuss this later. Right now, I want you to meet my family."

Quinn smiled at him, and he pulled her in the direction where he had left his family earlier. They were still there, waiting for him to reappear.

Seadon was all smiles as he approached. "Father, Mother, Wynne, Adda, this is Commander Quintessa Quimby."

Quinn smiled and offered her hand. Harper grabbed her and hugged her, taking her by surprise. Wilkins and the girls did the same.

"So nice to meet you all," Quinn said, smiling. "Shall we take this reunion to the city and a more comfortable place to visit?"

"Yes, please," Harper replied, still smiling from finding Seadon alive and well.

As the group of people moved to find transport for everyone, Quinn looked at Seadon who gave hand signals to the airship still hovering above. When his attention returned to her, she admonished him for his earlier stunt.

"What if you had fallen from that rope, Seadon?" she asked incredulously.

"I didn't. I guess it was divine intervention." He chuckled at the look she gave him. "All I could think about was you being here on the ground, and me up there unable to help you. Besides, it wasn't like I wasn't used to swinging from the ships rigging between the deck and the crow's nest."

Quinn smiled at him, knowing had it not been for her, he would likely still be up there in his beloved airship. Which meant she ranked highest in his life. Quinn smiled brightly to herself as they straddled a speeder. She wrapped her good arm around Seadon's waist, ready to head back to headquarters. Seadon's family was also seated on other available speeders and given quick instructions on how to operate them, since many of the officers were to march the large line of prisoners back to the city.

Seadon looked at the mass of jumbled ships laying on the dry, dusty desert floor.

"How are we going to explain this to King Wilberforth?"

"You might be surprised. He does know that these portals exist. Willa and I came through one, remember?"

"Yes, but I didn't know how much of that story you told him."

"We were kids, we pretty much told him everything." She laughed at the memory.

"Still, this is a far cry from people coming through a portal."

"True. This will likely make him more anxious now to implement Willamina's airship brigade."

"You have a point there." Seadon grinned at her and they sped away, followed by his family, as the line of prisoners made the three-mile walk beneath the hot desert sun.

As they made it back to headquarters King Wilberforth's car was parked outside. He and Colonel Manning, who had returned earlier, had been discussing the events of the day.

Quinn asked as they approached the king. "King Wilberforth, where is Princess Willamina?"

The king grinned a little before answering. "Shortly after we arrived, Captain Trent passed by on a float-cart headed to the hospital, so Willamina went to see about him."

Quinn nodded, knowing that she would be worried about their old friend. Still, it wasn't like her to go out of her way to check on anyone. She certainly had not come to the hospital to see Quinn, but the king did have her on house arrest at the time.

As Seadon's family entered the building, he introduced them to the king and the colonel.

"King Wilberforth, this is my father, Wilkins Brinley," Wilkins held out his hand and the king accepted it.

"Pleased to meet you sir. Commander Brinley has been a tremendous asset to our fair city."

Wilkins smiled. "Good to hear sir, though I doubt I can take credit for much of that. Our son had been missing these last eleven years. We've only discovered him today ourselves."

"Oh! Is that so?" The king asked incredulously, turning to Seadon. "You'll have to tell me more of your adventures Commander Brinley."

Seadon smiled. "Certainly, Your Majesty, at your earliest convenience."

The king turned to look past Wilkins, "And these lovely ladies are?"

Wilkins said, "Sorry, Your Majesty. This is my wife Harper, and my two daughters, Wynne and Adda."

"Pleasure to meet you all." The king nodded at them, and they responded kindly.

"Is this all of your children, sir?" the king asked.

"No. We are still searching for our eldest son, Bain, who also disappeared about the same time that Seadon did."

"Well, I certainly hope you succeed in your endeavors, Mr. Brinley, and if there is anything I can do to help you only need to ask." The king's graciousness was evident and welcomed.

Seadon said, "Please excuse us, Your Highness, we have a lot of catching up to do."

The king nodded and smiled as Seadon and his family took Quinn to see Doctor Breighton to make sure her arm didn't suffer any more damage. Then he made arrangements for a vehicle for them to go by the hanger to show them the new airship construction, but mainly to pick up Killer, who had been hitched to a post outside the building since Seadon and his crew had taken off in the airship. Seadon also introduced them to the crew and the others that were there, putting away equipment and seeing to the security of the building.

Quinn accompanied them in the vehicle while Seadon agreed to meet them at a local outdoor restaurant to catch up. He rode Killer back to his place to change out of his uniform and vest and put on a shirt. Then he rode killer to meet up with Quinn and his family.

When Seadon approached riding the massive, spirited animal Wynne and Adda cooed, going out to meet him.

Wynne exclaimed, "Seadon, he's beautiful!"

Seadon smiled. "He is, although he can be a pain at times."

Killer shook his head, turning toward Seadon.

Adda said, "He says you're the hot head."

Seadon smiled. He had forgotten that his sisters could telepathically communicate with virtually any creature.

As he dismounted, Seadon indignantly exclaimed, "Is that right? I guess that makes us a good match then."

Killer whinnied, shaking his head up and down. Everyone laughed. The girls each hooked their arms through Seadon's as they walked to the outdoor table where Quinn sat with his parents.

They all greeted him, and he took a seat next to Quinn.

Wilkins asked, "I've seen what you've been up to while here, Son. What else has transpired over the last ten years?'

Seadon filled them in on the parts of his life they had missed, leaving out a few delicate details so as not to distress his parents too much more than they had already been, especially after learning he had lived as a pirate for those ten years. They spent the remainder of the afternoon chatting about their lives and what each had been up to, also getting to know Quinn and hearing her story.

Wilkins was surprised to find out that she was the young girl he had spoken to all those years ago that had led him on the correct path to find Seadon. They were all amazed by the circumstances and situations that had led them all on the paths that had brought them back together again.

Quinn smiled and said, "It's no coincidence, it is the Creator's divine plan."

Wilkins smiled and said, "Seadon, I like her." They all laughed, but then he said, "Seriously though, if not for the Creator's plan and intervention in our lives, we might never have found one another again."

Seadon grinned. "I'm surprised you never left Chindaria to search for Bain."

Harper put her hand over her sons. "Why would we leave our younger son behind to search for our eldest? At that moment,

Seadon, you were more important. We knew you had been taken against your will. There was no way we would ever have left you behind. As far as Bain is concerned, he walked through that portal in Storm Valley of his own free will. Bain was older and had already lived on his own. We know that somewhere out there, he's safe and one day we will find him again."

Seadon smiled at her, grateful for his loving and persistent parents.

The afternoon dragged into evening, and everyone was growing tired after their long day. Realizing that his family had nowhere to stay, Seadon procured them a couple of rooms close to his own at the local hotel where he had been staying. Everyone said goodnight and Seadon went to his room, alone.

As he lay in bed, his mind wandered through the events of the day; it dawned on him at that moment that he had been living out of a hotel. He had been in Montesario-Belarusel for four months and had nothing permanent to show for it; except for Killer. He wasn't even certain that he wanted to stay here, even though he had a lot going for him at the moment.

Quinn was, of course, the main reason he would stay. The airship academy was just beginning and he had been given a commanding position as head over the entire project. He lived in a beautiful city which was ready to take the next big steps toward advancements in science and discovery; but was staying here really what he wanted?

Honestly, he wasn't even sure he could leave. He hadn't looked for, or seen, any portals during the very few storms that had taken place here. Seadon fell into a fitful sleep with the events of the day and the pondering of his future on his mind.

Chapter 22

Seadon woke the next morning, a bit tired, but happy. He got dressed and walked down to his family's room and knocked. Harper answered the door smiling brightly.

"Good morning, my son." She reached out and grabbed him into a fierce hug. She pulled back and smiled at him. "I'm sorry, I'm just relieved that it wasn't all a dream. I'm just so glad to see that you are all right."

Seadon smiled back as he walked into the room. "I'm fine, Mother; never better actually."

Wilkins appeared around the corner. "Good morning, Son. What's the plan for today?"

"Well, you've seen most everything there is that I could show you yesterday. I figured we could head over to the castle, and I'll show you around there."

Wilkins smiled. "Sounds good. Then what?"

Harper slapped him on the arm. "Wil, give the boy a break. He doesn't have to entertain us."

Wilkins laughed. "I know, but we all have to figure out what we are going to do from here on out."

Harper asked, puzzled. "What do you mean? We still haven't found Bain."

Wilkins answered, "Exactly. But just because we've found Seadon doesn't mean that he's going to just give up his life here to go storm-walking the world in search of his now eleven-years, older brother."

Harper turned concerned eyes to Seadon. "I never thought about leaving you again after finding you. I suppose things have to change. We can't all stay together now, can we?"

Seadon walked forward and took his mother's hands in his. "No, but surely there is a way we can find each other when we want to. There has to be signatures in the storms or the level of force they create to allow us to navigate the world and dimensions. Mother, you are a brilliant scientist. If anyone can figure out how to track time or find familiar traces in patterns, you can."

Harper smiled at her son, brushing his cheek with her hand. "You're absolutely correct there. The only problem with that is finding a place to work, the funds to support it, and designing the equipment to use."

Seadon smiled. "I might have an idea on that, and even a man who might can help build it."

They all finished getting dressed and went for breakfast. Seadon called on Quinn to join them, riding in the large headquarter-sanctioned vehicle so they could all ride together. After breakfast they made their way to Montesario-Belarusel castle to show them around, and so that Seadon could chat with King Wilberforth about his idea, and the further protection of Montesario-Belarusel from outside forces.

Once they arrived, Quinn took over introductions with Princess Willamina while Seadon was brought before the king in his private chambers.

The butler announced him. "Commander Seadon Brinley, Your Majesty." The butler bowed slightly and left.

King Wilberforth smiled brightly from his position behind his large desk. He stood as he spoke, walking forward to greet him, his hand extended. "Commander Brinley, so good to see you this morning. Tell me, what can I do for you, sir?"

Seadon accepted the handshake and said, "I have a proposition for you, Your Majesty."

"Oh? Another one already." The king chuckled.

"Yes, especially in light of what has taken place recently. You know about the story Quinn told you, and of course, where I come from is obviously elsewhere; not of this world. You see that not only can a few people suddenly arrive here in Montesario-Belarusel, but entire ships filled with men. Some are good, and some are not."

"Yes, I see where you are going with this. What do you suggest we do to stop the unexpected and unintentional invasions?"

"They may be unexpected and unintentional now, Your Majesty, but if more men find out that time-travel between worlds exists, and figure out how to traverse it through storms, it may lead to greater invasions and create many problems for the city."

The king listened thoughtfully, his understanding and concerned piqued. "What do you suggest, Commander?"

"As you know, my parents came through the portal yesterday on the *Sea Palisade.* My mother, Harper, just happens to be a brilliant scientist from our homeland. I believe sir that Montesario should fund a research center to study storm travel, learning how to tell when one will open otherworldly portals, not only to benefit Montesario-Belarusel, but to protect her from would-be invaders."

"Hmm, this sounds like a wonderful plan. I suppose as we add on to the airship school, that adding a science and technology center would be beneficial as well. There's plenty of land out by the hangers to add the centers. We'll call it the Willow Center for Scientific Educational Research and Development. Willow is Willamina's nickname from childhood. She always hated it. She said I was comparing her to a tree."

Seadon smiled. "How about we reference it as the S.E.R.D. Center for short."

"Yes, that is much easier to say." King Wilberforth chuckled. "Wonderful plan, Commander. I'll see to the commissioning of the building right away. Our cities seem to have blossomed since your arrival. For many years, I spent time in meetings, and peace talks. I should like the change of pace of staying home and tending to the safety and protection of Montesario-Belarusel for a change. Besides, we have a monumental job of cleaning up the wreckage in the desert and seeing to the hundreds of new men who have fallen upon our borders. Perhaps, Commander, you can see to figuring out what to do with these men. I know many are imprisoned, but many more are left with figuring out what they will do in this new world they've stumbled into."

"I can do that, Your Majesty. I assume that many will want to return to their world, should we find the opportunity and ability to send them back, especially the men of the *Sea Palisade*. Most have families, wives and children they will want to go home to."

"Yes, I see your point, Commander. We'll sanction this S.E.R.D. Center straight off. Ask your mother what it is she will need to begin her studies so that we may see if we can get these men home."

"Thank you, Your Majesty." Seadon nodded and bowed.

"No, no, thank you, Commander Brinley. Montesario has a much brighter future as we implement the many plans we've spoken about. It's an exciting new age, with my daughter Willamina leading us. I'm very proud of the decisions she has taken upon herself to implement. Soon, Montesario-Belarusel will be a formidable foe, or ally, for any nation."

Seadon smiled as he and King Wilberforth shook hands.

Seadon excused himself to go find his parents to tell them the good news. He also wanted to find Quinn and ask her to join him that evening for a private dinner, just the two of them. They had yet to discuss where their relationship was going.

It seemed like a week had passed since the revealing of the airships and the maiden voyage, him overhearing Quinn and Willamina speaking Chindarian and all that revealed, his anger at Quinn and the war in the desert, his parents appearing, and the realization that he was in love with Quinntessa Quimby when her life was threatened. It had all transpired in the last twenty-four hours. So much had happened in that short time.

Seadon needed some time just to process everything and get his head wrapped around all the plans that he was involved with now. Like his new commanding position over a new facility for the teaching and learning of airship building and flight. A new facility for further study and research for technological advancements of time-travel and weather study. The continued development of the float-cart harnesses for equine transport. The modifications for rough terrain speeders and water-travel speeders. The clean-up of the wreckage and placement of the men from the ships, his family suddenly being in his life again, and, of course, Quinn, the most important of them all.

He didn't know when or how he fell so hard for her, but she had completely invaded his heart and soul. Seadon's future was bright but also getting busy. Gone were the carefree days of sailing the oceans and skies. He would see to all things appointed to him, making sure that the people he loved were secure and taken care of. Then he would think about his forever future and where that might take him.

Seadon found everyone on the patio of the castle's receiving room, looking out over Montesario Lake and the mountains.

Wynne said, looking at the distant mountains. "I would love to walk those mountains and see what there is to see from there."

Quinn said, "Not those mountains to the right. Those are the Jaraphite Mountains. Exposure to the dirt for very long and you'll live to regret it. It causes a degenerative muscle disease that slowly deteriorates until it cripples you."

"Oh!" Wynne said. "I think first order of business should be learning about the region and its dangers."

Seadon laughed. "Yes, and there is this wonderful tasting berry which grows on a splendid looking tree all over Montesario-Belarusel that if eaten with alcoholic beverages will poison you."

Adda laughed, "Leave it to you to find that out."

Seadon sneered at her playfully. "I did, and I would have died if not for the dogged determination of one particular commander." He smiled at Quinn and winked.

She smiled back. "I knew he would be trouble the minute we found him lying in the desert."

They laughed and told stories for the rest of the morning and through lunch, at which time Willamina announced, "Commander Brinley, I'm going by the hospital now, should I give Captain Trent your best wishes for a speedy recovery?"

Seadon smiled. "Yes, you shall, and tell him he needs to heal quickly, for we are going to be very busy men."

"Oh?" she asked.

Seadon filled them all in on the newly sanctioned buildings and centers, and what he and the king had discussed. Everyone, especially Princess Willamina, was excited to get started.

"That sounds wonderful," she exclaimed. "So much to keep us all very busy."

"Yes, quite." Seadon's demeanor became more serious as he turned to Quinn. "I'd like it if you could join me for dinner tonight."

"You don't wish to spend it with your family to catch up some more."

"There's plenty of time for that. I want to talk to you. The last time we really spoke, we parted in anger."

Quinn looked at him with compassion. "Of course I'll join you. What time and where?"

"I hoped we could just meet at your place, have dinner, and talk. It's quiet and we won't be disturbed."

"That sounds perfect. How about six o'clock?"

"That's good. Shall I bring take-out?"

"That depends on when I get home."

"You still only have one good arm. And after yesterday, you're lucky Doc didn't cast it anyway."

"I know, I promise I'll take it easy, as long as there are no further invasions." She smiled.

Seadon smiled back. He looked from Willamina who was chatting amiably with his sisters who were both close to her age; not that he was old by any means; and then to Quinn. He couldn't understand how he ever thought he and Willamina would be good together. It wasn't necessarily that he had been in love with her. Sure she was a beautiful woman, but she in no way compared to Quinn. Quinn was the whole package.

Physically beautiful, smart, caring, kind, and she had control over her emotions. Everyone respected her, and she was interested in him of all people. A pirate. A once upon a time pirate, not by choice, of course. Seadon could see where the path of life had taken him, and how the decisions he had made had brought him here.

Perhaps the Creator had been guiding him; even though Seadon hadn't spoken or prayed to Him since the Three Army War so long ago in Zanchier. If Seadon hadn't experienced all the struggles and strife in life, he wouldn't be the strong, determined man he was today. Perhaps it had been the Creator's way to strengthen and grow him into who he would need to be. His goal had been to become a king. Now, he was content just being with Quinn, and wherever that life took them.

Seadon knocked on Quinn's door waiting impatiently for her to answer. He'd gotten himself all riled up that afternoon, thinking too much. Wondering if he was really the right choice for Quinn. Hoping she felt as strongly for him as he did her. He had begun second-guessing himself especially since Quinn had such strong faith. Seadon had done some terrible things in his past. Would she be able to forgive him those wrongs?

Quinn opened the door, a smile on her face. She was wearing a long, comfortable looking dress which billowed about her legs with each movement. The collar was a scooped neck which hit just at her shoulder bones on each side. The sleeves were simple and short, and loose, stopping just at the top of her bicep, leaving room for her sling to sit undisturbed. The shade was a soft lavender, reminding him of the first time he had ever laid eyes on her. As his eyes traveled the length of her he smiled when they landed on her bare feet.

"You look beautiful, Quinn." He entered the house, walking forward only a little as she closed the door.

She smiled, turning to face him. "Thank you, Seadon. I promise, I've dressed more for comfort than beauty."

He grinned, appreciatively, taking her uninjured hand in his and twirling her around. "Well if this is you not trying I can't wait to see you put effort into it."

They came together briefly, their smiles turning to more serious emotions. They stood there for a few seconds just staring into each other's eyes, their hands still locked together. Quinn quickly inhaled and stepped back. "Dinner is on the terrace."

"That sounds great. Shall we eat then?"

She smiled. "Yes. I'm starving. I think the antibiotics that Dr. Breighton has me taking makes me hungry."

They walked outside and sat at her patio table. The night air was cool and the breeze off the rushing river caused Quinn's hair to blow softly about her shoulders. Seadon wanted to reach out and run his fingers through it.

They had a pleasant meal, filling and light. Just as they were finishing up it began to rain and they moved inside on her couch with their glasses of wine and the dessert that Seadon had picked up on the way over.

As they got comfortable, Seadon sat his plate and wine glass on the table and turned to face Quinn, taking her plate and wine glass and setting them beside his own. He then turned back to her, taking her hand in his. He gently caressed the back of her hand, looking at the smallness of it compared to his own. He looked up at her and saw only tenderness in her eyes.

Seadon sighed heavily. "I first want to start off by saying I'm sorry for the way I stormed off yesterday morning."

"I understand, Seadon. That's why I struggled with telling you. I knew it would hurt and anger you."

"It did, but I'm not sure why. You didn't do anything to me. And I truly understand the reasons why you didn't tell me. The fate of a nation rests upon secrecy," he added jokingly, making her giggle.

His hand reached up and found a place against her cheek resting his arm along the back of the couch. His fingers intertwined through her straight, brown, silky hair. "When I saw you and Trent running through the chaos, it startled me at how scared I was."

Quinn began to protest but he stopped her and continued, his hand falling to her shoulder. "I know you're a skilled fighter. But, you are injured, and even if you weren't, that still wouldn't stop me worrying about you."

Quinn smiled, "Yes, so much so that you basically jumped out of a perfectly good airship."

Seadon smiled back. "Because I knew the kind of men who were running loose on the ground. I had spent the last ten years of my life in the company of those very men, and they were not the kind to be taken lightly; ever."

"Yes, I experienced that. And I'm so grateful you were there to save me."

"You were only in imminent danger because of me. Somehow Veramere knew you were important to me. I don't know how because I hadn't really figured that out yet myself."

"You were flirting with me earlier in the reception room after the flight ceremony."

"Well, yeah. I mean, I already knew I liked you; I just didn't know at the time that I had fallen in love with you."

Quinn sucked in a breath, sitting up slightly. "Seadon…"

He put his hand to her lips to stop her words. "I'm not done."

Quinn grinned and settled back down into the couch.

Seadon started again. "Tess." He looked at her and said, "That's my personal nickname for you. I hope you don't mind."

Quinn shook her head and grinned. "Not at all, I like it."

"Good." Seadon started again, "Tess." They smiled at each other. "I know that the life I led before coming here was bad. But being here in Montesario-Belarusel, with you, has changed me. It's not that I enjoyed being a pirate, but it was the hand I had been dealt, and I survived and excelled at it. I have done things I'm not proud of. I just hope that you can look past all of that and accept me for who I am now."

"Oh, Seadon," she said, touching his cheek briefly. "I'm no saint myself. I've told you that Willamina and I were taken by pirates. As girls, we were tormented nearly daily with threats. One man in particular tried to force himself on Willa and I grabbed his pistol and shot him dead. Right there on the ship." Her eyes fell to her lap. "The other men all laughed it off, but all I could do was stare into the face of the man whom I had killed. His lifeless expression haunted me for years afterward, along with the tortured screams of the girls who hadn't been so fortunate."

Seadon took her hands in his and forced her to look at him. "Did anyone hurt you?"

"No. No one tried again after that. It hardened me to the point that I became violent if anyone dared come near me, Willa, or any of the other girls. No one dared to strike us because the captain warned the men not too, since we were worth more on the slave market if we were healthy and unmarked. The only way to keep his prizes healthy was to leave everyone alone or I'd become livid with anger, to the point where I didn't care for myself at all. It was only when we fell overboard and came here was I able to change. The kindness and love of the people who took us in and helped me and Willa to heal. I have to keep my anger in check most days, and I do so with the help of the Creator."

"Well, as long as I am alive, I will protect you with everything in my being. I know it's not necessary, but I'm incapable of not doing so."

Quinn grinned at him and leaned forward, planting a soft kiss on his lips. She pulled back and said, "I understand. I feel the same way. I love you too, Seadon."

They spent the rest of the evening cuddled on the couch, just enjoying the quiet and peace of one another's company.

Chapter 23

Over the next year, Montesario-Belarusel grew into a city known for its militaristic and technological advancements. It became known as the protectorate of all of the country of Vondresonta, hailed so by many other nations.

The airship academy had been built and was in full term with many students training to fly and build the ships, adding another seventeen ships to the fleet, making twenty total with hundreds of people enlisted for flight and ground crew.

The Willow Center, S.E.R.D. for short, headed by Harper Brinley sought to understand and record storms in relation to time-travel. There were hundreds employed by the center in the fields of research, development of tools to aid that research, testing, and storm-hunting to collect data; keeping accurate records on storms, their coordinates, their strength and whether a portal appeared. No one dared enter a portal yet for fear of displacement, but much was being learned.

Wynne and Adda both volunteered to head up the burying of the dead and the clearing of the wreckage from the desert, always being interested in ships themselves, especially after bartering passage on the military ship, the *Sea Palisade,* for the last six months.

Captain Stratford and his men got busy righting the *Sea Palisade* into a dry dock position with the help of several airships, speeders, chains, ropes, and men.

The *Raik* was to be righted as well and rebuilt from the ground up, by orders of Commander Brinley. The *Reaper,* by order of Princess Willamina, was to remain broken on the desert floor where it rested. A stark reminder for future generations that the strange, and once thought impossible, was indeed possible, and that Montesario-Belarusel would stand vigilant and ready if anyone else ever came through a portal.

Harper, back at S.E.R.D., was also developing an alert system to let them know if anything passed through a portal, giving the city time to respond in the desert without bringing the fight inside the city walls.

Quinn was working with the military technicians on the development of the equine harnesses to be distributed to the Mountain outposts. She also pushed for speeders that could handle uneven or rough terrain, allowing the outposts to use them instead of horses if desired. A water speeder that could travel for short distances over calm water was also being created and tested on the lake.

Later that same year, Seadon and Quinn were married in the restored outer-garden gate on the south-western side of the castle. The one where Seadon and Willamina had first met. The garden had been restored by Trent as a surprise for his new bride Willamina, whom he had married earlier that year.

The garden had been Queen Revellia Margosa Belarusel Montesario's private garden when she had been alive, and since Willamina so enjoyed the seclusion and beauty of the forgotten garden and gate, he had restored it as a wedding present. The once forgotten splendor of the broken, iridescent-colored glass which had lain in the top and sides of the scrolled metal was replaced and reflected the light of the rising sun and the dappled light of day throughout.

The two side arches, smaller than the center, curved slightly in the opposite direction from the center arch, forming a slight S-shape. The center arch now displayed a large, beautifully carved bench beneath it with an inscription for the princess laid across the top of the back of the seat.

Large potted ferns graced the ends of both smaller arches and the beautifully intricate, thick, circular, tiled floor which laid into the dirt of the forest beneath and around the arches, was cleaned and restored to its natural glory. Roses and flowering shrubs were planted around the edges and along the pathway that led to the castle wall's gate.

Willamina had insisted that Quinn and Seadon use the beautiful garden for their ceremony and hosted the reception on the castle grounds just inside the gate to the garden. The event was one to be remembered by all. Quinn's gown was simple yet elegant, with small clusters of flowers stitched here and there, up the skirt, intermingling with the same on the bodice.

The whiteness of the flowers turned to shades of lavender, changing colors in the sunlight. Mr. Mardel, Trent's father, and the man who had raised her as his own, even for a short time, gave her away. Willamina was, of course, the maid of honor, and Wynne and Adda both were bridesmaids.

Seadon wore his official Commander's uniform with all of his sewn patches awarded for his contributions to the cities. Trent was the best man, Xavier Whiteclaw, and Reginald Terrabonne, formerly known as Cook, were the groomsmen. King Wilberforth, of course, officiated the ceremony.

In a strange turn of events, Rendel Sweetly and Xavier Whiteclaw became quite enamored with each other, which pleased Seadon as the young woman was persistent even after his marriage to Quinn. Xavier was just the man for Rendel. Both of them were red heads with fiery tempers, keeping each other in line. The only difference between them was that Xavier's temper was always in check, but he knew how to use it.

Everyone seemed to settle into a rhythm, finding something to keep them busy in their new, hopefully temporary, homes. Many of the crew of the *Raik* offered to work on the rebuilding of the ship.

Seadon had told them that once it was ready to sail again, they were going to work on finding a storm to allow the ships to return to their homeland, and any men who wished to return to the places of their birth, would be allowed to return. The *Sea Palisade* offered to return them as well, since they would be returning the recently taken young men the *Raik* had acquired.

At the end of one year, Harper had made some advancements in storm and portal finding, noticing another portal open in the desert where the ships had passed through. She was able to tell when a strong enough storm would appear, allowing the ships to return to the other side.

Captain Stratford, his first mate, and Seadon organized the preparations for the launch process of the *Sea Palisade* and the newly christened ship the *'Quintessa'* to be sent back through the portal to return people home.

Everyone assumed that Xavier Whiteclaw would captain the *Quintessa* upon its return. No one was prepared for the day they learned that was not the case. Seadon and Quinn made an announcement to the family.

Seadon stood at the counter of his and Quinn's home. "Father, Mother, Quinn and I wanted to tell you both that we will be returning to Chindaria with the *Quintessa* when she goes."

"What? Why?" Harper begged, distressed.

"Mother, as much as both of us love it here, we feel that our lives are meant to be lived elsewhere. Quinn is originally from Chindaria and would like to see her family again. And you know that as soon as you figure out storm travel, you, father, and the girls will be leaving here to search for Bain."

Harper sighed heavily. "You're right. We are doing all of this for several different reasons, but the biggest is to find Bain and make sure he's all right."

"You'll know where to find me, and perhaps you can even create a device that can travel over time where we can all stay in communication with one another."

Harper said, though her mind began to work, "That's a tall order, Son."

"And if anyone can do it, you can, Mother."

Harper and Wilkins smiled at Seadon and Quinn giving them both hugs, knowing that soon, they would both be back across the portal into Chindaria and off on their own adventures.

The day had come when it was time to send the rebuilt ships back through the portal into Chindarian waters to return the men marooned in Vondresonta, and the stolen, to their native homelands.

Large rolling tracks had been erected to pull the ships a good distance across the desert floor toward the soon to open portal. The tracks had been built up higher, and around the wreckage of the *Reaper* so as not to disturb the now historical site.

Many airships floated in the air above, with thick tethers attached to pull the two ships, the *Sea Palisade* and the newly sanctioned *Quintessa*, across the rollers on which they now sat. The idea for launching was to build momentum by pulling them and allowing their own force of motion to sling them through the portal and into the open waters beyond. Navigating such a task would be tricky as it was the first time it would take place.

Harper had pinpointed a storm which would hit the area, taking into account the force of the wind and rains, hoping that this particular storm would return them to the world from which they had originally come. Since the portal opened three separate times that they were aware of bringing people here, and they had recorded several other storms where portals had opened since then, they assumed that another such portal would return them to the same location from which they had arrived here in Montesario-Belarusel.

Twenty airships lined the sky, ten each per sailing vessel as a massive crowd of workers and those wishing to say goodbye gathered to watch the launch. Goodbyes were given and tears streaked many cheeks as Harper and Wilkins stood watching their son and daughter-in-law leave them for the foreseeable future.

Wynne and Adda smiled happily, waving to Seadon and Quinn and the many friends aboard the *Sea Palisade* and the *Quintessa* that they had made over the last year-and-a-half.

Seadon instructed the airships from a headset as he, Quinn, and most of the crew of the *Raik* which included Xavier Whiteclaw and his new wife Rendel, readied for launch. Also included in the new crew were several of the single men from the Montesario guard who wanted to seek adventure under Commanders Seadon and Quinn Brinley.

One such guard in particular was the young, ever-observant, watchtower officer Nuncio Angusdei. The twenty something young man was exuberant for travel ever since he started seeing people appear in the desert seemingly out of nowhere. Now that time travel was known to exist, the thirst for knowledge and adventure fueled many a young man's heart to see the known and unknown world.

Seadon watched from the Poop deck of the *Quintessa* and barked orders. "All airships ready and in formation?"

Replies came across the communications device. "Ready Ship One, Commander, Ready Ship Two, Commander..." And so it went as each captain replied in order, giving confirmation.

Seadon replied, "All tethers tight!"

The airships moved slowly in succinct motion as the ropes began to groan against the weight of the ships, tightening and stretching to their capacity.

Seadon bellowed to his crew, "Hold tight crew of the *Quintessa*. We are about to launch!"

Both ships began to move at a snail's pace until the airships had gained enough speed to pull them at a good pace. The storm brewing ahead was gaining power, and rain began to pelt everything and everyone. The heavens rumbled as lightning streaked from cloud to cloud, branching out to strike the desert floor somewhere in the distance.

The ships were now gaining speed and rolling at a decent, yet bumpy pace as the now opened portal glowed brightly. As the ships reached top speed and the airships could no longer stay tethered to them, the tethers were mechanically released from large hooks on both ships' bulwarks and the ships were flung through the portal, one after another, spaced apart so the last would not land upon the first on the other side.

Captain Stratford yelled to the men of the *Sea Palisade*, "Ready to get the ship moving men! We don't want to be sunk beneath the force of the *Quintessa* before we even get started!"

The *Sea Palisade* sailed through the portal first, hitting the water with such force that the ship bobbed up and down in the water, causing waves to break over the deck.

The men scrambled to move her hard to Port to avoid a collision with the *Quintessa* which broke through the portal just a minute or so later, crashing down into the turbulent ocean waters.

When both ships were settled safely in the water, loud whoops and cheers could be heard across both ships as everyone celebrated the successful launch and return home.

After the storm was over and the ships were sailing toward home, Seadon and Captain Stratford asked each person aboard the ships to sign a document agreeing to keep secret the coordinates and location of the portal into Montesario. Pirates still ruled the waters of Chindaria and they didn't want anyone trying to invade Vondresonta and the city of Montesario-Belarusel.

A week later, the two ships pulled into their ports of call. The *Sea Palisade* first returned the stolen boys whose families had sanctioned their voyage, while the *Quintessa* returned anyone who wished to go home to their homelands. The last port was Chindaria, Quinn's homeland.

After Quinn explained to her family what had happened to her she and Seadon took on new sailors to replace the crew who had chosen to leave, and they set sail across the waters for adventure and new ports; not only in the waters but across the open sky as well since advancements in sky sailing had also been set into place.

They had many adventures across Chindaria and other places and worlds. They even experienced other portals to other lands, fortunately landing in water instead of dry land. They even lost a few sailors along the way through unsuspected portals and rough seas which tossed the men overboard.

Nuncio Agnusdei was one such loss. They could only pray that the young man found his way to somewhere new instead of the depths of the sea.

Seadon and Quinn eventually settled down as life at sea was no place to raise a family. They chose a time when life was simpler and Seadon and Quinn could make their fortune with all they had seen and learned during their travels.

"Grandfather," Twenty-four-year-old Portland Aaron Bailey yelled from his position at the helm of the *Quintessa*, the privateer ship that sailed through the Japanese waters in the year thirteen-hundred-and-sixty-six A.D. "What's our heading?"

Captain Seadon Brinley called back, "Let's head home to England, Aaron." Seadon had always called the young man Aaron, after his father's father, never caring for his given name, Portland. "We've been at sea long enough this time, and I'm growing weary. Your Grandmother, Quinn, is ready for me to stay put on dry ground as well."

"Aye, Captain. By way of which coast?"

Seadon grinned. He knew that Aaron had fallen for a young woman off the coast of a small fishing village in Japan. Aaron had promised the girl he would come back for her, and Seadon supposed that he was now ready to make that promise a reality.

"The shortest one possible by way of the Japanese Izu Islands."

Aaron happily yelled, "To Mikura-Jima, Men!"

A shout went up around the ship as all the men of the *Quintessa* knew the young man's heart had been left on that island nearly a year ago. And they all knew that once there, he would be married to the young half-Japanese woman he had met on their last, unexpected stop to the islands. After marriage he would cart her off across the world to England.

Aaron's family had done very well in the shipping and transport business. His grandparents Seadon and Quintessa Brinley had also done well in creating useful technology and industrial equipment that was bought and sold the world over, becoming exceedingly wealthy in the process.

Aaron's father, William Bailey, married his mother Sadine Brinley Bailey, and had four sons. The eldest was named after his great-grandfather, Wilkins, the second was named, Bain after grandfather's only brother, the third was named Brinley, and then there was Aaron. Their father stayed on land and managed the family business along with Brinley. Wilkins captained another one of the ships for the Brinley line, transporting goods across the oceans. And Bain had set off on his own adventures years ago when he had turned old enough. Aaron's heart had always followed the sea like his grandfather Seadon, and he loved the stories and history with which his grandfather always regaled him. He had taken a job aboard his grandfather's ship and worked his way up to first mate. And how fortuitous it had been, especially when Aaron had first seen Kiyomori; he called her Kiyo for short.

Aaron and Kiyomori had fallen in love quickly, and Aaron having to leave the island had nearly broken both their hearts. He had promised Kiyo that he would return soon and take her away from her life as the village outcast. She had been ridiculed and shamed from birth because her mother had been ill-used by a sailor. Kiyomori's mother had grown ill over the years and was fading quickly when he first and last saw Kiyo. If her mother were still alive, he would bring them both back to England with him to their massive family home in an aristocratic neighborhood. Kiyo and her mother would never want for anything ever again, Aaron would make certain of it.

"Aaron, hurry, the baby is coming quickly," Quinn yelled from the door of the bedroom.

"Coming, Grandmother!" Aaron took the marble steps two at a time, reaching the bedroom on the third level of the house just as a baby cried out. He stopped for a moment as he and Quinn exchanged looks and hugs of tearful happiness.

Aaron walked into the room as his mother Sadine handed the now swaddled baby to a tired Kiyo. He approached the bed, sitting beside her as he marveled at the little life his wife held in her arms.

Kiyo smiled. "It's a girl."

Aaron grinned from ear to ear. "Have you chosen a name yet? I personally like the name Gabriele."

Kiyo smiled and giggled. "Well how about Gabriele Hannah Bailey. Hannah means splendid flower in Japanese."

Aaron smiled brightly as he scooped the tiny little girl from her mother's arms. "That sounds wonderful to me. What does Gabriele mean?"

Kiyo smiled. "Divine power."

Aaron's smile broadened as he lovingly looked at the precious bundle in his arms. "Welcome to the world little Gabriele. Your name suits you well. I'll never leave your side. And you and I will be as thick as thieves. I'm going to teach you everything there is to know about the world, and how to defend yourself, just in case you're called to a new, unexpected life. But most of all, I want to introduce you to, and teach you about, the most important person you'll ever meet. The Creator of the universe."

The End.

About the Author

SG Boudreaux homeschooled her three children for over twenty years. After which, God called her to write clean Speculative fiction. She still teaches her youngest, special-need's child. She enjoys music, especially playing the drums with her ladies group for special events, writing, creating new creatures for her books, learning new things, gardening, animals, and all things beach related. She and her youngest child live in the country in Louisiana; unfortunately not near a beach. She is the next to youngest of eight children; five older sisters, one older brother, and one younger adopted sister.

All her written works are published through Zanchier Publications, an imprint of S.G. Boudreaux.

You can find out more about her Blog, her books, and any current events at www.sgboudreaux.com. You can also see all current titles and their information at the publishers website at www.zanchierpublications.com

You can follow her on the listed social media accounts:
Facebook/S.G.Boudreaux, Instagram@sg_boudreaux, X@SGBoudreaux, Youtube,@SGBoudreaux , Tiktok@Sgwrites, or sign up to receive email notifications at - www.sgboudreaux.com

Her previous series of books are clean-reading, fiction, fantasy, and time-travel. You can contact her at the email address in the front of the books or through her website.

Get a free, downloadable novella for joining my email newsletter: This offer is for new email sign-ups only. Copy and paste the link in your browser, or type it in, to access the form.

https://sg-boudreaux-author.kit.com/099b8e5cfb

Thank you for your continued support, and I truly hope that you enjoy my line of clean reading, fiction, fantasy, and adventure novels.

Other Books by S.G. Boudreaux

Fantasy, Adventure

Fantasy, Adventure, Time-travel

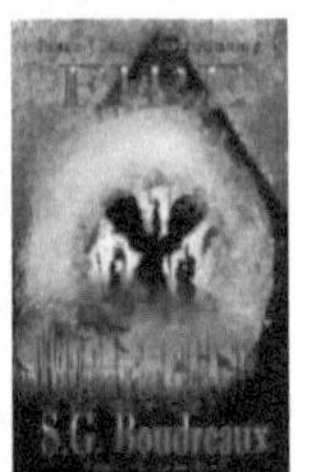

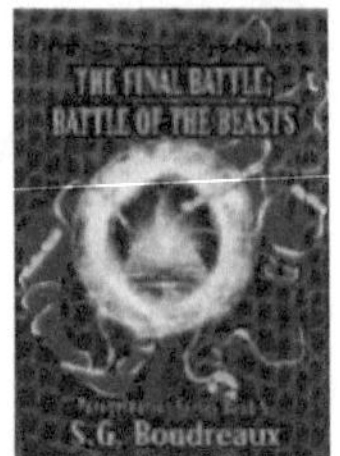

Post-Apocalyptic Romance

Bestiary-Companion book

Fantasy, Adventure, Time-travel

Non-fiction titles by Shawna Boudreaux

Self-help Health

Children's- Special Needs Awareness

Thank you for purchasing this book.

Scan the QR code to be taken to the "create an account page" on my website. Once you create an account you will be granted access to the private pages within a few days where you can download your free song, "The Stolen We", from chapter four of the book.
This song was created for the book and written by
S.G. Boudreaux.

If you have any issues with your free download, reach out via the website's contact me page or email me at
SGB@sgboudreaux.com